Carmen Posadas is the daughter of a Uruguayan diplomat, and has lived in many capital cities including Moscow, Buenos Aires and London. She is a prize-winning children's author and co-writer for film and television. *Little Indiscretions* was first published as *Pequnas Infamias* and won the coveted Planeta Prize in 1998, since when it has gone on to sell over half a million copies worldwide, and has been translated into ten languages. Carmen Posadas lives in Madrid.

International praise for *Little Indiscretions*:

'Dangerously seductive. Oh Carmen! How long must we wait till your next little crime?!'
Le Nouvel Observateur

'Told with incredible humour, and a combination of irony and wit with satire and parody . . . Guaranteed entertainment'
El Mundo

'A superb exercise in detective fantasy, to be savoured hot or cold'
La Marseillaise

www.booksattransworld.co.uk

‘A perfectly plotted novel to gladden the hearts of all amateur detectives . . . a glorious writer’
Le Monde

‘Perfect blend of Agatha Christie and Pedro Almodóvar . . . wonderful dark humour’
Figaro

‘A five star recipe’
Cosmopolitan, France

‘No rest for the reader . . . a denouement that takes you totally by surprise’
Madame Figaro

‘Carmen Posadas takes us into other worlds, specifically that of the upper bourgeoisie. Using different literary techniques, and working within the detective tradition, she has put together a perfect puzzle’
El País

‘Authentic entertainment . . . the author’s personal experience allows us a close-up view of the glamorous and putrid world of Madrid’s high society’
La Vanguardia

LITTLE INDISCRETIONS

Carmen Posadas

Previously published as
Pequnas Infamias

Translated by
Christopher Andrews

BLACK SWAN

LITTLE INDISCRETIONS
A BLACK SWAN BOOK : 0 552 77106 6

Originally published in Spain by Editorial Planeta 1998
First publication in Great Britain

PRINTING HISTORY
Black Swan edition published 2003

3 5 7 9 10 8 6 4 2

Set in 11/13pt Melior by
Phoenix Typesetting, Burley-in-Wharfedale, West Yorkshire.

Black Swan Books are published by Transworld Publishers,
61–63 Uxbridge Road, London W5 5SA,
a division of The Random House Group Ltd,
in Australia by Random House Australia (Pty) Ltd,
20 Alfred Street, Milsons Point, Sydney, NSW 2061, Australia,
in New Zealand by Random House New Zealand Ltd,
18 Poland Road, Glenfield, Auckland 10, New Zealand
and in South Africa by Random House (Pty) Ltd,
Endulini, 5a Jubilee Road, Parktown 2193, South Africa.

Printed and bound in Great Britain by
Cox & Wyman Ltd, Reading, Berkshire.

Papers used by Transworld Publishers are natural, recyclable products made from wood grown in sustainable forests. The manufacturing processes conform to the environmental regulations of the country of origin.

CONTENTS

PART ONE:
THIRTY DEGREES BELOW ZERO 7

1 Nestor, The Cook 9
2 Karel, The Czech Body-Builder 19
3 The Shout 25
4 i. A Visit to Madame Longstaffe's House 51
ii. From Mulberry & Mistletoe to Madame Longstaffe 55
5 i. The Woman in the Painting 59
ii. The Gentleman with a Crew Cut 77
6 What the Clairvoyant Saw 81
7 A Terrible Accident 93

PART TWO:
SIX DAYS IN MARCH 97

1 The First Day: Nestor's Notebook 99
2 The Second Day: Karel and Chloe 113
3 The Third Day 121
4 The Fourth Day:
i. Of Love and Blackmail 129
ii. Carlos and Adela, or Love in its Purest State 133
5 The Fifth Day 145
6 The Sixth Day:
Ernesto Teldi and Miss Ramos 149

PART THREE:
THE NIGHT BEFORE THE DEPARTURE 163

1 Nestor and the Woman in the Painting 169
2 Chloe Trias and the Ghosts 179
3 Serafin Tous and the Pizza 189
4 Karel and Madame Longstaffe Sing *Rancheras* 197
5 Ernesto and Adela in the Lift 203

PART FOUR:
THE MIRROR GAME 215

1 Arrival at The Lilies 217
2 Everyone Wants to Kill Nestor 233
3 The Dinner at The Lilies 249
4 A Door Shuts 265
5 A Ray of Sunlight on Nestor Chaffino's Body Bag 283

Part One

Thirty Degrees Below Zero

Be lion-mettled, proud, and take no care
Who chafes, who frets, or where conspirers are:
Macbeth shall never vanquished be until
Great Birnam wood to high Dunsinane hill
Shall come against him.

William Shakespeare, *Macbeth*, Act IV, Scene I

1

Nestor, The Cook

Sunday, 29 March (in the small hours) . . .

His moustache was stiffer than ever, so stiff a fly could have stepped out to the end, like a prisoner walking the plank on a pirate ship. Except that flies can't survive in a cool room at thirty below zero, and neither could the owner of the blond, frozen moustache: Nestor Chaffinch, chef and pastry-cook, renowned for his masterful way with a chocolate fondant. And that's how he was found hours later: eyes wide open in astonishment, but with a certain dignity still in his bearing. True, his fingernails were scratching at the door, but a dishcloth was tucked into the string of his apron as usual, though looking dapper is hardly a major preoccupation when the door of an 1980s-model Westinghouse cool room, two metres by one and a half, has just shut automatically behind you with a *click*.

And *click* was the last sound he heard before congratulating himself on his luck. Bloody brilliant, but it can't be true (since incredulity often precedes fear). And then: Jesus, why now of all times? The housekeepers even warned me about it before leaving, and there's a notice in three languages posted prominently in the kitchen, stressing the importance of not forgetting certain boring precautions like lifting the bolt so the door doesn't accidentally swing shut behind you. You can never be too careful with these old models. But for Heaven's Sake, I can't have been in here more than two minutes, three at the most, stacking away these boxes of chocolate truffles. No doubt about it, though, the door went *click*. You must have done something to upset it, Nestor, and *click* it went. Now what? He looked at his watch: four in the morning, said the phosphorescent hands – *click* – and there he was, in the pitch dark, inside the spacious cool room of a country house, almost empty now after a dinner party attended by around thirty guests . . . But think, think, for God's sake. Who could help me? Who's left in the house?

Let's see: the owners of the house, naturally. And Serafin Tous, one of their old friends, who arrived at the last minute. As it happened, Nestor had made his acquaintance a few weeks earlier, briefly though, very briefly. Then there were the two employees of Nestor's catering company, Mulberry & Mistletoe, whom he had asked to stay behind and help him clean up in the morning: his good friend Carlos Garcia and the new one (he never could remember his name). Karel? Koral? Yes Karel, the Czech boy who does weights, and is so handy around the place, the way he beats egg whites to a stiff peak and unloads a hundred boxes of Coke without working up a sweat, all the while singing a Caribbean *son*, *Lágrimas negras*, with his rather unfortunate Bratislava accent.

Who is going to hear him shouting and kicking the

door, bang, bang, bang, again and again, each blow resounding in his skull as if he were the one being beaten? Bloody *brilliant*, thirty years in the trade and not one accident, now this, just great! Who would have thought disasters could pile up like this, Nestor? A couple of months back you were diagnosed with lung cancer, and now that you're starting to get over the shock of it, you end up locked in a pitch-black cool room. Dying of cancer is unfortunate, but it happens to about one in five people in the end. Freezing to death on the Costa del Sol is just ridiculous.

Keep calm, it's going to be all right. Nestor knew that American technology, even the most dated, was designed to handle all eventualities. Somewhere, maybe near the doorframe, there had to be an alarm button that would ring a bell in the kitchen, and someone would hear it. The thing was to stay calm and think clearly. How long can a man in a short white jacket and checked cotton trousers survive at thirty below zero? Longer than you'd think; so come on, pull yourself together. His hand started to feel its way quite calmly (under the circumstances) along the wall, up a little, down a little. No! Not to the left – careful, Nestor. His fingers had just encountered something prickly and ice-cold. Holy Mary! There's always some sort of dead animal in these cool rooms, a hare or a rabbit with its bristling whiskers . . .

Suddenly, stupidly, Nestor thought of the owner of the house, Mr Teldi. He pictured him not as he had seen him a few hours ago, but as he remembered him from twenty or twenty-five years back. Not that Ernesto Teldi's famous moustache resembled a rabbit's long, sparse whiskers, then or now. It was smooth and elegantly trimmed, like Errol Flynn's. And it didn't so much as twitch when he saw Nestor reappear in his sitting room. Total indifference. But then perhaps that was to be expected; a gentleman like Ernesto Teldi has little reason to trouble himself with the domestic staff, so why would he remember a chef he had only seen once before, back in the seventies in the course of a terrible and traumatic afternoon.

Nestor's hand was feeling its way across another section of the wall. A little to the left now . . . but always trying not to wander too far from the door . . . This way, the life-saving button must be over here somewhere. Everyone knows Americans are practical people – there's no way they'd put the alarm bell where it can't be found. Let's see . . . but his hand seemed to be delving into an even darker abyss, so Nestor decided to give up the methodical search and go back to banging: six, seven, eight (thousand) kicks against the stubborn door. Holy Virgin of Loreto, Merciful Mother of God, Santa Maria Goretti and Don Bosco . . . please make someone wake up and come down to the kitchen for something to eat. There must be one insomniac among them. Adela maybe, oh yes, dear God, please make Adela come down.

Adela was Mr Teldi's wife. A banal thought ran through Nestor's mind (it can happen even in desperate circumstances): Time is so unkind to beautiful faces. Adela must have been about thirty when Nestor met her in South America. Such smooth skin . . . he stretched out his hand . . . Jesus! Those bloody dead hares again. There they were – yes, it was them, with their furry bodies and little white teeth glowing inexplicably in the dark like will-o'-the-wisps – but what about Adela?

No. She didn't seem to recognize him either, when they'd met to finalize the details of the evening, and that was much more surprising. Their paths had crossed on various occasions, at her house too, but of course that was all many years ago. More than once she had come in and found him chatting with Antonio Reig, the family cook, in that house of theirs in faraway Buenos Aires. 'So it's you, Nestor, back again?' she would say, or simply, 'Good evening, Nestor.' She always called him by his first name. Yes, that's what Adela used to say to him back then: 'Good evening, Nestor,' and sometimes she would even add: 'How are you? Well?' before disappearing from the kitchen, leaving an unmistakable fragrance of Eau de Patou while the two cooks carried on gossiping, swapping stories about her, as even the most discreet people do when someone vanishes with such a delectable trace.

A sound from outside made Nestor perk up and listen. He could have sworn he'd heard a noise coming from the other side of the door. And for someone with his long experience of kitchen sounds, there could be no doubt: it was the fizz of a soda siphon. Except that soda siphons disappeared from kitchens years ago, and anyway you wouldn't hear such a soft sound through the reinforced door of a cool room. Santa Gemma Galgani, Blessed Virgin Mary, Mother of God, he begged, please don't let the cold make me stupid. No nonsense, no hallucinations. I must stay calm to find this damn button that will save me. If this was the summer season, someone would have made sure there was a light that worked in this bloody cool room, and none of this would be happening to me.

But of course a blown bulb was hardly a priority in a house occupied for most of the year by an old couple whose idea of housekeeping is a cursory look around now and then to check there hasn't been a burglary.

People are so inefficient and sloppy in their work these days, Nestor thought. It's just plain irresponsible. But, no, he couldn't let the cold or panic cloud his thoughts. He had to carry on feeling around in the dark. The button had to be around somewhere. The housekeepers might be chronically slack, but the alarm was part of the system, and no self-respecting American engineer would design a cool room where a man could freeze to death like a sorbet . . .

Nestor heard the sound of the soda siphon again. He told himself it couldn't be, it was completely impossible, but it did remind him of a place in Madrid where they still used those old machines, along with all sorts of other gadgets: chewing-gum dispensers, old cash registers, gramophones playing teenybopper hits from the fifties and sixties . . . retro toys for men with certain tastes, and the gorgeous boys who work in those bars, where obliging gentlemen are only too happy to buy them a fruit juice and soda water . . . But such things are best not mentioned. Silence and discretion have always been his watchwords. Fruit juice and soda? That's Serafin Tous' favourite drink, thought Nestor, although he had a glass of sherry this evening, and spilt most of it on his trousers when he saw me. Such a respectable widower. No, no-one need hear of Nestor's little discovery. Least of all Adela and Ernesto Teldi: close friends are always the last to know the things that really matter, that's the truth. Not like you, old boy, he thought. All the little secrets you know about so many people, like Serafin for instance. But that's hardly surprising when you've been in the trade for thirty-odd years. Working in so many different places, you hear a few things. Nestor believed knowledge was power, so long as you never used it. Or rather, so long as you stayed in the background, listening and keeping it all under your hat, which was easy enough for him since no-one pays much attention to domestic staff, especially not to a professional cook who doesn't go in for gossip. But that didn't stop the stories from filtering into the kitchen, where they were blended with the meringues and set like nougat.

Serafin . . . what an appropriate name, he thought, smiling as he remembered his two encounters with the seraphic Mr Tous, and the memory of them made him smile. It was the last thing he should have been thinking about, but he couldn't help it. Fate has a weird sense of humour: *Serafin* . . . as in the holy, as if that harmless-looking gentleman had been fated to finish his days surrounded by cherubim.

A laugh. A clearly audible laugh on the other side of the door. Impossible. He was imagining things; it must have been the cold, seeping in now through his ears, his mouth, his nose – it felt like a fine drill trying to penetrate each orifice of his body, boring into his brain to knock out the neurons one by one. And the last thing Nestor needed right now were cold-deadened neurons. That's how people die in the mountains, numbed by the freezing temperatures, smiling stupidly. No, you fool, it's not a smile, it's a *grimace*, everyone knows that. But so what? Soon you won't even be able to think straight, you'll be going completely off the rails.

That's enough. Let's try and think this through methodically: who else is there in this house? Who else is around to save me? There's my assistant, Carlos Garcia – one in a million that boy – and there's Karel or Koral or whatever the hell he's called. And Chloe, his girlfriend, who insisted on coming along in case we needed an extra hand. Any one of them would do. Someone's bound to come along in the next few minutes, thought Nestor, for he was certain that with all his banging he must have pressed the alarm button at some stage – God bless the Westinghouse engineers! Surely one of those kicks or punches had set off the life-saving alarm. It was just a matter of time, the door would open. But meanwhile he had to do *something* to stop his neurons freezing or he'd lose his mind completely. If you can no longer think straight, you'll start to behave like an absolute moron. He remembered seeing a television documentary on Arctic explorers that said they'd been known to take off all their clothes and go running around stark naked like lunatics in the desert. Careful, Nestor, don't be silly, no stripping off, and don't even think of moving from the door. Not even a few centimetres, or before you know it, you'll have lost your bearings and you won't know which way is which. The darkness can be so treacherous. Don't budge, Nestor, and definitely don't give up. But the problem was the cold, seeping in through his mouth, his nose, his ears . . . *That* was what would kill him. It would drive him mad, Santa Madonna de Alexandria.

He looked at his watch. The luminous hands indicated four past four. How slowly, how terribly slowly time passes. And then he had an idea: he could block off his orifices, all of them . . . well, not the nose, of course, but the ears for instance. With what, exactly? With the only thing handy: paper. You mean from your little black book, Nestor? Obviously from the little black book, you dumb fool! And destroy an irreplaceable collection of dessert recipes, from all the countries of the world and the great houses of Europe? Worse still, you'd be destroying all the secret details of . . . Now there's proof your neurons are freezing up, you old fool. What use is all that to you now? And so Nestor extracted a thick notebook covered with moleskin from the inside pocket of his white jacket. Block out the cold, hang on a bit longer, and it'll be OK, his intuition told him, and his intuition had never failed him yet.

He heard a noise on the other side of the door. And another. The alarm button had worked! At last someone had heard him, and soon they would open the door. He was saved! That would teach him to work late in the kitchen on his own, and go marching into an old cool room in a strange house without taking precautions. But it's over now, it's over. The door's about to open . . . *click*. And again, *click*.

And not a moment too soon: just when the cold was getting to him, filling his head with stupid thoughts and fears.

2

Karel, The Czech Body-Builder

It was Karel, the Czech boy, who found him, but much later, at about four minutes to seven in the morning.

Karel was in the habit of getting up at dawn, so the hours people keep in Spain, and especially the hour they go to bed, struck him as obscene. 'It's *obscennie,* Nestor, truly' (when he got worked up his Czech accent was especially thick). 'It's really bad for you to go to bed so late, it gives you no time to recover.'

It was difficult for someone like Karel to change his morning routine after so many years – to forget the discipline of rising early that had been drilled into him in Moscow, where like so many other boys from the Eastern bloc countries who showed sporting promise, he had been adopted by the great military machine and trained, first in a 'pioneer camp', then in the Lefortovo barracks, in the south-east of the city. At Lefortovo, he was known as Karel 4563-C, an up-and-coming weightlifter, a future Communist star, chosen by destiny (and by the Julius Fucik Committee for Czech-Soviet Friendship), to outshine all others at the Atlanta Olympic Games, which were to take place ten years later in July 1996, the very month that Karel would turn eighteen. But a lot of unforeseen things were to happen before that long-awaited moment, most importantly the fall of the Berlin Wall in '89, an event that temporarily prevented Karel from going back to his country (after all, an investment's an investment, even if it is in the form of an athlete and is part of a disinterested exchange between two kindred nations like the Soviet Union and Czechoslovakia). But curiously, just a few months later, when the Russians were facing far more serious urgencies than winning Olympic medals, they were only too glad to cut costs, so they allowed and even politely ordered Karel and other Polish, Romanian and Czech sportsmen to go home. Karel was just twelve years old when he went back to Prague at the beginning of the nineties, so it wasn't hard for him to make the transition from weightlifting to a vocation more in tune with the new era that was about to dawn. 'Body-builders', that was what they were called, apparently, in the West, and according to his new classmates at the Sportovni Skola in Prague, the capitalist countries held major competitions and awarded prizes for the finest biceps and the most sculptured calves. And there was even the chance of getting your photo in the muscle magazines, which paid well, *splendidnie* even, although according to his friends from the Sportovni Skola – aspiring body-builders like himself – real professionals were few and far between, and didn't make much of a living.

Even so, what could be finer in life, sighed all those young dreamers, than the pursuit of the perfect body?

For Karel, only one thing measured up to body-building: cultivating the magical sounds of the human voice. And this was to be the other focus of young Karlicek's adolescent enthusiasm before his departure for the West.

It all began with the last gasp of Czech-Cuban fraternity (*Anno Lenini* 1992), when Karel was invited to compete for the José Martí medal for young sportsmen at the XXth Spartacus Games, a sporting event of great revolutionary value, held that year in Camaguey. It was there, among his comrades from The Most Beautiful Land (i.e. Cuba), that Karel succumbed, at the tender age of fourteen, to the rhythms of Latin music: the *son*, the cha-cha-cha, the bolero and the conga. The spell was so strong that from the moment he returned to the Sportovni Skola in Prague, his burning ambition was no longer to be a weightlifter, or even a body-builder, but one day to become a member of the fabulous Cuban *son* band, which was famous throughout Eastern Europe, and rejoiced (and still does) in the name of Los Bongoseros de Bratislava.

Sadly though, destiny does not often grant us our every wish, and so his musical vocation had to go on hold. Three more years went by: 1993, 1994, 1995 . . . until one day, an opportunity came up for him to emigrate to the West. He went first to Germany, a natural destination for Czechs, but things were not easy. So he flew a little further south to France (where things were no easier) and then further south again, to Spain, where there was no work as a body-builder, and certainly none as a cha-cha singer, and so had to make do with a job as motorbike errand boy and dogsbody for a catering company called Mulberry & Mistletoe.

But some adolescent obsessions leave indelible traces. Which explains why that morning, many miles from Bratislava, and several more from Camaguey, Cuba, as

Karel emerged from his room in the Teldis' house and went down to the kitchen in search of Haagen Daaz ice-cream to help him get going so early in the morning, he was jiggling and singing to the rhythm of a well-known forester's folk song.

When he saw Nestor inside the cool room, eyes wide open, and his left hand still seemingly scratching at the door, the song froze on his lips. There was a scrap of paper in Nestor's right hand, but Karel didn't notice it: there were far more urgent things to do, like finding out whether his friend was dead or if there was still some hope of bringing him back.

The long years of military training undergone by all elite sportsmen of the former Soviet Union can come in useful in a situation like this. Trainees were taught how to respond to all sorts of accidents. Karel Pligh had learnt, for instance, that freezing does not always cause immediate death but can sometimes induce a form of lethargy, similar to the effect of hibernation, from which the victim may be revived by a relatively simply procedure. After dragging Nestor out of the cool room, he applied this routine as best he could. First he gave him heart massage, pressing down rhythmically with his fists as required by the so-called Boris technique, then he tried mouth-to-mouth resuscitation, over and over, and not until the eleventh or twelfth attempt did he finally give up. Only then did he notice the piece of paper in Nestor's right hand.

Although Karel had been thoroughly trained in first aid, his education in television and film had, by contrast, been rather neglected. Otherwise he would have known, as everyone does, not to touch anything at the scene of an accident. 'Be careful, leave things exactly as they are until the police get here . . . Remember that anything, even the most insignificant detail, could turn out to be some kind of clue . . .' We know the cautionary words so well. But as soon as it was clear that Nestor was dead, Karel's priority was to notify the other people in the house. So, without giving it much thought, he pulled the scrap of paper from the chef's clenched fist. It tore in Nestor's tight grip, and all he could decipher were fragments of a list of desserts:

especially delicious with cappuci
lso be served with a raspberry coul
which prevents the mering
not to be confused with frozen chocolate
but rather with iced lemon

Poor, poor Nestor, poor dear friend, thought Karel, pondering death's curious habit of visiting the conscientious when they are absorbed in their work. A true chef, right up to the last, he said to himself as he took the piece of paper. Then he removed the dishcloth tucked into Nestor's apron string: a little quirk that death had underlined. The most respectful thing to do, he thought, was to ensure that these objects were properly laid to rest, now that their owner was sleeping eternally. And so, with great tenderness (and some difficulty) Karel managed to fold the frozen dishcloth. As to the list of desserts he had removed from the deceased's hand, he thought the most appropriate thing would be to put it in a cookery book, and it just so happened that over on the marble bench-top lay a copy of Brillat-Savarin's *Physiology of Taste*, Nestor Chaffinch's bible and constant companion through thirty busy years in the profession. Karel slipped the piece of paper between the pages of the book, shut it and placed the folded dishcloth on top, making a neat little pile. Only then did he go back to the door of the cool room.

With the light shining in from the outside, he had no trouble finding the alarm button that Nestor had been searching for. He pressed it. Nothing. He'd have to find some other way of waking up the others. Ringing the bell at the service door, for instance. But Karel's faith in electronic devices had been shaken. A good shout would be much more effective. So Karel Pligh shouted. He shouted with all the force of his well-trained lungs.

3

The Shout

Five people heard Karel Pligh's shout in the early hours of the morning on the 29th of March.

Serafin Tous, a friend of the family

When you haven't had a wink of sleep all night, the sound of a man shouting can have a decidedly odd effect on your mind: Serafin Tous thought it was a factory siren, and since he was a respectable independent magistrate with no links at all to industry, he rolled over and made the best of his last chance to catch a little sleep after a night of merciless insomnia.

He had spent hours worrying about that man. Was it Nestor? Yes, that was the fellow's name, according to his friend Adela. It didn't ring a bell at all, but there was no mistaking that moustache, even if he had seen it only twice, and both times only briefly. The first of these, three weeks ago at a club called Freshman's, was certainly the worst. And just as he always did when he remembered that very discreet little establishment, he had come upon quite by chance – he certainly wasn't seeking the place out – Serafin Tous tried to focus his thoughts on his late wife. 'Nora,' he said to himself, pronouncing her name out loud to feel the calming effect of those two syllables. Nora, darling, why did you have to leave me so soon?

All through that night at the Teldis', a night that was now nearly over, Serafin Tous had been telling himself a thousand times: If Nora were still alive, I would never have even thought of visiting a place like Freshman's. And he would never have seen that gossip-mongering chef appear there in the kitchen doorway, preceded by his moustache, or heard him chatting with the owner of the club (it sounded like they'd both been knocking around in the hospitality business for years). And if he had never encountered the owner of that moustache, he would have been sleeping peacefully now instead of suffering the effects of this terrible insomnia.

5.31, click . . . 5.32, click . . . While Serafin lay there worrying, his rather archaic alarm clock showed the time with square, phosphorescent numbers that flipped over like the pages of a calendar. Minute by minute. Like the artful drip-drop of Chinese water torture.

Forty-three years! Forty-three long years, perhaps not years of happiness exactly, but years of peace at least. That is what Nora had given him: more than half a life together, just the two of them. No children with whom to share their affection, no nephews or nieces, no adolescents. A long and peaceful adult life, from distant student days working as a piano teacher in a school run by the Christian Brothers to pay his way through law school, up till that afternoon when Nestor had spotted him at Freshman's. Forty-three years of perfect respectability: more than enough to make up for a moment of weakness. Forty-three years since his unforgettable last glimpse of the boy with the blue eyes and crew cut (where could he have got to now? What could have become of that waif-like fourteen-year-old with the downy blond knees?) up till the ill-fated moment when he crossed the threshold of Freshman's private club.

After a brief welcome and a few questions from the owner, he was shown to a room smelling of erasers and chalk dust. Perhaps there were rooms at Freshman's with different decor. Glancing into one on the left, as he passed, he thought he could make out an old American gramophone and a soda fountain, but the room he had been led to was more like a classroom and it did indeed smell of chalk and erasers, and of coloured pencil shavings too. The worst thing, though, was the upright piano against the far wall. He couldn't resist. He went over to the instrument and even dared to lift the lid and touch the keys. They were so smooth, as if someone had played on them every day for the last forty-three years. Dear God, so many impulses he thought were dead and gone had been simply lying dormant, for there he was, in a little room at Freshman's, stroking a piano and staring fixedly at the owner, who looked for all the world just like an arts-and-craft teacher.

'This way, sir, if you please. Perhaps it would be best to start by having a look through our photograph albums. The boys have been hard at work this year making them up, and they've done a lovely job as you'll see.'

The classroom with its smell of coloured pencils . . . the piano . . . and a man wittering on, while holding in his hands two large albums bound in red leather.

'Why don't you have a look? We are very proud of our boys. Go on, there's no need to worry, everything's above board here. None of the lads are under age, I assure you.'

The photos were set out like an old school album: row after row of diligent pupils. A large range of adolescent faces for Serafin Tous to admire: blond boys, dark boys, some smiling broadly with braces on their teeth to make them look younger than they really were.

'Take your time, sir,' said the arts-and-craft teacher. 'Take as much time as you like. We're in no hurry, me and the boys.'

More photos of bright-eyed lads, some wearing knee-length shorts, like his piano pupils back in the days before he had Nora's love (and her money) to provide for him.

'What do you think, sir? Perhaps you'd like to be left alone for a moment. It's often easier to make a choice that way. I'll go away and chat with a friend and colleague who's just dropped in to see me. I'll be back in a tick.'

Serafin felt calmer flipping through the pages on his own; he felt more able to concentrate on the multitude of young faces before him. Some boys were wearing spotless white sports gear. Three or four were dressed as explorers. He flicked back to look at the muscular young men with dirty faces and commando gear. Page after page of faces, until the click of the door almost made him slam the album shut: the arts-and-craft teacher had returned.

'No hurry, sir, please keep looking. Can I bring you something? A good old-fashioned fruit juice, perhaps, with a splash of soda water? It's very good the way we make it here, you know, just like the old days . . .'

And suddenly, just like the old days, there it was, that face. Well, perhaps it wasn't *exactly* the face he had loved. Serafin sat back in the chair – it couldn't be . . .

but how could anyone resist those eyes, that limpid gaze, that blond crew cut? You couldn't see his hands, but Serafin was sure the fingers would be jittery, like the thin fingers that had once entwined with his on the keys as they played a simple sonata. He preferred not to think about what happened afterwards, that day and so many other days, throughout the course of that ruinous year. Serafin shook his head. No, no. There are memories that should remain securely locked away.

'How are we going? May I take a look, sir, if you don't mind? So Julian has caught your eye, has he?' he heard the owner of the establishment saying. 'Excellent. I'll go and call him.'

And he disappeared before Serafin could say a word.

We'll just have a drink together, he promised himself as he sat there waiting, when suddenly he felt an imperious urge to bite the nail of his index finger. What would his wife have thought if she could have seen him? Just a couple of drinks, I swear, Nora, he thought, mentally trying to reassure her. I'll have a fruit juice with soda water, like in the old days, and I suppose he'll have a Coke.

And that was exactly what happened. He bought the boy a drink, and that was it. So that fellow with the pointy moustache, Nestor or whatever the hell he was called, had no right to be spying on him from the kitchen door as if he were some kind of criminal. Serafin Tous had a clear conscience.

But now that they had run into one another once again at Teldi's, what if the chef were to reveal how they first met? What if this Nestor fellow took it upon himself to tell Ernesto or Adela or one of their friends? It's a sad fact, thought Serafin Tous, that what actually happens in life doesn't matter half as much as what people say about it, and it's safe to assume that they rarely err on the side of generosity.

6.05, click . . . 6.06, click. Every time the numbers flipped over, it was like a reminder or a warning: he was that much closer to the moment when he'd be forced to confront that loathsome man with his pointy moustache. No-one gossips like a cook. What a squalid profession it is: scurrying around among pots and pans like cockroaches, thought Serafin, with a bitterness quite out of keeping with his normally mild personality. They're like insects creeping in through cracks, turning up everywhere, carrying filth from house to house as they please. That's how they end up knowing all about other people's private lives.

All we did was have a drink together, Nora. I had a fruit soda and he had a Coke. I swear by all our years of happily married life, you have to believe me. Those forty-three years were a new life for me, without the music I once loved so much, without the memory of childish fingers on piano keys. I haven't touched a piano since then. You changed my life, darling, and I let you do it. We were so safe in our grown-up world, Nora, a world without temptation where a grown man has little likelihood of coming across a boy in flannel shorts with a crew cut.

But then Serafin stopped. What are you saying, Nora dear? Something about my visit to that tarot reader the other day, the famous Madame Longstaffe? Please, don't think I'm looking for . . . You're wrong, I swear you're wrong. It's just that I'm so lonely . . . Look, he added, no longer sounding quite so contrite, I don't mean to be reproachful, darling. I know I should be grateful for all the years of peace you gave me. But really, with all the unpleasant people there are in the world, nasty types who would be better off dead and buried, why did you, my love, you of all people, have to go and die so soon?

Chloe Trias, the kitchen hand

Chloe also heard Karel's shout from the kitchen, but she still slept deeply like a child. She stirred for a few seconds, and reached across to the side of the bed where her lover should have been. Instead of Karel Pligh she found a reassuringly familiar hand, one that for many years had kept her company at night. Then she rolled over and went back to sleep, with her chestnut-brown hair, cut in a bob, falling across her face.

Seeing her half-asleep like that, you wouldn't have thought she was almost twenty-two, especially when she curled up with that invisible hand, which was in fact nothing more than a lump in the sheets. Other nights, a corner of the bedspread or a pillow case would do the trick: a strong enough longing can easily transform cotton or linen into human skin. So holding the imaginary hand of her brother Eddie, Chloe lapsed again into a deep and innocent slumber, as if outside it were still the black of night.

Sometimes, like that morning of the 29th of March at the Teldis', she dreamt that Eddie was coming to take her to visit Neverland. But Neverland, that island-haven for boys who refuse to grow up, has changed a good deal since the days of Peter Pan and Wendy, of Mr Smee and Captain Hook: no more crocodiles going tick-tock or pirates stealing lost boys. True, the coastline is still skull-shaped, it is after all the same island she used to visit as a child, flying off after her brother's shadow. And yet, for some time, or to be more precise since Chloe met

Karel and Nestor Chaffinch, a treacherous wind had been blowing her off course, so that she never quite knew where she would end up.

And on this occasion, her visit to Neverland was completely wrecked by Karel Pligh's second cry for help from the kitchen.

Cries from the real world have a tendency to distort the dreams they disturb. Some can even turn peaceful idylls into nightmares, and so this second shout, though it did not succeed in waking Chloe, provoked a string of memories she would have preferred to leave undisturbed. She pulled her hair across her face, trying to shake off the bad dreams. A relatively inoffensive childhood memory came back to her: a banal scene, at least it was to begin with. 'But darling,' said a voice, 'what extraordinary names to have chosen for your children. Oedipus and Chloe, truly! . . . Another one of your *caro sposo*'s whims, no doubt. Psychiatrists do come up with the strangest ideas. It might seem amusing at first, but what about later on, when they grow up? Imagine going through life with a name like Oedipus. Just as well it didn't occur to your *caro sposo* to call the girl Electra while he was at it.'

Amalia Rossi, better known as *Carosposo* (in fey homage to Jane Austen whose novels lined their wall), was one of those neighbours who obligingly inform a child of all his or her family's darkest secrets. As far back as she could remember, Amalia had always been popping in and out of the house: a fat, blond woman, quite a bit older than Chloe's mother and three times divorced, the last husband being an Italian actor who had left her his surname as well as an exasperating habit of joking about serious matters.

It was Amalia, wicked witch that she was, who, some

years later, had taken Chloe to the bottom of her Italian garden, and told her that her brother Eddie had just died. And in her dream she suddenly saw the whole scene again, every detail intact: Amalia Rossi's ring-laden fingers running through her brown hair, snagging every time, while Chloe, in a state of numbness, pulled leaf after leaf off the box hedge, thinking: It isn't true, it *can't* be true. Get me out of here . . . somebody help me!

Thankfully, in the dream, that ugly hand would suddenly be transformed into its opposite: the beloved hand that snatched Chloe out of the Italian garden and took her flying, flying away to Neverland, or anywhere, anywhere at all, as long as it was away from there.

Come on, Chloe, fly with me a little while longer, said the hand, while down there in the garden Amalia's voice seemed to choke on its own slimey words of commiseration, like a myopic boa constrictor strangling itself in its own tremendous grip for lack of prey. Fly higher, Chloe, come on, up we go . . .

When she flew away with her brother in a dream, she could believe it was all a lie. A lie that happened on the 19th of February seven years before. A lie that Eddie had borrowed his father's Suzuki 1100 to try it out on a straight stretch of the La Coruña highway. And a huge lie that he had lost control of the bike going round a bend, just where the 22-kilometre marker happened to be waiting. Twenty-two: his age then, the age Chloe was about to reach. But Eddie, like Peter Pan, would never be a minute older: forever young, forever identical to the photo Chloe carried with her since the day he died, though she never looked at it. It was a good thing to carry around pictures of the dead, but it was better not to look at them, it hurt too much.

For a moment she thought she could see Eddie's face on the bedside table. But no, it couldn't be. She must have been imagining it. The photo was in its usual place, in her bag, hidden away in a little red leather case, somewhere under her sports gear and the Led Zeppelin and Pearl Jam CDs. Chloe never took it from its case, but she knew every detail by heart. She had taken it herself, they'd been laughing and Eddie looked so handsome on that afternoon of the 19th of February, just before he went away for ever. Every one of her brother's features, so similar to her own, was fixed in her memory: only their eyes were different. Eddie's were very dark, almost black, while hers were blue, but apart from that, his hair, cut short, was the same colour as Chloe's, the lips were the same, and the shape of the face. Everything about the photo reminded her of that last day, even the clothes he was wearing: his father's motorcycle leathers, peeled off down to the waist. It was an incongruous sight: a boy with sensitive, almost feminine features disguised as a biker. That was what they had been laughing about that morning.

'And where do you think you're going, Eddie?'

Her brother had never been especially keen on motorbikes (or anything else to do with his father) and yet that day . . .

So it's easy to understand why Chloe preferred not to look at the photo of her brother. Luckily, there were other images filed away in her memory, more faithful reflections of his true personality. Eddie looking very serious with the tip of a pencil in his mouth, for instance, and she only had to concentrate on this image to make it expand and come alive like a film in Cinemascope. Then she could see Eddie typing something on an old computer. She could see the short hair on the back of his neck, and those lively eyes that sparkled whenever he got onto his favourite topic: literature.

'Are you writing a novel, Eddie? What is it? I bet it's a story with adventures and romance and crime and stuff, isn't it?'

But Eddie didn't let her see what he was writing.

'Not yet, Clo-clo. I'll let you read the next one, I promise you.'

(Chloe hated that nickname: it made her sound like a chicken. But Eddie was her brother, and he could call her what he liked, even Clo-clo.)

'One day I'll let you read what I've written, but not this; it's garbage. I've still got a long way to go. The problem is,' he said, sucking the pencil-point as if that might help him solve it, 'first of all, you need to find a good story to tell.'

'Oh, come on, Eddie, I bet you can think up something really good, something brilliant . . .'

Eddie kept running his hand through his hair, over and over, as if he might find the secret in there, the key to a good story. But then he ran out of patience.

'Well, there's no point racking my brains, Clo. I guess there's only one way to come up with a really good story, and that's to live fast, have loads of experiences, get drunk, fuck hundreds of girls, kill someone or something – live on the edge, and look death in the face. It's just a matter of time. I'll get there some day, Clo, you'll see. I promise you . . .'

'And what happens to a writer if he doesn't have any interesting experiences?' asked Chloe, who, like a lot of fourteen- and fifteen-year-olds, was always on the lookout for some patient soul to bombard with rhetorical questions: And what if this happens? And what if that doesn't? . . . 'And what if you don't get to fuck hundreds of girls or live fast and look death in the face? What if it turns out you don't like getting drunk and you don't have the guts to be a killer, Eddie?'

'Well, then Clo-clo I'll just have to steal someone else's story, won't I?' he replied, sick of her stupid questions.

They never got to talk about it again. Of all the experiences he had wanted to have, Eddie was granted at least one: living fast and looking death in the face. There at the edge of the La Coruña highway, the 22-kilometre post was waiting to send him off to Neverland.

'Come on, Chloe, come fly with me . . . Let's fly higher, let's dream again . . .'

A racket of voices from the stairway burst into her dream. Startled, she let go of Eddie's hand. What the fuck? Jesus!

Eddie wouldn't have liked to hear her speak like this. He wouldn't have liked her new haircut either – a short bob, shaved up the back of the neck – or her clothes, and he certainly wouldn't have approved of her pierced tongue and lower lip, not to mention her left nipple (and various tattoos). In fact, there were a lot of things he wouldn't have liked about the new Chloe, who was almost twenty-two now, like him. Only he was gone. He had left her alone with her psychiatrist father and her self-absorbed mother . . . He had gone and he only came back from time to time, at night, to take her by the hand and whisk her away through the window, although she knew those nocturnal escapades were no more than dreams, so why pretend? Neverland doesn't exist. It's a story for children, and stupid children at that. All she knew for sure was that Eddie had died seven years ago and the world had gone on without him.

So how come the photo of her brother was sitting on the bedside table? Chloe was certain she hadn't taken it out of its red case, she never did, and yet there he was, her brother Eddie, looking at her with that smile she had tried to imitate so often in front of the mirror. Eddie standing there smiling silently in his father's leathers with the sleeves tied around his waist, not knowing he only had minutes left to live.

'Tell me a story, Eddie. Don't go; stay with me.' That's what she should have said that afternoon, but she didn't say anything, and Eddie jumped onto the Suzuki 1100 and went off in search of stories, because he was only twenty-two years old and nothing worth writing about had happened to him yet.

'And what if you get old and you still haven't had any experiences worth writing about? What then, Eddie?'

'Well, Clo-clo, then I'll just have to kill someone and steal their story, won't I?' he said, and off he went, for good.

From the stairway came a clamour of voices and general confusion. Chloe decided to get out of bed and see what was happening, but she took her time. No point in hurrying, she thought, nothing ever happens anyway. And that was the truth. Since that 19th of February seven years before, nothing had happened. Abso-fucking-lutely nothing.

Ernesto Teldi, the owner of the house

People say you can get used to anything. You can even get used to nightmares if they come back night after night, relentlessly, for twenty years. Maybe it was even longer. 1976 to 1998: twenty-two years; a whole lifetime, for some.

Karel Pligh's shout from the kitchen didn't wake Ernesto Teldi, but surreptitiously took its place among the other shouts that inhabited his dreams, one among many, and not the most terrible.

Just as he had learnt to live with his nightmares, Ernesto Teldi knew that the persecution would cease the minute he woke up. It was a perfectly reasonable arrangement – calm days in return for troubled nights – and that was how it had always been, both when he lived as a young man in Argentina, and since his definitive return to Europe several years ago. Not once in all that time had he been bothered by an unpleasant thought or a scare during his waking hours, not even now that he had to travel quite often to Buenos Aires to look after some new business. Occasionally while on a trip he would hear news that someone suffering nightmares like his own had finally talked. Some of these had written books, while others opted for prime-time television, like that bald, sweaty army officer called Serenghetti or something, whose public confession Teldi had happened to see one afternoon in the Hotel Plaza. The fellow had multiple chins and reminded him of those Shar Pei dogs with their folds of cinnamon-coloured flesh. He hung his big bald head and explained to the interviewer that the worst thing was simply walking down the street. 'Because, you see, there are all those young people, and you can't help looking at their faces.'

Having said that, he wiped his canine jowls with a fat, trembling hand as if belatedly trying to stop the words coming out of his mouth.

'What I mean is, well, say I go out for a walk,' he

continued, 'and I'm minding my own business, walking down the Calle Corrientes for example. Suddenly I realize I can't look at anyone under twenty-five without thinking, that boy or that girl, that gorgeous blonde, maybe she was one of . . . she'd be just the right age, you see.' Then Serenghetti paused and turned to the interviewer, who was looking at him with a highly professional and screen-friendly air of disgust. 'And then,' he said, switching at this point to the second person in a hopeless bid for compassion, 'you remember what you did to their parents when they were just babies, the age their own kids are now, and you hear the motors of the Hercules drowning out their shouts, not completely though, you can still hear them and you can't forget the terrible look in their eyes, and you can see that look in the faces of the boys and girls on the Calle Corrientes or Posadas or whatever. You see what I mean? They're looking at you, and you're trying to keep calm and wondering what they know behind those eyes. The truth is, they don't know anything. They were just babies when we went around giving them out. And the way I saw it back then, well, it was the most humane thing to do. Poor kids. Anyway now they have other parents who love them, who brought them up, wiped their noses and comforted them in the first months when they cried at night for their real mothers. But by then their real mothers,' said Serenghetti, sniffing and breathing noisily through his Shar Pei nose, 'were at the bottom of the river under several metres of dirty water; and that's where they are to this day, at the very bottom, dead but not buried, and there you are walking down Corrientes thinking you can still see their eyes every time one of those kids looks at you.'

Serenghetti wiped his own nose after coming out with

all this on prime-time television. A moment of silence. A couple of coughs. The interviewer seized the moment and wrapped up the show with a highly professional combination of pity and loathing, and the fat guy probably went home thinking now he could breathe a bit more easily having publicly confessed his sins. True, many people would despise him after what he'd said, but they already did, before they knew exactly what he'd done. And now maybe a few would feel sorry for him. Why not? Deep down, in some dark corner of our souls, we all feel comforted to know that our little cruelties pale into insignificance beside what others have done.

Ernesto Teldi, however, was of quite a different mind. A public confession was certainly not on his agenda. In any case, what did he have to confess? Nothing. His situation was totally different. He'd done a little deal and it was all over in a night. No-one could honestly say he had collaborated with the army or even had anything to do with those stupid arseholes. His only sin – if you could call it that – was to have maintained polite but distant relations with the colonel in charge of the barracks near the town of Don Torcuato. They had known each other for a good while, almost since Teldi had arrived in Argentina. Minelli always called him 'Teldi the Spaniard', with a certain respect. Teldi, for his part, thought the colonel was a good sort. One night, just that one night, mind you, it must have been in '76 or thereabouts, not long after the generals took power anyway, Minelli asked him a favour: he wanted to borrow Teldi's light plane.

That was all he knew. At the time, anyway.

'Look, Teldi,' said Minelli, 'best not to ask any questions. You do a bit of trading on the black market, don't you? You bring tobacco back from Colonia and land in the field just across the way. It's a good little business and you wouldn't want it messed up, would you? We really don't give a damn what you do. Listen, here's the deal: I'll turn a blind eye, and you don't ask any questions. Got it?'

So Teldi the Spaniard asked no questions, because in those days nobody did.

He only started asking two or three years later, very quietly, very timidly at first, when rumours began to spread in the towns along the estuary, rumours about planes that were loaded up when they flew out over that part of the Rio de la Plata, but always came back empty. There was talk about what happened out there, and screams in the night, but it was better to forget all that or at least push it to the back of one's mind so it didn't get in the way, because Minelli was a good sort after all, he kept his word and always turned a blind eye to the smuggling. In return, Teldi kept his side of the deal.

So now Ernesto Teldi could go for a walk on Calle Corrientes or Posadas without a worry in the world, because he hadn't asked any questions. Not then, not later, when it was all over, when he had given up smuggling cigarettes and had used his already considerable fortune to embark on a new career as an art dealer in Buenos Aires. It all worked out for the best.

And yet, two years after his little conversation with Minelli, when he was still trading on the black market, something happened. Something truly strange, although it was probably no more than a figment of his imagination. In any case, one night as he was flying his plane across the river to Colonia, he thought he heard a shout coming up from the water, then another, and another. It was crazy, it couldn't be . . . With the noise of the engines you can't hear a thing, especially flying at that altitude. He looked down. The black waters of the river were as quiet as ever: no movement, not a sign of life. Impossible, he said to himself, lighting a cigarette to smoke the fright away, and he didn't give it a second thought. But those shouts took up residence in his dreams. And they were still there twenty-two years later; very reasonable guests really, since they never bothered him during the day and only made their presence felt at night. And you can get used to anything in the end, even living with ghosts.

That is why the shout coming from the kitchen of Teldi's country house that morning seemed to be just one of the many that inhabited his dreams. He didn't wake up until Adela came in from the bedroom next door to get him. She had to shake him repeatedly before he opened his bleary eyes, dazed by the light of the real world. The first thing they registered was a letter lying on the bedside table. There it was, a fat envelope addressed to 'Teldi the Spaniard', his name written in green ink. It had arrived the night before, in the mail, without a sender's name or address. Before looking at Adela, Ernesto stared at that little paper packet that logically should never have emerged from the world of his dreams. Shit, he thought, it's still there. I'd almost convinced myself it was just another nightmare.

Adela Teldi, the model hostess

As soon as Mrs Teldi heard Karel Pligh's shout, she thought something irrevocable had happened. And if it was irrevocable, why hurry? Adela didn't leap out of bed or rush into the corridor screaming. She had never been able to understand what it was that impelled people to go running around when they found out something over which they had absolutely no control: a patient in hospital whose brain scan has gone to a flat . . . a drowned child floating in the sea . . . they start rushing around, as if by getting in a flap they could outrun death and rewind the film, back through those crucial minutes. Back to when the brain scan was still showing signs of life and the child was safe on the top of the cliff, under his mother's watchful eye, a few seconds before he gave her the slip for good, and she went running, flying, hurling herself at a small body that she knew was irreparably broken.

Since the previous night, Adela had known that something was going to happen. There was no specific reason for her hunch, except that strange tingling sensation in her fingers. *By the pricking of my thumbs, something wicked this way comes* . . . Adela was not a great reader of Shakespeare's tragedies, but those lines had provided the title of a novel she remembered from her Agatha Christie phase. She had enjoyed that one, and it was true, too, about the pricking. Just before something awful happened she could always feel it in her thumbs. For Shakespeare, of course, and Agatha Christie, only the worst kind of witches had prescient thumbs, but what did that matter? she told herself. Life isn't a novel in which everyone has to play a predetermined role and stick to it. In real life, you end up playing all the roles. Sometimes you're the victim. Sometimes you're the hero. Or the schemer, or an extra. And so on right through the cast.

Now it's your turn to play the witch, Adela, she said, gazing at herself in the mirror. She certainly looked the part. Fifty-two years of narrowing her eyes in that charming way. More than half a century of smiling charmingly to display her faultless teeth. The sun of a thousand beaches too. A moderate amount of whisky. Many sleepless or almost sleepless nights (not to mention countless personal setbacks, which she had borne with serenity, aided by an Existential philosophy of indifference). All this amply accounted for the dreadful Hecate-like apparition in her bathroom mirror. Slowly Adela's hand moved over that scene of devastation, her face, then down to her neck and chest. She decided to put on one of her bathrobes, the finest, smoothest one. She didn't intend to get properly dressed, but only to cover up a little, so that when she went running out into the corridor or down the stairs to see what Karel Pligh was shouting about, she would look like a mature but, my word, still a very good-looking woman, caught unawares, charmingly *déshabillé*. She brushed her hair a little, not too much, then came forward and peered at herself in the mirror with her blue, short-sighted eyes, absently stroking her cheek with three fingers and her neck with another, as if she were wanting something . . . but there was a good deal of deft cosmetic repair work to be done if she was to achieve the desired effect, and on this occasion her touch did not revive the memory of that boy's kisses, kisses that had, in the last two weeks, turned her whole world upside down.

And yet every one of Carlos Garcia's caresses was imprinted deeply on her skin, on her temples, on the unflattering creases around the corners of her mouth, which had resisted the expertise of her plastic surgeon. A cyclone leaves a trace of its passage even on the hardest rock, and a beach hit by a tornado will never recover its former shape. Something similar had happened to Adela's face: since the unleashing of that passion, it was the same face, yet somehow different.

For heaven's sake, Adelita – that old Nat King Cole song had taught her how to laugh at herself and her name, which was so much at odds with her personality. For heaven's sake, my dear, anyone would think you'd never had a lover before. She laughed. The mirror on the wall kindly reflected what was still a quite lovely smile. Dear oh dear, Adela, she added, an old trooper like you, with a service record – to use a military metaphor, and what could be more appropriate? – that would have impressed even good old Nat King Cole. A boy comes along, young enough to be your son, and look at you: head over heels! There was no denying it, the encounter with Carlos had turned her world upside down. It had been totally, overwhelmingly *devastating*, she might have said, if she hadn't been allergic to self-dramatization. Yet devastation had been wrought: every last trace of her former loves had been swept away. All gone. She looked at herself long and hard in the mirror, but nowhere on her seasoned, worldly skin could she find the tiniest memento of those other affairs, even the truly scandalous ones. Those secret affairs, including one that had done such terrible damage, and after that, the brief, passionate escapades and various bits of fun: all completely wiped from her memory. Looking at herself in the mirror, the only thing Adela could remember was an inexperienced hand trembling as it touched her body, as if it were venturing into unexplored territory. A hand that was slightly moist and had that sweet smell of very young skin. That was all.

Adela Teldi contemplated the little hollow at the base of her neck. No doubt one of his kisses had left a trace of love's perfume in that fragile, wrinkled little cup: witch's flesh, old skin, like all the skin on her body; but strangely its texture had never seemed to bother him, not even that afternoon when they first met.

The way it had all begun was truly odd. She and Ernesto were planning a party for some of his business associates at their country house, so on one of her visits to Madrid, she decided to visit a catering firm that had been recommended to her. But when she arrived at Mulberry & Mistletoe, she was annoyed to discover that the owner, a certain Mr Chaffinch, was out, so she had no choice but to deal with his assistant. Which turned out to be more than satisfactory. The assistant was a charming, conscientious young fellow. They started talking about broccoli flans, then they considered various wines to accompany the dishes, discussed the finer points of goat's cheese on salad leaves followed by vol-au-vents with meat, or perhaps some fish? Then they came back to the question of the wines . . . but Adela soon realized that with all the talk about food and drink she was feeling ravenous and parched, so she asked the charming young fellow if there was 'a place nearby where perhaps we could finalize the details of the dinner over a drink . . . I'm sorry, I've forgotten your name, what did you say it was?'

After repeating his name, Carlos suggested the Embassy, which was nearby. When they got there, they ordered two tomato juices and a few chicken sandwiches, and went on talking food, whether it would be better to have two sea bass for the buffet, or a salmon and a sea bass; yes, yes, definitely a salmon with dill as well as the sea bass with tartare sauce . . . And so the conversation continued, accompanied by more sandwiches, smoked trout this time, and they talked on and on, still about catering, even after they had paid and left and were walking together towards the Plaza Colón, at which point they realized that they hadn't even considered dessert.

There was nothing for it, dessert would have to be discussed. And they can't have quite sated their appetites at the Embassy, because soon they were heading for the Phoenix Hotel to have a last drink.

In the bar at the Phoenix, the tomato juices became Bloody Marys (not one but three, and strong) and Adela wasn't looking at her watch any more. What did it matter what time it was? To hell with meeting her husband at such and such a time. To hell with the party for thirty guests at her country house on the Costa del Sol. To hell with everything, because by this stage Adela couldn't even remember how she had ended up in a room at the Phoenix Hotel where, as she sat on the bed taking off her black Woolford stockings, first one leg . . . then the other, just like Mrs Robinson in *The Graduate*, it was impossible to know what the boy was thinking as he watched her, but he was certainly better looking than Dustin Hoffman, by a long shot, and younger too: Adela suspected her graduate was not even twenty-two years old, twenty-three at most.

Now standing in front of her dresser, Adela applied the subtlest touch of eyeliner, putting some depth back into her gaze. All she needed was a layer of powder and the effect would be perfect, without it looking like she was wearing any make-up at all. How much time had gone by since she heard Karel Pligh's shout? Five minutes perhaps, no more. In fast forward, memories tumble past in no time at all . . . but maybe it was longer, ten or even twelve minutes, for suddenly Mrs Teldi heard another shout. Had it come from her husband's room? Ernesto Teldi often cried out in his sleep. She knew what caused his nightmares. Although they never discussed his past, it held no secrets for Adela.

Likewise, they never talked about that other incident, her own dark secret, something that had happened a few years after she and Ernesto had got married and moved from Madrid to Argentina. When was that again? In 1981, or maybe '82? Adela had tried to forget, but the best she could do was to muddle the dates. Suddenly, stupidly, she started singing: 'If Adelita eloped with another man.' In the mirror, her eyes had a feverish look, which was quite unusual since their mistress was not inclined to let them betray any sign of weakness. Self-control was the key, the self-control she had maintained for more than seventeen years, ever since the day her sister Soledad died.

If Adelita eloped . . . but Adelita never did. That was her punishment. As well as knowing that the price of an unblemished reputation is silence. Or death. But now you're getting all melodramatic, my dear, she thought, casting a final look at her arms and hands, applying the finishing touches to her artful look of early-morning informality. It's sheer melodrama to suppose that all your problems, past and present, could be solved by a death. Highly unlikely, too, despite the strange tingling in your thumbs, you old witch. Time to get moving; you'd better go out and see what's happened, can't put it off much longer . . . but first, my God, I nearly forgot, I have to go next door and tell Ernesto. What's the bet he's sleeping like a log?

Carlos Garcia, the waiter

From the servants' quarters on the top floor, Carlos Garcia could hear Karel shouting in the kitchen. But he didn't mistake the shout for a factory siren, as Serafin Tous had done. He didn't ignore it, like young Chloe, or think it was part of his nightmare, like Ernesto. Just as Adela had done on the next floor down, when he heard the shouts Carlos got out of bed, but rather than indulging in some leisurely morning grooming, he made straight for the door, hesitating only for a moment to look at the deep hollow left in his pillow by the head that had rested next to his.

He couldn't remember at what point Adela Teldi had left his room; it must have been a good while ago, certainly before dawn, but . . . Come on, hurry up, something was urgent from the sound of it – you can worry later. Better get down there and see what's going on.

Which is what he did.

There was no-one in the kitchen except Karel, and Nestor's body stretched out on the floor. The room seemed perfectly tidy, with nothing to indicate what might have happened. Without asking questions, Carlos knelt for a moment beside the body of his friend. He felt no pain or sorrow or even incredulity. There was something impersonal about the whole scene, as if that body had never been Nestor. The corpse of a friend is already a stranger, and just like any other corpse. Who had said that? It was all too true. But it wasn't the moment to be probing his memory.

Nevertheless, during those long minutes of confusion, before the others came bursting into the kitchen, with only Karel crouching down, impassively like a ventriloquist's dummy awaiting manipulation after raising the alarm, Carlos Garcia had time to recall many scenes in which his dead friend had figured. And he relived those scenes: things they had been through together, shared secrets, laughter, little mysteries and the odd premonition, beginning with the time, two weeks back, when they had gone to see a certain fortune-teller. And yes, maybe that was where it all began: the chain of events that would lead to Nestor's death.

4

i. A Visit to Madame Longstaffe's House

A parrot or perhaps a lorikeet with red and blue plumage, a green breast and a very tatty tail looked at them with one eye. The other eye, also asquint, was looking up at the ceiling, contemplating a corner miraculously free of decorations or knick-knacks of any sort.

They shut the front door behind them. Nobody had actually opened it for them, but a sign saying 'Come in and wait your turn in the little aquamarine sitting room, thank you' directed them to the second door on the left. They went in, greeted the three people in the room, and sat down to wait with the patience required of those who frequent such establishments.

After a little while, Carlos Garcia looked at Nestor as if to say: Do you think I could take a newspaper from this um . . . magazine rack? And his friend's moustache, which fitted in perfectly with the decor of the house, replied: Of course. Carlos was about to delve into that multicoloured plaster imitation of a doctor's bag and make his choice among the glossy magazines and newspapers when he noticed the head of a roman tribune peeping out. He promptly withdrew his hand and decided to look around the room instead.

He had heard about fortune-tellers' houses: they were always weird. Some, no doubt, were decorated *à la Chinoise*, with little coloured lamps, and yins and yangs everywhere, even on the bathroom tiles. And Cuban faith-healers probably had their places done up like Bacardi ads, with drums and sea shells everywhere, and statues of Babalú-ayé and Shangó and the Blessed Saint Barbara. But Madame Longstaffe, the famous clairvoyant, was Brazilian. She hailed from the peerless city of Bahía, and her house defied imagination: a natural response to such surroundings was to take flight.

'Let's go.'

'*Cazzo* Carlitos,' said Nestor. (*Cazzo* was the Italian for 'dick', but Carlos still hadn't worked out if it was meant affectionately or as an insult.) '*Cazzo* Carlitos, you're the one who insisted on coming, and now that we're here, we're going to stay.'

Aside from the novelty magazine rack, the most disturbing decorative feature in the room was a stuffed white Maltese terrier perched on an alabaster column. But it didn't seem to be bothering any of the other clients waiting their turn. An elegantly dressed woman was sitting on the sofa on the right (threadbare Aubusson tapestry with little Indian cushions), a Rastafarian was leaning against a Japanese screen, and cleaning his fingernails with a large knife, a nervous woman hiding behind sunglasses had chosen a seat in front of the window so that only her silhouette was visible, like Fedora in the Billy Wilder film. None of them seemed the least bit surprised by the presence of a mummified dog on top of a column. Carlos observed that the animal had its ears pricked and its little pink tongue hanging out as if it were smiling. On one side of the column, a bronze plaque provided an explanation: 'Dear Fru-Fru, you will always be in my thoughts. Day and night I will remember the patter of your tiny paws following my weary footsteps.'

'Let's get out of here,' said Carlos, with the natural impulsiveness of a twenty-one-year-old, but also, truth be told, with a superstitious fear of what he might discover about himself and his future. Yet if he didn't want to find out, why had he asked Nestor to come with him to the clairvoyant's house? His friend was right.

'Eh *cazzo*, it was your idea to come and find out about your imaginary lover, and if you think you can back down now, after pestering me for days about it at Mulberry & Mistletoe, you can forget it.'

4

ii. From Mulberry & Mistletoe to Madame Longstaffe

There is something about stoves and ovens that makes people confess their secrets. Take a young man, put him in front of a pan full of simmering syrup with orange blossom and pieces of pumpkin and other such flotsam in it. Next thing you know, he'll be baring his soul to friend or mentor, whoever happens to be present, like a young bard confessing himself to a druid. Not that there was anything bard-like about Carlos Garcia – slack first-year law student turned part-time waiter – and far from being the green homeland of the Celts, Mulberry & Mistletoe was a very exclusive catering business, owned by Nestor Chaffinch. 'Home and business catering,' said the card. 'Dinner parties, cocktail parties and other social occasions. We specialize in desserts. Visit us for a free quote.' As for Nestor, well, maybe there was something druid-like about him: not so much his appearance (an Italo-Argentine cook with a pointy blond moustache is hardly the spitting image of Panoramix), but there was a certain wizardry to the way he stirred his pots and pans, and somehow it made people feel like opening their hearts to him.

And that was why, in the course of a long winter afternoon, while helping to prepare large quantities of morello cherries soaked in cognac for one of Nestor's famous desserts, Carlos timidly began to reveal his secret.

It all started with a casual remark, one of his philosophical observations on a subject that would never even occur to most people, let alone a waiter rushed off his feet, with not a moment to spare for idle speculation.

And yet it had occurred to him.

'No, honestly, it's something I've noticed time and again, Nestor: when you're working as a waiter, you reach a point when you realize that people have lost their heads,' he confessed over the syrup they were making before the customers arrived. 'Don't get me wrong. It's not that you start thinking they're all crazy, though there's that too,' he added, laughing. 'No, there you are, busy serving the wine, and all you can see are the details, like they're not whole people any more, just *bits* of people.'

'Pass me the cognac, will you, Carletto,' said Nestor, interrupting, 'and stop eating the cherries.'

Carlos, who didn't drink, was discovering the magic effect of cherries soaked in cognac, which are even more conducive to the revelation of secrets than the stirring of pots.

He went on to explain to his friend how, since he had started working at Mulberry & Mistletoe, he had discovered a whole new way of looking at the world: the way you see things when you're carrying a tray full of glasses. 'And from that vantage point,' he said, 'it turns out people have no faces. No, seriously, it's true: when you're serving drinks, you don't look into their eyes to see who asked for whisky and who asked for grapefruit juice. There are other ways of telling. And when you're out there taking orders, and everyone's milling around and making a racket, you can only recognize people by very specific physical features. Do you see what I'm getting at?'

Nestor said he hadn't the foggiest idea what he was talking about and Carlos had to make a special effort to explain a point only fully understood by people who constantly deal with large groups of strangers.

'What I mean, if you'll listen for a minute instead of looking at me like I was a lunatic, what I mean is that, however important these people you're serving are, when you're trying to remember who's who, you don't remember their names or their faces, not even if they're film stars or government ministers. It's some insignificant detail that tells them apart. A gold tooth, a tell-tale scar left by one too many visits to the plastic surgeon, whatever . . . sometimes it's a piece of jewellery, an old Cameo, for instance. It's not as if you're looking for these details, but something just catches your eye. And if you happen to see one of them in the street later on, you won't recognize their face, but you'll be thinking to yourself: Look, there's that woman with the arthritic fingers and blood-red nails who will only drink vodka and lemon . . . And the fat man with the wart on his neck? He's the one who asked me for matches to light his cigar – those moist lips were made for smoking big cigars. Do you see what I mean now, Nestor? For me, people come in pieces, eye-catching details that sum up their personalities. It's one of the things you discover as a waiter, and then, of course, you start doing it in your private life too. I suppose that's why I've started thinking about her again . . .'

Nestor stopped stirring, and pricked up his ears at these last words.

'Her?'

Carlos carried on. He wasn't consciously sharing a secret with his friend, it was more like talking to himself.

'Not that I ever stopped, I mean there were days when I thought about her all the time, but the problem now is, since starting this job, when I look at a woman's hands, I keep thinking they're *her* hands, or I stare at the neckline of a woman I've never seen before because it looks like *her* neckline. Nestor, have I ever told you about the woman in the painting?' he asked. 'No, I suppose not. I haven't told you or anyone else for that matter. Well, I'm not going to start now. There's no point.'

Nestor was silent. He kept stirring the syrup, but one more cherry soaked in cognac was all the prompting Carlos would need to launch into the story of a very old secret, a secret that went right back to his childhood.

5

i. The Woman in the Painting

'Can you imagine . . . ?' said Carlos, feeling he had found the perfect introduction to his story. 'Can you imagine spending your whole life looking at mouths and lips, hoping to find a smile you've never seen? And if I told you I spent all my working hours, and the rest of my time for that matter, looking out for things like a shadow falling across a woman's neck or the curve of an earlobe, you'd think I was mad, wouldn't you? But I keep a special eye out for details like that absolutely everywhere I go.'

'Come on, Carletto,' said Nestor in response to this outpouring. 'It's all right; don't be ashamed. Some of the things that go through our minds seem totally insane, but there's no room for nonsense in the book of Fate, if you see what I mean, Carletto.'

Carletto didn't see at all, and he didn't understand why Nestor's curious accent kept coming and going, shifting from Spanish to Neapolitan and back again, depending on his mood and what he was saying. Alone with Nestor on that fateful afternoon, in the kitchen at Mulberry & Mistletoe, having finally resolved to tell his story, Carlos didn't give a hoot (as Nestor would have put it) about his friend's wandering accent. It could roam the whole world over for all he cared. He was too busy finding the right words to tell the story of an old obsession, one that went back almost to his birth.

Carlos began to explain why it was for many years now, but especially in the last few months, he had been haunted by the image of a woman, and why a pair of adolescent lips could have such a hypnotic effect on him – he'd stop whatever he was doing and follow their curve, or perhaps it wasn't so much the lips themselves as the smile that played on them, for the mouth that obsessed him was always smiling. In his mind's eye he could also see a pair of rather inexpressive blue eyes, neither cold nor still, just absent. Then the hair, platinum blond, and tied back so you could just make out the shape of an unadorned ear. And, further down, the shoulders where his gaze could have lingered for ever had it not been drawn immediately away by the hands, so different from each other: the right hand, serenely held with fingers apart, as if they were about to alight gracefully on a veranda rail; while the left was holding something close to her chest: a little sphere, a jewel or some sort of cameo, intensely green in colour.

It was, of course, a portrait he was describing. A painting of a woman Carlos knew nothing about: a painting that had always lived in his grandmother's flat in Madrid. He had only been there twice before the flat became his as part of an inheritance. On his third visit, not long before joining Nestor's staff, a mass of childhood memories had come flooding back.

When no-one is around any more to report what actually happened, family secrets stay hidden. Only the walls could have explained why Carlos's grandmother and his father hardly ever spoke to one another. Father and son lived far from Madrid, in a small town near the Portuguese border. Carlos's father, Ricardo, was a quiet and content family doctor, who had drifted through life without causing any disturbance apart from the inevitable flutter provoked by a handsome doctor in a white coat. The grandmother, Teresa, was Ricardo's wife's mother. His wife, Carlos's mother, was called Soledad. She had been dead for many years.

In fact, Carlos was not yet four when his mother died, and that was so long ago now that all he could remember of her was the *ching ching* of her bangles, a sound that should have been cheerful but wasn't. In his memory it was accompanied by words that he was never sure he had actually heard, they could easily have been part of a bank of early memories fabricated in hindsight from what other people had told him. In any case, he associated the *ching ching* of the bangles with a voice whispering in his ear: 'Carlitos, give your mother another kiss, she's going on a trip. Another kiss, darling.' That was all. His memory had not retained a single detail of her face. Soledad was faceless. It would have been simple enough for the obliging fabricator of false memories in all of us to restore her features, one by one, since Carlos kept several framed photographs of his mother in his sitting room. Some of the frames were wooden, others silver plate. And on each frame was inscribed a name, a date and a place: 'Soledad, San Sebastián, 1976', 'Soledad, Galicia, 1977', and so on, up to the most recent: 'Soledad at her parents' house, 1978.' She always had the same smile, but the person Carlos saw in those photos was not at all like him, since his mother's hair was very dark, and her straight, attractive eyebrows were darker still. Ricardo Garcia turned up in some of the photos too (though he was never in the inscriptions), always standing or sitting near his wife. Those photos showed Soledad with a calm expression. 'Soledad, San Sebastián, 1976', for example, had them in summer clothes, sharing a beer, while in 'Soledad, Galicia, 1977', they were laughing, arm in arm, in their own little world, while a woman to their right looked like she was trying to get out of the picture. Any one of these images could have provided him with a false memory, or at least a face to go with the tinkling of the bangles or the cloudy recollection of a voice asking for a kiss. Despite all of this, he could only remember sounds, a voice perhaps, but definitely no face.

Apart from the sitting room with its reverently displayed photographs, the house in which Carlos had lived with his father had all the virtues and vices of an exclusively male household. When a father of a young son loses his wife, he usually looks for some way to fill the gap she has left. Either he marries again or, sooner or later, he ends up delegating the more tedious domestic tasks to a female relative, a sister or a second cousin, who looks after the day-to-day running of the household and occasionally resurrects the memory of the departed wife, sometimes with fondness, other times not. So the legacy of the deceased woman lives on in her house, rekindled by her female successor. But this is not what took place in the Garcia household.

It was clear from the start that Ricardo Garcia was not going to follow convention. He never showed the slightest desire to remarry (although he did become almost conjugally fond of eau de vie and, later, anisette) and was quick to reject the offers of two distant cousins who would have been only too happy to help him out. He mourned Soledad in a very private and undemonstrative way: by building up a collection of framed photographs.

In the end, the housekeeping problems were solved quite simply by hiring help. As soon as Carlos was old enough, he was packed off to boarding school, and the chores were taken care of by local girls who came in to cook, change the sheets and give the rooms a quick dust. So, little by little, all feminine traces were wiped away from Carlos's life, including the living memory of his mother. The dead are all too easily reduced to anonymous photographs that grow dim in their frames on the mantelpiece unless a special love or hate exists to keep them alive.

Quite a different fate, however, awaited the girl with long fingers and blond hair whose portrait hung in Carlos's grandmother's flat. Perhaps it was because, unlike his mother, this girl did have a face. He remembered precisely how he had discovered her. What's more, he could relive every detail of the scene. It was his earliest childhood memory, and there could be no doubt that it was genuine, and certainly not constructed afterwards from other people's stories. It must have happened just as he remembered, because no adult would have bothered to tell him about it. Only children are interested in such things.

He was sitting on the floor, playing, tracing the arabesques in the carpet with his finger, when suddenly unfamiliar feet approached and a pair of hands put a painting down against the wall beside him: an oil painting of a young woman with blond hair. A few moments later, the same hands put another picture next to the portrait, but it was much less interesting: a drawing of what appeared to be a tree or maybe several trees. In any case, it disappeared soon afterwards. It was lifted up and hung high on the wall, just where the blonde lady had been previously, in a spot so high up that Carlos had never been able to see her before.

But now he was face to face with her . . . and those blue, indifferent eyes were smiling at him. He could have put out his hand and touched that deliciously white hand, delicately grasping something in its fingers. His contemplation was interrupted by murmuring voices engaged in a long, unintelligible conversation. He looked up briefly but without properly tuning in, fascinated as he was by the strange picture in his eyeline from the carpet, in a world where young women with long fingers and smiling blue eyes are unknown and only the seamy underside of the adult world is visible: chair and table legs, heating pipes, a cobweb beyond the reach of the fussiest feather duster, and the feet of those who move in the grown-up world above, disdainful feet that seemed to be pointing at the picture of the girl, and women's shoes standing on tip-toe as if to stress a point, or so it seemed. Meanwhile there she was, with her curious smile and her look of indifference. It didn't seem to bother her at all being down there on the ground, a talking point for so many opinionated feet.

A few minutes later she vanished. This time four arms and as many unfamiliar hands – strong, fortunate hands – reached down to the young woman and hoisted her up into the adult world, and out of his sight.

If Carlos had finally worked out that he had first seen the portrait in February 1982, it was because a few days later something else happened, something which, unlike that fateful meeting, had since been overlaid with a multitude of false memories: he learnt of his mother's death. Despite the gravity of the event, he could not for the life of him visualize the scene. Soledad had died unexpectedly, a long way away, on a trip to South America. So there was no agonizing illness to remember, no corpse to kiss goodbye, not even a funeral, or if there had been one, someone had decided it would be better for such a young child not to be present. Some sensitive soul had spared him the sight of his mother disappearing under a pile of white flowers, and spadefuls of earth thumping on the wood of the coffin. Spared him the Our Fathers. And the Hail Marys.

But Carlos did remember the days that followed, a short week that felt more like a century, crammed as it was with memories, some true, some false, none of them pleasant. Moist kisses from strangers and anonymous, pitying voices saying, 'Poor thing.' Such a weight of tears, the wailing and sighing. Then the trip back to the village, just him and his father: the end of an era. For Carlos, who was less than four years old, it seemed like the end of childhood. Remembering his cousins, whom he had met briefly at his grandmother's flat during the days of mourning, and all his friends from the village, he supposed he must now be an adult, and he was sure nothing so grown-up had happened to any of them.

Years went by before his second encounter with the woman in the painting, though just how many was hard to say. Carlos knew it occurred during Holy Week, but was he seven, eight, nine or ten when he went to Madrid that holiday? He did not know. What he did know was that his father was overseas at the time, and that was why he'd spent those weeks at his grandmother's flat. His father hardly ever left the village; it must have been the first time he'd gone away since the tragic trip to South America with Soledad. For the first few years after her death, when Carlos was younger, Ricardo never mentioned the long journey that had taken him and his wife to Uruguay, Argentina and Chile, but suddenly, around the time of Carlos's second visit to his grandmother's flat, he began to talk about it more often, especially when he had a few more spirits than usual. On such occasions (Carlos particularly remembered a long conversation on the train to Madrid) Ricardo would go over everything he and Soledad had done in Buenos Aires: the places they had visited together, how happy she'd been, and so on, in great detail, all recounted with a strange, almost pedantic insistence that Carlos would only begin to understand many years later when he had grown up and learnt to deal with his own unwelcome memories. He realized then that his father's insistence had been motivated by a secret desire to wear down that painful part of his past, as if he were compulsively putting on the same article of clothing day after day, unconsciously hoping it would soon fall apart, at which point he would consign it to a box to be forgotten without further thought for ever.

As to the exact dates of Carlos's second visit to his grandmother's flat, if he had asked his father (which he had not done and could not do now), perhaps he would have been told that the visit had taken place in April 1986, when he was just eight years old. Eight: the age of exploration, of ghosts and secret forays; when mysteries lurk behind every curtain and every wardrobe opens into a magical world, when you may enter at any moment, but who knows when you will ever return.

His grandmother's flat was especially rich in untold mysteries.

It was only many years later that Carlos would come to wonder why his father had been barred from entering the flat that day, and why, instead of kissing her son-in-law, Grandma Teresa had rather coldly touched his arm. But that was grown-up stuff, and he was busy with mysteries of his own.

And there were so many secrets to uncover in that flat.

For a start, you could see straight away that it belonged to someone rich, quite the opposite of all the houses Carlos had ever known: his father's lonely house and the homes of all his friends, that smelled of boiled vegetables and were badly in need of a coat of paint. Nothing like this flat at Number 38, Calle de Almagro, with its huge windows and high ceilings. Number 38, his grandmother would call it, talking about it as though it were a person.

'Be good, Carlos. I'll come and pick you up as soon as I get back.'

'Yes, Dad.'

'Eat all your food and try to get up a bit earlier on Sunday.'

'Yes, Dad. Of course, Dad.'

'Listen to your grandmother and do what she tells you . . .'

Addressing herself directly to Carlos and deliberately ignoring his father, Teresa said: 'Let's get one thing straight, young man: at Number 38, you'll have a siesta every afternoon,' at which point Carlos looked her in the eyes for the first time.

And then a thought occurred to him, or rather, a fledgling thought began to develop over the few days they spent together: Grandma Teresa was just like her flat, full of corners. Both were large and angular, both had unexpected nooks and crannies. People are a lot like their houses, at least from a child's point of view, so Carlos soon came to identify his grandmother's moods with the various rooms at Number 38, which varied in appearance depending on whether the doors to the corridor were open or shut, and whether it was raining or dark outside. Some sunny mornings, for instance, Grandma Teresa seemed to resemble her dressing room, and when you came to think of it, they both smelled of lavender. His grandmother seemed so fragile, the deep darkness of her eyes offset by the almost metallic blondness of her hair. And the dressing room corresponded to her perfectly: its walls were a pale ochre, contrasting with the darkness of the two windows, which were always kept shut. But at night a hard gleam came into his grandmother's eyes, banishing any hint of fragility. At such moments, Carlos thought she was like the entrance hall: a damask-hung tunnel, and predominantly red. Yet all these childish impressions were like preparatory sketches for a fuller picture: Grandma Teresa in perfect communion with the decor of her yellow sitting room.

Teresa spent most of her time in that round room, with its one window opening onto a balcony and a stretch of sky, not always blue. She hardly entertained any visitors there, but would sit alone with a vague smile on her face playing solitaire by the fireplace, ignoring Carlos, hardly even glancing up from her cards when he came in to kiss her. Rather than look at him, she seemed to lose herself in the contemplation of a dull painting on the opposite wall – a landscape with a tree – while her elongated fingers placed a jack on a queen, then a seven on an eight . . . all the while saying not a word to her grandson. But that, as Carlos soon discovered, was the best thing about his grandmother and her yellow room: they were both remote but still gentle. Only around three o'clock did they liven up briefly: the room would light up with watery afternoon sunlight and without fail Grandma Teresa would intone a stern refrain: 'As you well know, young man, here at Number 38, you have a siesta.'

And it was during the siesta one day, as Carlos was investigating the contents of a room at the back of the house, that he once again encountered the young woman in the painting, only to be caught a few minutes later by Nelly, the maid. The siesta was an ideal time for escapades and secret exploration, and Carlos had been making the best of it for several afternoons when, quite by chance, he came upon the portrait of a woman he remembered only too well from his first visit to the flat. But now the painting wasn't in the sitting room, or in any other room, and Carlos would never have found it had he not heard Nelly's steps approaching and tried to hide in a wardrobe. There it was, among various dusty bits and pieces, barely visible, half covered by a blanket. Just then Nelly opened the door of the cursed wardrobe, but she could scold him and yell at him all she liked. Filled with a strange new sensation, he was busy removing the blanket to reveal the woman's bust. Before Nelly could extract him forcibly – 'Naughty boy! Get out of there, you little devil!' – and get hold of his ear – 'Don't you think you can run away from me' – he managed to reach out and stroke that dust-covered neck. His fingers slid down to the neckline of the black-and-white dress, a little further down, and then to the right to touch those long, slender fingers holding a greenish sphere. 'Just you wait till your grandmother finds out what you've been doing during siesta-time, you stupid child,' shouted Nelly. While he was being told off, the woman in the painting seemed to be watching him with her blue eyes, as though heartily amused by it all. And that's what gave him the courage to stand up to Nelly, stick out his tongue and yell with fearless insolence: 'Stupid? You're the stupid one, Nelly. Stupid Nelly! Smelly Nelly! I've been a good boy.'

All the same, what he had done must have been very wrong indeed, because from that day on, the door of the room at the back of the house was kept securely locked, and his grandmother wouldn't hear a word about the portrait, not even when he came into the yellow room and found her smiling at the particularly happy result of a game of solitaire. Are you listening, Grandma? Please, Grandma . . . But the most he managed to get out of her one day was: 'You're quite mistaken, young man. A woman in a wardrobe? What *are* you talking about? There's no such thing in this flat.' And she smiled again at an ace of hearts, or maybe it was a king of clubs, but the smile disappeared as she added: 'If you keep on about these bad dreams, I'll have to tell Nelly not to give you stew at lunch time. Besides, with this lovely warm weather we're having, it must be time for summer food, and salads.'

That was the only time Carlos ever heard his grandmother give instructions about the running of the household, except regarding the siesta, which continued to be obligatory at Number 38. Curiously, it was thanks to that much-resented nap that Carlos, after first coming upon the portrait, was to make a second great discovery. He learned that during the siesta, a boy may be visited by a peculiar sort of dream from which he will awake all hot and bothered, breathing heavily, and with a strange warm feeling between his thighs that will disappear much too quickly, like the fleeting image of three long, very white fingers, holding what? Carlos didn't know, but perhaps he would be able to glimpse it in his next dream, and perhaps he might be able to caress that blond hair too, which sometimes made him think of other hair, but whose? Was it Nelly's? His grandmother's? There were so many mysteries, too many, and yet, at the age of eight, there were still important lessons to be learnt.

Such as how to keep your mouth shut.

Thirteen years later, his grandmother was dead. The deep-red entrance hall, the ochre dressing room, the yellow sitting room and everything at Number 38 now belonged to him. He didn't inherit any money, not a bean; all those years of solitaire and keeping up appearances must have eaten up all her savings. Since that Easter holiday long ago, Carlos had turned into the sort of young man he had always shown signs of becoming as a child: more interested in dreams than reality, more often to be found at the cinema than at school (though, in his own way, he was a conscientious pupil – he repeated his first year of law three times). In fifteen years, he had grown as tall as his father, and had developed the same dark, slightly wasted look, as if fate had used him for an experiment: take the look and bearing of a typical nineteenth-century hero and put him in a pair of Levi's. He had curly hair, long sideburns, and skin so pale you could see blue veins on his temples. His father's nurse once said to him: 'If you'd been born in the last century, you'd have made a great Hussar.' She might not have known much about military history, but she had seen a lot of historical romances on television. But the nurse had moved on, her services were no longer required. It would have eased Doctor Garcia's mind to know that Teresa had left the flat in Madrid to him and his son, but he had already been dead ten months when the will was opened.

All Carlos had to do now was move permanently to Madrid and take possession of Number 38. How he wished his father could have been there with him; no-one would have kept him at the door this time, or given him an icy welcome and a reluctant embrace. But Carlos moved out of the village on his own. When he got to Madrid he discovered his inheritance was in a sadder state than he had anticipated. Everything was covered up with white sheets: the old beds, all the furniture and fittings he had seen on his last visit. In all those years, no-one had been bothered to change a thing. Not even the ashtrays had moved; as if they were held in place by the will of the departed, as if the whole house were a derelict tomb. Carlos, however, was not bothered about the furniture. Like a little boy loose at siesta-time again, armed with his grandmother's bunch of keys, he went hunting for the forbidden door, and then the wardrobe, and there she was, just as before, the woman in the painting, wide-eyed among piles of useless junk. Carlos lifted up the portrait just as those anonymous hands had done almost twenty years before. He carried it to the yellow room and put it back where it belonged, in a space usurped for so long by the landscape with trees his grandmother had always stared at while playing cards. It was only then that he fully realized what the inheritance meant. Number 38 was now all his. There was nothing valuable in the flat, but that didn't matter: after the sale he would have far more money at his disposal than ever before. Until then, he said to himself, it was just a matter of being careful and finding a part-time job that wasn't too demanding so that he would have time to continue with his Law degree (in theory, at least). And while he was looking for a buyer, he could live there and take time to discover all its secrets.

'So let me get this straight, *cazzo* Carlitos,' said Nestor in the kitchen at Mulberry & Mistletoe, interrupting his employee at this point in the story, while a copper pan full of cherry syrup came perilously close to boiling over. Carlos's confession had been so long in the telling that Nestor felt he was losing the thread, and was forced to stir the syrup backwards, something you should never do, unless you want your morello cherries to turn sour. 'You have just moved to Madrid after inheriting a flat, but there's no way you can afford to maintain it. And to complicate matters, you don't know anyone here, but you're having a romance with a woman who lives in a wardrobe. Is that it?'

'Oh come on, Nestor!'

'What you're telling me about is an unexpected inheritance, a childhood dream, a delirious romance . . . You sound like a typical wide-eyed country boy who's just arrived in the big city. Seriously, next you'll be telling me you're going to see this mysterious woman while out walking the dog in the Retiro park, or eating a hamburger at McDonald's. The vapours from that cherry syrup must have gone to your head, eh Carlitos?'

'I know I'll never meet her, I'm not that stupid. But I

swear I keep finding *pieces* of her everywhere,' said Carlos.

And then he had to explain all over again that since joining Mulberry & Mistletoe, he had realized how working as a waiter allowed him to gather together fragments of his lost love: the ivory skin revealed by one woman's low-cut dress, another woman's engaging smile . . . and that was enough. After all, he didn't know who the woman in the painting was, when she had lived, whether she was even a real person or just an artist's idealized image. For Carlos, these were insoluble mysteries.

Alcohol, however, was working its old magic, and Nestor, who was normally so careful, was feeling its effects as well. Once he reached a certain degree of tipsiness, the chef's attitude changed unexpectedly. 'This business with your ideal woman,' he said in an impetuous rush, 'I'll let you sort that out for yourself, but there are such things as omens, and that's the bit I'm interested in: the twists and turns of destiny.' Then, lowering his voice as if he were about to pronounce a strange spell, he added: 'Come on, Carlos, don't tell me you wouldn't like to find out who that woman was. Why don't we try? It's all so romantic, this search for her features in other women. But don't you think it's pretty silly when you could be looking for the real thing?'

'But I actually *see* her features,' said Carlos, who was as drunk as his boss. 'Don't forget I own her now, and I can look at her every day if I want to, even if I'll never know who she is or why she is holding that green jewel.'

Nestor, however, had something more practical in mind than the worship of a picture. He whispered to his friend what it was, finishing off with a reassuring pat on the shoulder, as if to say: *Forza*, Carletto, we've had a bit of cognac and a few cherries, sure, but that story of yours is a gem. So listen, don't you worry: I know a way of finding out family secrets when there's no-one left to ask . . .

5

ii. The Gentleman with a Crew Cut.

'I got one question for you, man – and don't you be lying to me now. What time you seeing Madame Longstaffe?'

The Rastafarian, who had been leaning against the Japanese screen cleaning his nails for hours, eyed Nestor suspiciously, while Carlos emerged with a jolt from his daydream.

'Wouldn't be five o'clock, would it?' he asked with a challenging air. 'Cos I'm telling you now: that's when she is seeing *me*.'

As he said 'me' he pointed to his chest, visible in the opening of his skin-tight shirt, with one long fingernail. Carlos seized upon it with his waiter's eye. Had he come across this character again in the street, he might not have recognized his dreadlocks or his teeth, which were disconcertingly white given the general squalor of his appearance, but he would certainly have recognized the single long fingernail.

'At five, it's my turn, man. Five o'clock on de dot.'

Nestor beamed him a charming smile and told him not

to worry, it was quite all right, their appointment was for five-thirty and they were happy to wait. No problem, man.

The Rastafarian smiled back and was about to resume his position in front of the Japanese screen when he was blocked by a very nervous gentleman who, on emerging from Madame Longstaffe's room, had gone past the exit onto the street and walked straight into the waiting room by mistake.

He stopped abruptly, looking to his right and left, first at the lady on the sofa, then at the lady by the window. He seemed relieved not to know either one of them. Nor was he bothered by the Rastafarian, but he was noticeably taken aback when he caught sight of Nestor.

'Goodbye, Mr Tous,' said the chef, as if he knew him vaguely, but the man beat such a hasty retreat that all Carlos could recall later was his air of respectability and his grey crew cut.

'Be patient, Carlitos,' said Nestor with a sigh, referring not to the fleeting appearance of that short-haired gentleman, but to the leisurely pace at which Madame Longstaffe was conducting her divinatory skills. It was already a quarter to six and there were still three clients ahead of them in the queue, including their Rastafarian friend. 'We'll just have to be patient,' he said, before lapsing again into the tranquil hush he had felt ever since entering the clairvoyant's house. So Carlos went back to pondering what his friend had said to him while the cherry syrup was simmering:

'Yes, yes, this story of yours is a-very romantico' (Nestor's accent seemed to become more Italian with each liqueur-soaked cherry) 'but like I tell you: getting nostalgic about some woman who doesn't exist, falling in love with a ghost and looking for her face in other women, this is a-crazy, Carlos, and not at all practical. Let me tell you my theory, Carletto. It's much more logical. Obsessions like this always foreshadow something, you see what I mean? That woman in the picture isn't a real girl, and even if she is, what do you care? She's probably dead, or if she's alive she's an old woman by now. But if you're so fascinated by this picture, it must mean that somewhere there's a woman just like her, exactly the same, and you know what?' shouted Nestor, who was quite worked up by this point. 'We are going to find her!'

Then he declared that he knew a way of finding out old family secrets and summoning up characters from childhood fantasy. It was very simple, he said, all they had to do to solve this mystery was to pay a visit to Madame Longstaffe, the famous clairvoyant.

Yet as soon as he had made this statement, and in spite of his tipsiness, Nestor Chaffinch started back-pedalling, as if fear had suddenly sobered him up.

'You know I'm joking, don't you, Carlos? It's a silly idea, consulting a clairvoyant. All that stuff about the spirit world, it's a load of rubbish . . . just forget I ever mentioned it, all right? You're not going to tell me you believe in witches now as well as ghosts, are you? Look, no spell has ever been able to turn a fantasy woman like yours into living flesh and blood, honestly . . . No, don't insist, I'm not coming with you. It's a scam, the whole thing. I don't believe in spells. They're fakes and con-artists all of them . . . and what makes it really dangerous is they're all so devilishly *cunning*. And Madame Longstaffe is the worst of all, believe me . . .'

Maybe the cherries were to blame. Maybe there's something too irresistible about a good romance. Or maybe there was another reason for Nestor's sudden capitulation, one that can't be revealed just yet. In any event, Carlos finally did overcome his friend's reluctance. And so there they were, the two of them, waiting their turn in that confined aquamarine room. And that was why Nestor had been so forceful with Carlos when they first arrived.

'*Cazzo* Carlitos, you're the one who insisted on coming to see this witch, so that's what we're going to do, but be warned: I take no responsibility for whatever happens as a result.'

6

What the Clairvoyant Saw

Madame Longstaffe, lying flopped on a *chaise-longue*, addressed them in her thick Brazilian accent: 'I'm so tired, young man, completely *exowsted*.' Naturally: it was past eight-thirty and she had been drawing on all her reserves of human and esoteric energy to light the way for four very hard cases (especially the mysterious woman who remained by the window, a truly *exowsting* client), and all that effort had knocked her flat, as Nestor and Carlos could see from where they stood in the doorway, not daring to enter. Only her legs were visible, wrapped in fine green muslin, resting delicately crossed on the *chaise*, while her feet, encased in slippers that would have provoked the envy of a Venetian Doge, quivered intermittently.

'What a frightful afternoon! Come in, gentlemen. I'll see to you in a few moments.'

But she didn't stir. Carlos and Nestor crept in and sat down on two chairs at the back of the room, next to the bureau from where the fortune-teller plied her trade. And an imposing pair of thrones they were; the short-legged Nestor was left with his feet dangling. Just as well: a few seconds later, a small fluffy white dog appeared and began to manifest a lively interest in the chef's ankles. Quite a fixation, to judge from the way he was barking and molesting them, while Nestor, having recoiled into the chair, didn't know whether it was better to wait out the siege or shut the mutt up with a well-aimed kick.

'*Fri-Fri, tais-toi,*' said Madame Longstaffe from the *chaise-longue*, then 'Sit!' and '*Raus*!' Her polyglot performance would no doubt have greatly impressed the two friends, had they not been busy giving each other knowing looks while conducting a silent dialogue that might have run something like this: 'Nestor, did you hear what she called that fluff-ball?' 'I'm afraid I did: Fri-Fri, son of Fru-Fru, no doubt.' 'Poor animal! Thank God they have no idea of the awful things going on around them . . . I mean, can you imagine?' 'I agree, I agree, don't start me: just the thought of having one of my relatives (my father, maybe) mummified and stuck on top of an alabaster column with a name-plate . . .' 'And knowing you might end up like that yourself one day.' 'It's shocking, isn't it?' 'Isn't it just?'

And they concluded their telepathic conversation with a mutual shudder.

The memory of the stuffed Maltese terrier in the aquamarine waiting room prompted them to look around and find that the room they had entered was a splendid example of the inimitable Longstaffe style of interior decoration. It was dimly lit by a single Bloomsbury lamp, but what little light there was permitted them to make out various dead animals, watching them with blind, glass eyes from a series of display cases: one or two large iguanas, what appeared to be an owl, a vixen with a glaucous stare, and no doubt other witnesses to Madame's love affair with taxidermy. But before they had a chance to inspect the rest of the glass cases, they were cut short by the clairvoyant, who rose (not without a good deal of effort) from her divan and came towards them, with outstretched hands.

'Good evening, gentlemen.'

The most interesting thing about the famous fortune-teller was not her impressive mass of blond hair, or the tunic of transparent green muslin in which she was wrapped, or even her height, nearly six feet, but another characteristic altogether, one which neither of them noticed straight away.

'It's up to you,' she said, in a lilting Brazilian accent completely at odds with her distinctly Germanic appearance. 'What would you like: shells, tarot cards or crystal ball?' And as she said 'crystal ball' she swivelled her head around so that on seeing her front-on for the first time, Carlos noticed how much she resembled the Marbella socialite Countess Gunilla von Bismarck.

'So, what's it to be?' she asked snappily, wearied perhaps by how her appearance always made strangers gawp. 'I don't have all night, you know, and I'm too *exowsted* for the shells, so take your pick, sir: tarot or crystal ball.'

Then, seeing Carlos hesitate, she added, more sweetly: 'All the ways of fortune-telling are pretty much the same in the end, you know. I have an eclectic method, so you can choose whichever way you prefer, only don't take too long about it.'

'I just don't know . . .' Carlos said slowly. 'Maybe the cards—'

But he didn't get to finish the sentence, because Nestor, who had decided to take matters in hand, launched into a concise and accurate summary of the story of the woman in the picture, to which Madame Longstaffe listened in attentive silence, interrupting only now and then to say 'What a charming story!' or 'How delightful!' or sometimes '*Que beleza*.' She had picked up the Maltese terrier and put it on her lap. She stroked its head as the story unfolded, and when Nestor was through, she sighed and twisted around to the left as if she were looking for something in one of the desk drawers.

As she did this, Carlos noticed something very odd about the fortune-teller, a quality quite unique among human beings: Madame Longstaffe's face had two completely different aspects. Now, for example, looking down, with her hair pulled back, she no longer resembled Gunilla von Bismarck. A sudden and unaccountable metamorphosis had transformed her into the spitting image of Malcolm McDowell: a nasty shock for Carlos, who had recently seen *A Clockwork Orange* on television. He did a double take and stared incredulously, but there it was, that terrifying face – all that was missing were the stiletto and the single false eyelash under the left eye – and it belonged to Madame Longstaffe, who was rummaging intently through the drawers of her desk. Then she found what she was looking for (a pile of well-worn cards), and turned back to face them: Gunilla von Bismarck again, a much more comforting sight.

'To cut a long story short, madame,' said Nestor, who had broken the awkward silence by repeating the end of his little speech, 'that's why we came to see you. Like I said, the boy doesn't really need a tarot reading to find out about his future. What he needs is a love potion, you know what I mean, some kind of spell that will help him find a woman like the one in the picture, or one as much like her as possible. I know it sounds mad, but I've been told, madame, that you can work wonders.'

'Have you now? And what exactly have you been told?' asked the clairvoyant, interrupting sharply, as a look of fear flashed across her Barbie doll's face (if one can imagine an ageing Germanic Barbie doll). 'You seem to know a great deal about all sorts of people. Too much, if you ask me . . .'

Nestor smiled, reaching out across the bureau to the soothsayer's arm and complimenting her. But then his grip tightened, as if to express something that good manners forbade him from putting into words.

'All right, all right, as you wish,' replied Madame Longstaffe, caught off guard and unaccustomed to such treatment from her clients. 'Forgive me, I don't want to be a busy-body, but . . . but,' she added, suddenly more animated, swivelling her head again so that she looked like Malcolm McDowell once more, 'there's something I want to tell you, and it won't take long. Just forget about the boy for a minute. Let's talk about you: I think I can see something happening, something you should know about.'

Before Nestor's menacing grip could tighten again on the fortune-teller's arm, she continued in the same tone of voice: 'You're suffering from an incurable disease. It's been diagnosed, hasn't it? Cancer, yes? Well, you'll be glad to know that you're not going to die of—'

At this point Nestor began tapping firmly on Madame Longstaffe's arm, as if he were sending a threatening message in Morse code, and it must have read something like this: 'For God's sake shut up, you old witch, don't say another word,' because she pulled her arm away in surprise, as if one of her stuffed birds had pecked at it.

Yet only a few seconds later, like a boy scout, honour-bound to tell the truth in all circumstances, the two-faced fortune-teller added: 'At least let me warn you, sir. Are you sure you wouldn't like to have a little chat about the state of your lungs, or the perils of cool rooms and stacking chocolate truffles? And dessert recipes? What about a little moleskin notebook? No? You're not curious about that either?'

The old bat's totally lost the plot, thought Carlos, though of course he didn't say a word.

If Nestor sent another message in Morse code, Carlos missed it, because Fri-Fri's yapping and licking distracted him, and the next thing he heard, a few seconds later, was: 'Very well, there's no point in trying to help someone who simply refuses to listen. Anyway,' and now she seemed very tired again, '*isso não é comigo* – why should I care? It's getting late, so let's wrap this up: now then, what can I give this young man?' Then she began delving in her drawers again with a professional air of authority.

This time Carlos didn't find the metamorphosis so striking. He must have been mistaken before, when he thought the old woman could transform her face with a sudden turn of her head, because now, with the tip of her tongue peeping out between her lips to show how hard she was concentrating, Madame Longstaffe still looked exactly like the Countess von Bismarck – not a trace of *Clockwork Orange*. Just as well.

'Here it is,' she said, rising from the depths of her drawers, enveloped in a cloud of dust that was anything but magic. '*Esta bom*,' she added as she sat up straight, and set on the table a tubular bottle the size of a little finger, which she then offered to Carlos, saying, 'Listen carefully, *filhinho*,' and instructed him to drink four drops every night of the full moon until the bottle was empty.

'And by the time you've finished the treatment, young man, things will be looking up: the spell will have taken effect. It's child's play, this one.'

'Really? Have you had a lot of cases like this?' asked Carlos.

Madame Longstaffe waved her green sleeves at him, wearily. 'You know, sweetie, if there's one thing I hate about this job, it's the monotony. It's so dull these days. When clients come with love problems, either they're after a spell to help them find the perfect match, or a spell for holding onto someone who's trying to escape. Of course every now and then something unusual does come up. Like someone who wants to blot out the memory of a terrible passion or an unspeakable desire,' said Madame Longstaffe with an absent look, as if she were not so much talking to clients as thinking aloud about the day's events. 'Did you see that very proper-looking gentleman who left just now, the one with his hair cut like a German soldier in the First World War? Well *he* was one out of the bag. He wants to rid his heart of an unwelcome urge,' she added (this inexcusable lapse of discretion can only have been caused by extreme fatigue) while stroking the fur on Fri-Fri's little head into the shape of a crew-cut. Then, realizing what she had said, she pulled herself up short. 'Enough of that, Marlene.' (Marlene? Was that the famous clairvoyant's name: Marlene Longstaffe?) 'All I meant to say is that there's not a lot of variety with these love problems, because you see, searching for the living image of your ideal woman, well, it's hardly very original, is it? But if that's what you want, darling, here it is. That'll be fifteen thousand pesetas, and now, if you don't mind, let's call it a night.'

That said, Madame Longstaffe rose from behind the bureau with a good deal more agility than before and flopped back into her *chaise-longue*, muttering something that was not so much a goodbye as an articulated sigh: 'Santa Maria, it's been a long, long day.'

But to judge from the slight Afro-Brazilian accent, she may have been addressing her faithful Fri-Fri rather than her clients.

Their visit had disturbed the quiet mystique of the fortune-teller's room. The noise of rummaging in drawers rattling with tiny bottles like the one Carlos had taken away had broken the ambience. But once Madame was comfortably re-ensconced in her *chaise-longue*, everything was just as it had been before.

The dim light of the Bloomsbury lamp . . . the glassy eyes of the animals . . . it was all so cosy. To linger there after their appointment was over would have been like profaning a church. But there's nothing quite so tempting as a little profanation, and Nestor just couldn't resist. He put a finger to his lips to stop his friend from speaking.

'Just a couple of minutes,' he hissed urgently, 'then we'll go, Carletto. It's not every day you get to observe a witch in her den, I'm telling you.'

'Hang on, you're the one who didn't want to have a bar of her prophecies.'

'That's right, I don't. I'm just curious to find out what witches do when no-one is watching them. She'll probably pull out a mobile and I bet she won't be ringing the Spirit World.'

The chef put his finger to his lips again. 'Shhh,' he said, 'just a couple more minutes.'

On the other side of the room, Fri-Fri had leapt up and made a hollow for himself in the folds of his mistress's tunic: it was a charming scene. Madame was lying stretched out and, just as before, all they could see were her legs, or, more precisely, her right foot, which, bare inside its slipper, was bobbing up and down in time with some imaginary music. Everything else was still. Her slipper, rubbing precariously against the edge of the *chaise-longue*, looked as if it might fall onto the carpet at any moment.

'Come on, let's go,' urged Carlos. 'This place is scaring me. What are we waiting for, anyway?'

Just then they saw Madame Longstaffe reach over to a small trestle table beside the *chaise* and pour herself a tiny cup of pleasantly scented tea, like a prostitute treating herself to a quintessentially bourgeois pleasure after an afternoon's work.

'Let's get out of here. That ugly little dog's going to sniff us out any minute now.'

But the dog remained oblivious.

The aroma of the tea quickly filled the room, wafting round the furniture, making Fri-Fri sneeze and Madame Longstaffe sing. She sang an old song that went '*Mamba umbé yamamabé*,' or something like that, in a mezzo-soprano well past its prime that grated on the ears of the two spies still lurking in the shadows. '*Omi mambambá, amba umbé yamamabé*,' she continued tunelessly. What with the song and the strong scent of the brew, for a moment Carlos thought he saw a glint of life in the eyes of a moth-eaten vixen in the glass case to his left. He gripped the witch's little bottle tighter – the last thing they needed was for him to drop it accidentally (or out of fright) and alert Madame Longstaffe, who was still sipping her tea from a cup so tiny she had already refilled it three times, as Carlos had noted. It was while she was pouring out the fourth cup that the fortune-teller began to speak. But at no point did she turn to face them, remaining supine on the *chaise*. All she did was make her Venetian slipper bob a little more vigorously, so that it seemed to have a life of its own, or at least to be speaking like a ventriloquist's doll: 'He who believes he is mortally ill shall not die by illness but by ice, and he who believes that words can kill should not keep them so close to his heart.'

Carlos looked at Nestor, who no longer seemed amused.

And then a laugh rang out and filled the room, coming not from the talking slipper but from the ventriloquist herself.

'I knew you couldn't just walk away,' she said out loud. 'Even those who say they don't believe in omens like you, Nestor, can't resist the temptation to find out what destiny has in store for them. Isn't that right? But destiny loves to play tricks on us . . .'

Madame Longstaffe was now sitting up on the *chaise-longue*, her legs folded beneath her so that her feet and the talking slippers were no longer in view. In that position, she looked like a legless torso or a talking figurehead attached to the prow of the *chaise*, cup of tea in hand.

'No, don't go yet,' she called to Nestor, as if she could read his thoughts. 'I want to leave you with just one piece of advice, and if you follow it, you'll be grateful to me, I assure you.'

'Sometimes it's better not to know what the future

holds, madame. Especially when you know there's nothing you can do about it.'

But the old woman insisted: 'Listen, all I will say is this: Nestor shall not die – do as you please, enjoy yourself, my friend, fall in love, write a scandalous novel, learn to play the bassoon, do whatever you like. But don't worry about your future, because Madame Longstaffe has seen it clearly: Nestor has nothing to fear until four Ts conspire against him.'

The chef tried to protest, but the witch, sitting up even straighter, held her little cup out in front of her as if all the world's mysteries were floating in it.

'You're suffering from an incurable disease, but that's not something you need worry about, I promise you.'

'All right, madame . . .'

'. . . too many coincidences,' she continued. 'For your luck to turn, four Ts would have to join forces, and that could never come to pass, could it? Although coincidences do occur, the gods are fond of practical jokes.'

Madame Longstaffe laughed again, and her small dog seemed to be laughing with her. Then she added: 'You shouldn't have hidden there behind the door.' She had stopped laughing. 'You really shouldn't have done that, you know. If what you were after was a love potion for our young friend, you'd have been better off going somewhere else. Any clairvoyant could have given you that, it's money for jam, but you wanted something else, didn't you? Yes, that's right, what you really wanted' (the Afro-Brazilian accent had come back in force, as if she were not a white fortune-teller at all but the Brazilian priestess Mae Senhora herself, or even Aspasia Guimarães do Pinto, the famous *Yarolixá* from Bahía, but without the imposing African aspect) 'what you wanted was to discover your destiny and now you have,' she said, bidding her clients good night with an impatient flick of her hand. 'Until that fourfold coincidence occurs, you have nothing to fear.'

'Four Ts,' she repeated, with a hooligan's street-wise air, 'Four Ts.' (Or was it teas?) 'What an evil brew.'

The voice might have belonged to Madame Longstaffe or Mae Senhora, or even Aspasia Guimarães do Pinto, but the face . . . it was definitely the face of Malcolm McDowell in *A Clockwork Orange*, no doubt about it this time. She even winked at them as she said, 'Nothing to fear.'

7

A Terrible Accident

Lying, deceitful, crafty, and the worst thing is, sometimes she's actually half right and that's what pulls you in, it makes you think all her predictions will come true. Despicable, cunning old witch, stealing people's hopes and dreams.

This is what Carlos was thinking as he knelt beside the body of his friend Nestor, while the Teldis' kitchen filled up with people and noise. Poor Nestor. There they all were, staring at him. Little Chloe Trias, in her bare feet and possibly naked under a large T-shirt with 'Pierce my tongue, not my heart' written on it. Behind her was Serafin Tous, a friend of the family, prudently keeping his distance, as if he were afraid the deceased might suddenly spring back to life like some kind of Lazarus. And there was Karel Pligh, too, trying to explain to the Teldis when and where he had found the chef. Beside him stood Adela – so beautiful, even at this hour of the morning, thought Carlos, with her freshly washed face and a knowing look in her bright eyes, as if none of this had come as a surprise to her – while

Mr Teldi listened impatiently to Karel's explanations, itching to take control of the situation. He was the boss, after all.

'All right, all right, let's calm down. There's been a terrible accident, that's all,' he said. 'In any case, we'll have to call the police. There's no way around that . . . May I borrow your pen? Where did you leave the telephone? As it's a holiday, they probably won't even answer. You can never rely on the military – I mean the police – it's the same all over the world.'

Teldi was talking with the phone in his hand, ready to dial, and tapping the lid of the pen on the kitchen table. The line was engaged. As he redialled, his gaze wandered over the table where he noticed a perfectly clean egg-whisk, a complete set of brand-new knives, and a copy of Brillat-Savarin with a dishcloth folded neatly on top of it, like a ceremonial cloth on a pagan altar. You had to admit the fellow was a first-class chef, he thought, and a bastard, an absolute bastard. Somehow this opinion had escaped from the confines of his dreams, but he locked it away again promptly and dialled: 0 . . . 9 . . . 1, then more quickly 091, maybe this time . . .

'Police? Are you ready to take this down? Ernesto Teldi speaking, I'm ringing from The Lilies on Oleander Road, number 10b. There's been an accident, no . . . nothing dramatic, I mean, it could have been much worse, it could have been a member of the family.'

While on the telephone, Teldi removed the dishcloth Karel Pligh had so carefully used to cover the copy of Brillat-Savarin, and as the conversation dragged on, and he was put on hold, and then switched from department to department, he rubbed the lid of the pen up and down on the book's cover. For a cookery book, he noticed, it was remarkably clean: not a spot of grease or a pastry crumb, clean as a missal.

'You what? You want the name of the house again? Oh, I see, the computer's being rather slow. It's called The Lilies, as in the flower.'

The lid of the pen was beginning to wander over the book's cover, tracing around the gilded letters, pressing into the leather's smooth furrows, before going over the side and down the edges of the pages, where it ran into something that was sticking out: the sheet of paper Karel Pligh had hidden in the book after finding Nestor's body.

'No, number 10*b* on Oleander Road. There's an *a* and a *b* and this is 10*b*, got it? That's right, it's off Rockrose Road . . .'

And Teldi toyed with the protruding sheet, plucking at it with his finger like a guitar string, but nobody was watching him. They had better things to do. Serafin Tous was suggesting someone open a window, while Chloe Trias shrugged her shoulders (after a pointed look from her boyfriend, Karel) and went upstairs to put on some trousers. Meanwhile, Adela was using the opaque glass of a window (the kindest of mirrors) to adjust her hair before glancing over at Carlos, who was the only one thinking about the dead man. He had removed his jacket to cover Nestor's face.

What a pity it isn't big enough to cover all of him, thought Carlos. Nestor's body, spread-eagled on the floor, seemed larger now, as if his limbs in thawing out had uncurled like the petals of a funerary flower. Even his fingers had opened, although his blue-stained right thumb was still very stiff. Poor Nestor, Carlos repeated again (it was becoming a litany). Perhaps, before the accident, he had used the pen Teldi was playing with to write something down in his notebook. Perhaps in the quiet of the small hours he had taken the time to jot down a few lines in that moleskin notebook he always carried with him. Where could he have left it? It must be around somewhere, on the kitchen table or near the stove. I'll have a look for it when Teldi gets off the phone, thought Carlos. He would have liked to keep it, as something to remember Nestor by.

'What?' fumed Ernesto Teldi. 'You don't know Rockrose Road either? I don't believe this. The village *idiot* knows where it is and you're telling me . . . Very well, young lady, it comes off the Coín-Ojén road, near the twenty-four-kilometre post . . . That's right, now we seem to be getting somewhere. What other information do you need? So you didn't get that down either? Well, I'll just have to tell you again, won't I? My name is Ernesto Teldi, no not Seldi, I said Teldi, T E L D I . . . yes, that's right, T for tortoise.'

Carlos looked at him with a sad smile: his tone of voice, the way he was carrying on, that pathetic sarcasm. It was just the sort of thing that would have made Nestor laugh.

Poor Nestor. He looked around the kitchen again, but he wasn't thinking about the notebook or Teldi. The others were right: there were more important things to do. Yet that voice filtered back into his thoughts, and it sounded almost as if Teldi the Spaniard had become Teldi the Argentine, improvising the lyrics to a weird sort of tango: 'Frozen to death, what a way to go. It's the luck of the draw, life's a bitch.'

Part Two

Six Days in March

Soothsayer: Beware the ides of March.
Caesar: He is a dreamer, let us leave him: pass.

William Shakespeare, *Julius Caesar*, Act 1, Scene 2

1

The First Day: Nestor's Notebook

A few weeks before Nestor's body was found in the Teldis' house, before Madame Longstaffe proffered her highly oracular (some might say fraudulent) prediction of the events that were to take place, the characters in this story were leading their separate lives, and it might have seemed unlikely that their paths would cross. 'Coincidences do occur,' Madame Longstaffe had said that afternoon when Carlos and Nestor went to see her, 'the gods are fond of practical jokes.' But that was just part of her witch's patter. Both Nestor and Carlos had soon forgotten what she had said. Not all of it, though: they remembered the spell for finding the woman in the picture, or her double, and although Carlos didn't carry out the instructions with all the recommended blind faith, he did take four drops of the prescribed love potion each full-moon night.

In any case, what with all the little tasks involved in the day-to-day running of Mulberry & Mistletoe, the rest of what they had heard that afternoon at Madame

Longstaffe's house was soon forgotten. And the management of the catering business was an unpredictable affair, with months of frenetic activity, especially in summer and spring, followed by months of dead calm, in February and March. There were only three permanent staff: Nestor, Carlos Garcia and Karel Pligh, the Czech body-builder. Chloe Trias had also recently joined the team – a rather eccentric extra hand perhaps, but also very economical, since she hadn't asked for any pay at all.

Mulberry & Mistletoe somehow managed to survive from peak season to peak season and through the months of hibernation (as Nestor called them), owing mainly to the owner's consummate skill for desserts and tarts, often bought up by famous Madrid restaurants and passed off as their own. But when business was slow and the telephone didn't ring, Nestor Chaffinch would pull down the metal grille over the shop-front muttering *porca miseria*, give his staff the afternoon off and sit there staring at the white tiles on the wall.

Everything was dazzlingly white at Mulberry & Mistletoe: a bright, well-located establishment consisting of two rooms. The kitchen at the rear was the main room. It was spacious and had good sunlight, with three windows looking onto the street, so that passers-by could see how spotless the food preparation area was. From outside you could see a large room lined wall-to-wall, including the benches, with white tiles, waiting to be transformed into a hive of creative activity. Copper pots and pans hung on one wall, and, laid out on the large stainless-steel table in the middle was an array of the finest kitchen accessories, each patiently waiting its turn, accompanied by a little instruction card. Cleanliness, order, impeccable hygiene: these were the fundamental principles of the realm of Nestor Chaffinch, a realm which extended to the smaller front room, used as a waiting room or reception area for clients. The ambience there was more Bohemian. Nestor, who had spared no expense in fitting out the premises, had decided to give the waiting room a certain *Ritorna a Sorrento* feel, or that, at least, is what he used to tell his clients. And although they didn't quite understand what he meant, they had the impression of having stepped into a scrupulously prepared theatre set, part Sicilian villa, part trattoria (minus the tables but still with a gastronomic feel) and, subliminally, the convivial atmosphere of the room set them off dreaming of the delicious things that might emerge from the adjoining kitchen. While the kitchen at Mulberry & Mistletoe was spotless, the waiting room was charming. While the back room was scented with raspberry syrup and one of those upmarket cleaning products named after a fairy, the front room smelt of the most expensive wood and metal polish. All expense was justified, given the quality of the furnishing. The waiting room was bedecked with knick-knacks and mementoes from exotic trips: a model ship with *Sole mio* inscribed on the poop deck, a poncho draped artlessly over a sofa for the clients, a collection of Murano glass paperweights over to the left, and over to the right a collection of seashells, a cluster of little boxes and pictures of saints. Watching over all of this was a sizeable collection of photo-portraits autographed by more or less famous people, more or less forgotten, and more or less dead, but all of whom had one thing in common: at least once in their lives they had enjoyed the marvels of Nestor Chaffinch's cooking.

The photos in the waiting room at Mulberry & Mistletoe smiled down from the walls at visiting clients (when there were any, that is; at the moment there were none). There was a photo of Aristotle Onassis inscribed with the words: '*Epharistos*, dear Nestor, *epharistos*, your Churchill sorbet is a splendid invention.' And one of Ray Ventura: 'Ah, *ton bavarois, mon cher, ça vaut bien mieux que d'attraper la scarlatine, dis donc*.' And Maria Callas: 'Bravo, Nestor, bra-vo!' Now *there* was someone who really appreciated my chocolate fondant, thought Nestor as he sat there alone in the afternoon, checking the accounts after his staff had gone home, faced with the evidence that February had been an even slower month than January. He put the calculator back in its case and sighed. Hopefully the good weather wouldn't be long coming, then the first communions would begin, and the outdoor parties, and soon it would be Easter (Callas loved the surprise of an Easter egg, and Nestor's eggs were quite exquisite) but Easter, alas, was still a good way off. '*Porca miseria*,' he muttered again.

It must have been at such a moment, while waiting optimistically for a customer and reminiscing about his favourite clients, that the idea came to him: he would write down a little compendium of culinary secrets in his moleskin notebook. At that point no-one even knew about it apart from the staff. In a tiny, impeccably neat hand, he began to write – three secrets per page, plus diagrams where necessary – and this is how the text began:

Little Indiscretions
(A Book of Culinary Secrets)

By Nestor Chaffinch, Master Pastry-Cook

Prologue

All around the world, chefs will tell you that there's no point in giving recipes, because it's not the recipe that makes the dessert, it's the chef's talent. You have to have 'a feel for it', and when the recipe says a pinch of ginger or vanilla, it might just as well say a dash or a smidgin. Let me be perfectly frank: pastry-cooks, like chefs, always withhold something, a tiny, crucial secret that will make all the difference, and these little tricks of the trade are what I propose to reveal to the world.

Little Indiscretions
Part One: Cold Desserts

Special tricks for the preparation of cold desserts and how to avoid the errors most commonly made by novice pastry-cooks.

You must remember that to make a perfect *Ile flottante*, the use of fresh eggs is absolutely essential. You can beat them by hand or with an electric beater. To make the whites stiffen into peaks, some people use a pinch of salt, but the truly infallible method is to use a coffee bean. This is how to do it—

Having got this far, Nestor interrupted the composing of this curious opus to write a letter to an old friend.

Don Antonio Reig
The Three Anchovies Boarding House
Sant Feliu de Guíxols

Madrid, 1st of March . . .

Dear Antonio,

No doubt you will be surprised to receive this letter after so many years, and especially when I tell you that by the time you read it, I will be dead . . . or almost.

Nestor bit the cap of his old fountain pen, a 1954 Parker of blue bakelite with gold-plating, which he had bought on a whim at the San Telmo market in the company of Antonio Reig, his friend and colleague, back in the days when they were both living and working in Buenos Aires. It wasn't easy for him to write this letter; he had been putting it off for weeks. 'By the time you read it, I will be dead . . . or almost.' It sounded like something out of a novel, especially the 'almost', but there was nothing fictional about his lung cancer, and all he could do was prepare himself and tidy up things a little before the time came. In a way, this eccentric cookbook he had begun to compose was his last will and testament. No doubt it would have been considered an act of high treason by the secretive freemasonry of chefs – and pastry-cooks in particular – who never provide exact recipes for their creations. He liked the idea of calling his compendium *Little Indiscretions.* The title had a literary ring to it that appealed to him and it suggested a certain treachery in his enterprise. The idea was to go public with the tricks of the trade: the subtle touch that is the difference between a proud, upstanding soufflé and a flop, all closely guarded secrets that transform the pleasures of confectionery into a veritable art.

. . . Since I don't know how long I have left to live, given the state of my health, I would like to send you this little culinary testament in instalments. At the moment I'm writing it in my spare time, in a notebook, but I plan to send you ten or twelve tips in each letter. I would be grateful if you could compile them for posthumous publication. Don't you think it's a delicious way of taking revenge on those famous colleagues of ours who stop at nothing for a fourth star in the Michelin guide, but won't give the public even an inkling of the simplest tricks that you and I use every day? Little Indiscretions *. . . what a splendid title, don't you think? The other day I was talking to my staff about it and they got completely the wrong idea, poor lambs. 'So you intend to reveal the shameful secrets of all those famous people you worked for before you set up on your own?' Chloe asked me this (she's the new girl I've got working for me) and I let her think she was right. Given the highly sensitive nature of my subject, it's not a bad idea, as I'm sure you'll agree, to keep people in the dark about what I'm really up to, which is something far more significant (and dare I say it, yes I do: heroic) than gossiping about the foibles of Mr X or Mrs Y. Can you imagine what would happen if you and I started coming out with all the things we've seen and heard in our careers? Just think of the scandal we'd create! For instance, do you remember back in Buenos Aires . . . what was the name of that couple you used to work for? Seldi? Teldi? What's become of them? Funnily enough I was thinking of them only yesterday, not*

because I was planning to write to you, but because I was trying to remember the recipe for that perfect summer pudding I used to make for them. You must have a copy of it. Would you mind sending it to me in full? I've forgotten some of the ingredients. So there I was racking my brains, when this Chloe girl I was telling you about came and interrupted me: 'Go on, Nestor, tell us what you're writing, tell us one of those shameful secrets.' Then I remembered that we happened to have a catering job to do that day for the Seldis or whatever they're called, and that gave me an idea. I said: 'That's right, dear, my Little Indiscretions *is a book about people's shameful secrets, but not famous people, no, it's not like the gossip you get in the glossies. When you're a bit older you'll learn that people who seem utterly normal on the surface often have something far worse to hide than those trying to shake off the paparazzi: poke around in their closets and you may get a nasty surprise.'*

You're probably wondering why I lied to her like that, saying I was writing a book full of scandal and gossip, when the thought had never crossed my mind. Well, I only did it to conceal my secret plan. Young people can't help blabbing . . . But the thing is, once I started lying, I went on, making my story more and more elaborate. I couldn't help it. Maybe it's because I'm a pastry-cook: you start something, even if it's just telling a fib, and before you know it, you're decorating it all as artistically as you can, like a big wedding cake – a few flakes of caramel here, a raspberry coulis there. Meanwhile Chloe's hanging on my every word, so I look her gravely in the eye, and add, 'You're still very young, but some day soon you'll find out that there are many people in the world who have done something shameful in their lives. I don't mean anything heinous: a little affair on the side, say . . . a betrayal of trust . . . a petty theft . . . maybe even a one-off homosexual experience. In other words, an act they're ashamed of, but which is really perfectly forgivable . . . The problem is that often, later on, sometimes many years later, in order to keep their shameful secret hidden, they have to do something far worse, even commit a real crime, do you see what I mean, my dear? Oh, you'd be surprised how often it happens: I've come across several cases myself.' You should have seen the look on her face. She was absolutely convinced that this little notebook of mine was full of juicy secrets instead of dessert recipes. So much the better. That way she'll never suspect what I'm really up to, and I can keep her sweet by promising to tell her about some old scandal that no-one cares about any more and no-one will remember after I'm dead.

But how to make a perfect chocolate fondant? Now there's a secret I'm duty-bound to hand on to posterity, don't you think, Antonio? So will you accept my offer? If you agree, I'll start sending you recipes in the next letter.

Anyway, you might be amused to hear what happened with this Chloe girl: she just went on and on at me, so in the end I had to tell her a little secret, and since I was already thinking about you and the time when we were both in Buenos Aires, the first shameful secret that occurred to me was one that you know all too well: that business with Mrs Teldi. I tell you, Antonio, I felt like that character in Tintin, Oliveira da Figueira, whose storytelling creates a distraction and keeps a crowd of listeners spellbound with a juicy morsel of old gossip. There I was, yours truly, telling the tale of Mrs Teldi or Seldi or whatever the hell she's called. My audience consisted of the wide-eyed Chloe, Carlos Garcia, my trusty sidekick, and Karel Pligh, the Czech boy who's been helping out with the deliveries. There's been hardly any work the last few days, unfortunately, so I could take my time, and I have to admit I was so proud of the exciting way I described that accident (shall we call it), that happened at the Teldis' house back in '82 or thereabouts, when Mrs Teldi's younger sister and her husband came to visit. Of course I didn't mention any names – as you know, I've always preferred to err on the side of discretion – but I did tell them in some detail about the visit of your employer's sister-in-law and her husband from Spain, beginning with a little description of the visitors themselves: she was beautiful, I said, but with a melancholic air about her, yes, that was the word that sprang to mind, almost mournful . . . and her husband seemed to be one of those rare specimens: a man who is handsome but doesn't know it.

Then I went on to tell them how we all noticed Mrs Teldi flirting with her brother-in-law. But adultery was no big deal back then in Argentina. It was almost par for the course and nobody made much of a fuss about it: we certainly didn't and neither did her husband or anyone really . . . except, of course, the betrayed sister. 'Because one fateful day, my dears,' I told my rapt audience, 'she found them together in one of the upstairs rooms, where nobody went as a rule, since those rooms were no longer in use . . .'

You should have seen them gape and stare when I told them all this. Isn't it funny, Antonio, how people go on being fascinated by stories of adultery, even the young people today, with their busy sex lives and all sorts of affairs: straight, gay, even incestuous sometimes? And yet there is something irresistible about love stories from another era and another world, the kind that reek of mothballs and secrets. I should say too that I was particularly inspired that afternoon, for instance the way I explained in such close detail how, a few hours later, we found Mrs Teldi's younger sister dead, 'lying crushed on the paving stones of the back patio, as if the poor thing had quietly, ever so quietly, let herself drop from that upstairs room, the scene of defeat.' Then I added: 'Her face was destroyed by the impact, and yet, as we stood there looking at her, we could still see clearly the pain in those eyes, that had witnessed something intolerable. Relationships between siblings are always complicated – I don't know if you have brothers or sisters, but it's not like any other relationship. There's so much unfinished business: "It's mine . . . you always try to take it from me . . . no, it never belonged to you . . ." The strong sibling versus the weak one, the same thing over and over, until one comes out on top . . . Anyway, in this story the strong sister obviously ends up with a guilty secret on her conscience. That brief affair, one silly fling among so many others, would never have mattered in the least if her sister hadn't opened the door of the upstairs room. But death can blow even a little indiscretion like that right out of proportion. And ever since that day, the brother-in-law and the surviving sister had to live with the image of those accusing eyes looking up at them from the patio below, her skull broken on the paving stones, and her skirt riding up obscenely, exposing a pair of innocent white legs that never should have climbed the stairs to the top floor.'

But what am I doing rambling on? This isn't what I meant to tell you. You know the story from start to finish, Antonio, so it isn't going to have any effect on you, but you should have seen those kids when I came to the end. They were very impressed, I tell you. Carlos kept staring at me, Karel was speechless, while Chloe was hungry for more details: 'And what was the name of the sister who died? Maybe she suspected they'd been shagging for ages, since before she married him, eh Nestor? And what about the other husband? Sounds like he didn't give a shit, all this going on under his nose, maybe they both had their bits on the side, like my folks do.'

'That'll do, Miss Trias,' I had to tell her, 'enough chatter for today.' She pulled a face. On anyone else you'd hardly even have noticed a frown like that, but Chloe has these two metal rings, one in her lower lip and one in her tongue, which you can see when she smiles (they say it's the fashion, I think it's pretty disgusting) so the result was really quite frightening. 'It's just an old story that doesn't matter to anyone any more,' I said. 'I was only telling it to fill in time.' She didn't answer and just stared at my little notebook, as if it concealed untold treasures. She's an odd one, that girl, and if I actually were writing a book about people's shameful secrets, I'd have to put her in it. Not that I think she's done something truly shameful, she's too young, but over the years I've developed a sense of what destiny has in store for certain people . . . Anyway, I'd better not drone on and on, this letter's becoming epic. If I had time and could be bothered, I'd tell you what I know about Chloe Trias, but it's hardly worth it. She's a typical poor-little-rich-girl-turned-rebel, I'm sure you know the type. This one's a

punk with an apathetic attitude and a Czech body-builder for a boyfriend, nothing very unusual, really, and besides what do we care about other people's private lives? We've had enough of that over the years . . . So let's get back to business, shall we? Here's something I know you'll love, my little trick no. 3, for making chocolate mousse. Something just occurred to me, though: don't you think some people are rather like desserts? I admit it's incongruous, but if someone asked me to describe Chloe, I'd say she's the human equivalent of a mint-flavoured chocolate mousse, made with very bitter chocolate and too much tangy mint. There's an observation for my little notebook – spot on, if I say so myself.

2

—

The Second Day: Karel and Chloe

'It's gotta be straight on the edges. Look, I'll show you, give me the razor. Hey watch it! Don't move, I could slash your jugular. And don't even think about looking in the mirror, OK? I feel like I'm shearing a sheep now. You'll look *so* cool. Give me a break, will you?'

Karel Pligh leant his head back against the chair and tried to concentrate on counting the number of times Chloe said *cool* in the course of the conversation, to keep his mind off the super-sharp razor blade scraping at the skin under his lower lip. He had already learnt something that day: the transformation of a common or garden beard such as he had been sporting since his arrival from Prague into a minimalist goatee is a delicate and time-consuming operation. In the twenty-five minutes it had taken so far, he had counted seventy-three *cools*, thirty *wickeds*, not to mention a good deal of fucking-this and fucking-that. It's a good thing the vocabulary is so limited here, thought Karel Pligh, before replying with a *cool* to one or other of Chloe's questions. At this rate, he thought with a certain satisfaction, I'll be speaking like a native in two or three months.

And so he was. Thanks to his girlfriend, Chloe Trias, and his undying passion for Latin music, a few months after his arrival in Spain, Karel could express himself fluently in a curious modern Spanish that blended the coolest hip-talk with quaint turns of phrase from old boleros and congas.

He had more difficulty, however, mastering the secret code of Western love. Chloe was not the first Spanish girl to have burst into his life like a meteorite, catching him off-guard. The situation wasn't totally unfamiliar (this had happened with Czech girls too): before he could ask what was going on, there she was, making herself at home. And the preliminaries were pretty much the same as back home: you go to a club, you go up to a girl, ask her to dance, she offers to buy you a drink, you let her, and before you know it, you're in a strange bed full of soft toys or little pink pillows with 'You have to kiss a lot of frogs before you find a Prince Charming' written on them, while Brad Pitt or some other capitalist movie star watches your every move from a poster on the wall, just to make sure you're acquitting yourself like a man. That much was familiar, but there were other things about Western love, other points of etiquette, that were harder for a recent immigrant to understand. For instance, the kind of kiss that signals the difference between a bit of fun and true love.

'Now don't even think about moving, K – this little Michael Douglas dimple you have here is very sexy, but it's a bitch to shave, so hold still for a bit, will you?'

Chloe had started calling him K the first time she had given him a true-love kiss, and Karel had been touched by this apparent homage to one of his most famous compatriots. Quite a few weeks went by before he discovered that Chloe didn't associate K with Kafka but with a brand of shoe polish that bore a vague resemblance to his first name. By that stage, however, they were in love. They had met a few months before, and rushed through the early stages, the exquisite exploration of each other's bodies, and in all that time their lips had never met, for, as Karel had been rather stupefied to discover, in the West, you can touch countless bodies, lick and kiss them from top to bottom and penetrate various orifices in between without even imagining a kiss on the lips.

'No, man, no. It's not that things are really all that different here,' a drunk apprentice philosopher told him one day in a bar, confessing his intimate secrets as men do only in the company of complete strangers. 'The thing is, the girls these days, the young ones, they've gone weird. Sex: not a problem, whatever you like. But try and get them to give you a tongue kiss and you've practically got to pull out an engagement ring. It's fucking mad, I tell you. My theory is they all went off the rails after seeing that stupid scene in *Pretty Woman*. So now a bit of spit swapping is supposed to mean, "I will love you for ever and ever, amen." Well, fuck that!'

And perhaps that explains why it was only after working their way right through the *Kama Sutra* that Chloe said to Karel, 'Kiss me, K.'

'Jesus, careful! This razor's really sharp, you know . . . what if my hand slipped?'

Chloe's hand was steady enough, but she couldn't always hold her tongue, and one night it really got the better of her. Karel often thought about that night. Since they'd met one morning in a supermarket – Nestor had sent him out in an emergency for nutmeg, and she was buying a bag of cheese-flavoured crisps and two bottles of Coke for breakfast – she had told him many things about her life, all of which had turned out to be true: that she and two Moroccan friends had been subletting an attic room without electricity for two weeks, that she liked Led Zeppelin and Pearl Jam, and AC/DC, sort of (pity she had such eclectic taste), that she hated her parents, didn't care about money and had never been on a motorbike. But one unforgettable night, when Karel had already befriended Chloe's roommates, Anwar and Hassem, who were observing Ramadan, he would make some disconcerting discoveries about his new girlfriend. All because of Ramadan and a kiss.

'Let's get out of here,' Chloe said to him that afternoon in her attic. 'The guys are really boring when they're on this fasting-and-praying trip.'

And that's how Karel found out about the other side of Chloe's life. She insisted they take a taxi, even though he had his motorbike parked outside. It was getting dark when they pulled up in front of the sort of house Karel had only seen in old Hollywood movies. Before they could knock at the door, a servant appeared and took care of the taxi fare, while Chloe asked him, over her shoulder, if the folks were in.

The folks must be her elderly parents, thought Karel. And that's what he went on thinking until the day he actually met them: she was forty-something and looked like Kim Basinger, while he could have been the Marlboro man. So there's something else I've learnt about the ways of the West, thought Karel: rich, rebellious girls have walking ads for parents.

Why Chloe, who had a house bigger than the Sportovni Skola in Prague, chose to live in a dirty attic with a floating population of cockroaches, newspapers for carpet and *lebdas* of dubious cleanliness laid out several times a day in the direction of Mecca, why she lived on crisps and Coke: these were no doubt among the inscrutable mysteries of the capitalist world. But that first night he spent with Chloe at the old folks' house, a far more troubling ordeal awaited him: the first, long-delayed, this-is-serious kiss. Months later, forced to sit still by his girlfriend who was determined to make him look presentable ('You've got to get rid of this prehistoric growth. Just sit down there and I'll fix you up. You'll look *so* cool, I promise'), Karel looked in the mirror, but instead of scrutinizing the tailored remnant of his beard or the very long, thin sideburns Chloe was beginning to shape on his jaws, he remembered that momentous kiss.

First the moist, yielding feel of her mouth, and then a metallic taste, a mixture of copper and tin perhaps. Am I up to this? he wondered. Here goes, he thought, and pushed his tongue so far in he thought for a moment it would tickle her tonsils. But he stopped himself just in time and opted instead to explore Chloe's perfect teeth with the tip of his tongue: molars, canines, incisors. Too clinical, he thought: meticulous and unromantically exact. But how the hell are you supposed to kiss a girl with one ring in her tongue and another in her lower lip?

Unsurprisingly, Chloe's bed was full of teddy bears. No pillow with instructions for kissing frogs, though, and instead of Brad Pitt, all three members of Nirvana on the wall, casting a critical eye on Karel's performance at this crucial moment.

The door shut behind them. They had sneaked into Chloe's parents' house and, for the fist time, Chloe had given him a true-love kiss. 'I love you, K,' she said to him. 'I want us to be together for ever and ever. I don't ever want to come back to this awful house, not even to visit. You're all I have in the world. Can I come and live with you? Could I get a job where you work? I can cook. I can wait on tables, too. I'd do it for free. I don't care about money. I just want to be with you. Do you think your boss at Mulberry & Mistletoe would take me on? Please say yes. Listen, to prove I really love you, I'm going to show you something. This is a secret; I've never told anyone,' she continued breathlessly, diving into her backpack to find a small, red, rather battered case. But she must have had a sudden change of heart, because all she pulled out was a pair of Pearl Jam CDs.

'What's the fucking point,' she said.

Karel was curious to know what she had chosen not to show him. Perhaps a photo of a former lover; girls always keep pictures of what they love most, even when it's dead and gone. But in the end, he didn't dare ask. Nor, while she was still wielding the razor, did he dare ask her if she really thought it looked *so cool*, what was left of his poor beard: a little doormat of fur under his lower lip and sideburns like ants marching single file. Had Karel known the old proverb about what to do when in Rome, this would have been a good time to remember it. Instead, what he thought was: I've still got a long way to go before I understand how things work in the West. But in the meantime, he was determined to help Chloe however he could. If she was prepared to work at Mulberry & Mistletoe without pay, it wouldn't be hard to convince his boss to take her on. He could say he needed help with the deliveries, and it wouldn't cost anything. Nestor wouldn't mind, he was a good sort.

'Do you know how to ride a motorbike, Chloe?'

'You know what you can do with your fucking motorbike,' Chloe shot back. But then switching abruptly, as she often did, from anger to tenderness, she added: 'Kiss me, K. Kiss me again.'

And he did, not just because her words reminded him of a bolero, but also because, by then, he had grown accustomed to the sweet taste of her mouth.

3

The Third Day

Little Indiscretions
Part Two: Desserts Made with Eggs

You can't make an omelette without breaking eggs.
(Popular saying)

(A note for my dear friend Antonio Reig, to be sent with the recipes.)

I'm very tired tonight, Antonio. I haven't made much progress. It's late and I don't feel like writing. What happened was I went to see a fortune-teller – God knows what got into me – and though I don't believe in that nonsense, I have to admit it's a bit spooky. Do you think it's possible to read a man's destiny and see how he'll die just by looking at his face? I know it sounds mad but . . . Anyway, to get my mind off all that superstitious stuff, I'm going to send you a recipe, just one this time. It's an idea that came to me while I was observing Madame Longstaffe's clients, or rather one in particular. (Madame Longstaffe, as you will have guessed, is the name of the fortune-teller I went to see.) It's a delicacy I thought I'd call Oeufs Intacts. *What do you think? A little paradoxical, of course, but then it's meant to be. There's a lot of it about, you see: people dying for an omelette, but too scared to break an egg. But enough private jokes; here's the recipe:*

Oeufs Intacts:

Take two very fresh eggs and . . .

OEUFS INTACTS, OR SERAFIN TOUS BUYS A PIANO

That day, after leaving Madame Longstaffe's house, Serafin Tous decided to walk home. It was six in the evening, early still. He could have called a friend to see if they had plans for dinner, a close friend, so he wouldn't have to be good company, or even polite, someone who wouldn't mind if he dispensed with the customary questions about their health: he didn't feel like making an effort. He knew that Ernesto and Adela Teldi were in town. He didn't like Ernesto, but he'd known Adela for a long time, and over the years they had shared a good many secrets. He could have been alone with her – that would have been the perfect balm for his agitated state of mind. He could have called her, there was no danger: she wouldn't have probed him about anything he didn't want to reveal. His mobile phone was in his pocket, all he had to do was choose a number from the memory, the third one, to be precise, and . . . 'Just wondering if you were free tonight to put up with one of my silent moods.' But instead of calling Adela or anyone else, Serafin switched his phone off as if making a resolution. Put up with it yourself, like a man, he thought, and kept walking down the street.

At the first corner he came to, he turned, leaving the Plaza Celenque where Madame Longstaffe lived, and took the Calle del Arenal, heading west towards the Palacio Real, all this without any idea where his steps and his thoughts might be leading him. Recently steps and thoughts alike seemed to have a mind of their own: disquieting, to say the least. A few weeks ago, they had led him to the door of Freshman's, and now, in the same unconscious way, they had taken him to Madame Longstaffe's house, although this time he did not regret it.

'We have come,' he had said to the witch, as if speaking on behalf of himself, his steps and his thoughts, 'to ask you for help, madame.' And he went on to tell her about his unsettling visit to the club, ending with a plea: 'There must be a way, there *has* to be some way of turning me back into the sensible person I was before my wife died. It doesn't make sense, does it? Why should I suddenly start feeling those um . . . inclinations again? It must be an illusion, mustn't it? It probably happens all the time, no? You come across a photograph of a boy, say, who looks just like someone you remember from years ago and it stirs up all these . . . inappropriate emotions. But that's all in the past, I swear to God, madame. All that is gone and forgotten. I mean, it's nothing, is it? This feverish feeling I've had since the day I visited that horrible club, it won't last, will it? Tell me it won't. You must have something that will turn me back into the sort of man Nora wanted me to be. Nora was my wife, did I tell you? She died just a few months ago, a terrible loss . . .'

The Calle del Arenal was noisy and full of traffic. The jostling crowd swept even the most pensive pedestrians along, like corks bobbing in a stream. Tourists in sandals consulting maps, would-be artists hurrying off to a café, pickpockets, strollers, con-men and beggars, all moving together, a fluid mass of humanity channelled between the road and the walls of the buildings, sometimes diverted towards the window of a wig shop or a Seven Eleven.

'And why do you want to forget this boy?' Madame Longstaffe had asked, without waiting for him to finish his plea. 'Hmm? I notice that monsieur takes good care of his lovely long fingers, pianist's fingers . . . Monsieur is a very respectable man, a gentleman.'

It seemed that Brazilian fortune-tellers (a curse on the lot of them!) sometimes addressed their clients in the third person, with the deference generally reserved for VIPs. Not that it made Serafin Tous feel important, or even respectable. Had he really been respectable, he wouldn't have felt that pang whenever he remembered the boy from Freshman's. It was as if he'd come face to face with his past. Look at yourself, Serafin, you're just the same, he thought, you haven't really changed at all. This is exactly how you felt when you first met Pedrito Martínez. You were barely eighteen at the time, and you spent a whole year playing sonatas with him (among other things) behind closed doors in a mezzanine flat in Calle de Apodaca. Martínez, that was his name, your young piano student: Pedrito Martínez, such an ordinary name, but what a beautiful body . . . The agony of guilt, but oh, the ecstasy too . . . Admit it, Serafin, the ecstasy, the passion and . . . no! You didn't want to live like that, a sordid, fearful existence, always scared of being found out. *Martínez*, he was still a child, really. What would your dear parents have said if they had found out? And your friends? You know only too well: queer, faggot, shirt-lifter, turd-burglar, poof, poof, poof.

In the Calle del Arenal there is a wedding shop with shiny satin gowns and a myriad little artificial flowers for the headdresses. Nora would never have chosen one of those gowns for her wedding. She wore a wonderful simple raw silk dress that made her look taller, almost beautiful, even. And she was graced with the serenity of a woman who knows how to make her husband happy. So few women are capable of that. How lucky he had been to find her just in time. Intelligent, companionable Nora. Love gave her unfailing intuition: she never had to ask, she always knew, God bless her. You don't seem to understand, Madame Longstaffe, she was perfect, perfect for me, don't you see?

But Serafin Tous had left Madame Longstaffe's house behind him, and it was not the fortune-teller now, but the human torrent carrying him along the Calle del Arenal that replied: 'Let yourself go, boy . . . don't hold back. Accept what you are for once in your life.'

What sort of nonsense was that? He wasn't a boy any more, and he didn't want to let himself go. That was precisely why he had gone to see Madame Longstaffe. As she had sat there looking at him with her head tilted to one side and her blond hair falling over her left shoulder, he had thought, My God, what's going on? For viewed from that angle, she looked very much like a man. In fact, she was the spitting image of an actor whose name Serafin couldn't recall. Don't look at me like that, madame! Help me! You must have some way of warding off ghosts. It's the ghost of a man I chose not to be, coming back to haunt me after all these years. Imagine it, at my age: turning into an old queen, maybe even a paedophile, who knows . . . Luckily, just at that moment, the shop windows of the Calle del Arenal came to Serafin's rescue. He saw a sign that read 'Religious Objects'. Immediately he felt calmer: this was a lifeline thrown to a drowning man. On sale were small plaster figurines of various saints: Anthony of Padua, the great miracle worker, and St Jude the apostle, champion of lost causes and intercessor for those in desperate straits. Desperate indeed.

'Monsieur's problem is very interesting,' Madame Longstaffe had said, at which point Serafin thought he saw a glimmer of hope. But then the old woman added: 'I'm sure you'll understand if I don't prescribe anything today. An unusual case like this will require careful consideration. Don't worry, I'll ring you shortly to arrange another appointment.'

'But, madame, I would really prefer not to have to come back. I am a judge you know, and our public image is at stake. I wouldn't want to be associated with your . . . divinatory arts (which are, I'm sure, quite outstanding). But you see, someone may recognize me and think . . . You must realize I'm risking a great deal by coming here.'

'Oh be quiet, *meu branco*. Just wait for my call,' said Madame Longstaffe, shifting from the formal third person to a completely inappropriate Brazilian familiarity. Then, with even less respect, she added: 'Stop being such an old woman, will you? Off you go, shoo!'

As pedestrians make their way along Calle del Arenal towards the Plaza de la Opera, they will sometimes find themselves falling into step with the rhythm of a bossa nova or a samba. Or a tango, or a waltz. They come from a dance school with its window wide open onto the street, sending out its music, accompanied by the crisp one-two-three of the instructor.

'You can't send me away so soon, madame, without some sort of help. Surely it wouldn't be so hard to prescribe a potion, one of your famous little bottles. After all, I only want to forget, madame. I only want to forget a pair of young hands on a piano, a boy's fingers dancing on the keys.' Serafin's words came back to him as the rhythm of the bossa sped up. Fortunately, the sonatas he used to teach Pedro Martínez on the Calle de Apodaca were nothing like the old Brazilian crooner Viricius de Moraes' earthy tones which he could hear with such clarity from the dance school, so Serafin continued on his way, following his thoughts and steps, leaving all musical memories behind. He kept walking down the street past a pyjama shop, then a Pans & Co fast-food place; beyond that he passed the elegant old Café del Real and a bar from which an electronic jingle emerged, indicating that someone had hit the jackpot on a poker machine. I'm all right, Serafin told himself, I'll be fine. The flow of the crowd is carrying me away from the music at last, helping me forget. I'm sure I'll be able to hold out, at least until my next appointment with Madame Longstaffe. Stay calm, Serafin, in a few seconds all this anxiety will subside into the unthinking, unfeeling, unspeaking numbness that has beleaguered you out for years. It's all right now, soon the memory of Freshman's will fade away, like the memory of that boy with his crew cut, his melancholy eyes and nervous fingers, like the memory of Pedro Martínez in that sad refuge on the Calle de Apodaca until your beloved Nora came to save you, bringing with her a period of such love and peace. The flow of the crowd quickened his pace now, as the Calle del Arenal suddenly narrowed into a new pedestrian zone. And there, waiting mutely in a shop window, was a piano.

When, two days later, two handsome young men delivered the piano, manoeuvring it into position in the sitting room near the fireplace, Serafin found himself looking at a photo of Nora that one of them – the irony of it! – had placed on top of the piano, as if that were its natural place.

'Don't jump to conclusions, Nora, it's not what you're thinking,' he said to the image of his wife. 'I didn't mean to go to that music shop. Somehow my steps and my thoughts led me there . . . Anyway, it's only on loan, my dear. These days they even let you try out grand pianos. It will only be in the house for two or three days. Think of it as a kind of exorcism. That's all it is, I swear. Believe me.'

'Sign here please, sir.'

The young fellow was wearing blue sleeveless overalls. He didn't have the arms or the hands of a pianist, but Serafin couldn't help staring as he held out the clipboard: muscles tensing under young skin, smooth forearms covered with blond, boyish down.

'Here's something for all your trouble,' said Serafin. And, having slipped a few notes into the chest pocket of the young man's overalls, he gave it two delicate pats, as if it were a little bird that might escape at any moment. 'You've been so kind . . .'

4

The Fourth Day

i. Of Love and Blackmail

Don Antonio Reig
The Three Anchovies Boarding House
Sant Feliu de Guíxols

Madrid, 14th of March . . .

My dear friend Antonio,

I can't tell you how sad I was to read your letter. A chef of your stature ruined, banished from the kitchen, condemned to cook what he can on a primus stove in the bathroom of a run-down boarding house. It's just awful. You told me about your arthritis – sadly, it's not uncommon among the practitioners of our art. Destiny has seen fit to spare me that curse, which is something to be thankful for, I suppose.

I'm afraid I can't offer you any work, Antonio. My modest business barely covers its costs, especially at this time of year. But don't worry, we'll find something for you soon. You also asked me to help you get hold of the Teldis' address, that couple I was telling you about the other day. (Poor Antonio, the arthritis shows in your handwriting: there's so much pain in those wobbly letters, despite your elegant green ink.) What do you want their address for? To see if they will help you out, I suppose. At the moment I don't know how to get in touch with them, but how about this for a coincidence: a couple of days ago I saw a photo of them in one of those glossy foreign magazines. Remember how he looked back in the seventies, when he was beginning to build up his fortune? Teldi the Spaniard, they called him. Well he hasn't changed much, physically at least; he still has that distinguished but rather sly look about him. Why are you so curious about him? You kept mentioning him in your letter, but I don't know what else I can tell you. He did always strike me as an odd character, Ernesto Teldi. The Argentine upper crust held him in high regard, even back then, but you always said there had to be something suspicious behind that smooth, refined exterior. If you ever found a skeleton in his closet, you never told me, and besides, by now it would be a very old skeleton, hardly worth getting worked up about. The sins of the rich are easily forgotten, aren't they? Peccata minuta, *Antonio. For what it's worth, here's what I found out about him in the magazine, maybe it'll be of some use to you: he's become a well-known art dealer now and a generous patron of the arts, dividing his time between Argentina, Spain and France (his main base). In fact, in the photo I mentioned, he's wearing the little ribbon of the Legion of Honour on his lapel. Just like him, isn't it?*

He's obviously done well with his paintings. He was just getting into the art business when you were working for him in Argentina. I used to come round now and then and we'd brew up a pot of mate *and chat, remember? But I mustn't keep going on about the old days. What I meant to do in this letter was cheer you up and tell you what I found out about Teldi, since you seem to be so keen to locate him. Right now I have no idea where he could be, but that's exactly why I'm sure we'll find him. This may sound mad, but for a while now I've had this feeling that my life is running on a track, like a train, and there's no getting off it. Not just my life, the people around me too. The things that are happening are like pieces of a puzzle, and though the pieces are all shaped differently, one by one they're falling into place. I don't know how else to put it. I think it has something to do with going to see Madame Longstaffe, the clairvoyant I was telling you about in my last letter. Did I tell you what I was doing there in the first place? I really just went along with one of my staff, Carlos Garcia, to give him moral support. What he wanted from the witch was a magic potion to help him find the woman of his dreams, in the flesh. I know, I know, I think it's all bogus woo-woo too, but the thing is, honestly, since that day, I keep feeling that destiny – or my destiny at least – is playing tricks on me, setting up coincidences. For instance: I happen to see a complete stranger in a compromising situation. A few days later I run into him again in equally odd circumstances, and putting two and two together, I discover his dark secret. You see what I mean? It's very strange. And then there's Madame Longstaffe's prediction about my health, which she volunteered without asking my permission. I know it's hard to believe, but it's coming true too. She said I had no reason to fear the cancer that's eating away at me, and, much to the surprise of my doctors, since that day, I've been feeling a lot better. So much better, in fact, that if I weren't a natural sceptic I might think I was actually recovering. Now all we need is for Carlos to find his dream-woman and for me to run into Ernesto Teldi in the street . . . But it's no more than a bizarre series of coincidences, it has to be. You're a rational person, so tell me: Do you really think destiny likes playing Chinese boxes, taking odd bits of people's lives and fitting them together to make some weird sort of puzzle? No, I don't either. It's just my imagination, I know, and that's why, despite what I just said, I'm still assuming I don't have long to live. Cancer is no joke, so I have to keep working on my secret project. But I've prattled on again, so I won't be sending you a recipe this time, Antonio. Next time, I promise. My book of little indiscretions is getting bigger every day, and now you'll have to excuse me, the phone is ringing.*

'Mulberry & Mistletoe, who's speaking? . . . Yes, who's speaking? . . . Hello? . . . Pronto? . . . What do you mean the number I've rung doesn't exist? I didn't ring any number, *porca miseria*, somebody was ringing me. *Porca miseria*,' Nestor repeated impatiently. 'Bloody telephone! Bloody government! It was probably an important customer.'

4

---

ii. Carlos and Adela, or Love in its Purest State

Adela hung up the phone. It was the third time she had called and the third time a computerized female voice had informed her that the number she called was not in service. But she knew she hadn't made a mistake. The friend who'd recommended Mulberry & Mistletoe ('The very best, my dear, I wouldn't even think about a do without consulting my old friend Nestor – he's a genius when it comes to organizing parties, he takes care of *everything*') had repeated the number so that she could check it. But the computerized voice was implacable: the number you have called is not in service.

For a moment, Adela considered going there in person. After all, the address on the card, at the corner of Ayala and Serrano, wasn't far from where she was now, in the Calle Miguel Angel. She looked at the card again, not that she really needed to: yes, yes, she could walk or take a taxi and sort it all out in a matter of minutes. That would be best, really – she told herself – it's always a good idea to talk to people face to face with this sort of business. Just then, a taxi pulled up a few yards away to drop someone off, as if the driver had read her mind. It was starting to rain, and that decided her. As soon as the taxi's free, I'll hop in, she thought. First she would stop at Mulberry & Mistletoe. She'd ask the driver to wait while she went over the details of the party she was planning to have at her country house, and she'd still have time to get back to the Palace Hotel and meet her husband before three. Madrid is not a nice city in rainy weather. Now she just had to wait for the passenger to get out of the taxi.

A great mass of blond hair emerged from the inside of the car, followed by a foot encased in a silk slipper. Strange footwear for this time of year, thought Adela, but she said nothing. Over the years she had learnt to remain indifferent to all kinds of extravagance.

'Excuse me,' said the passenger, and for a moment they paused and exchanged glances. 'Excuse me, but could you tell me if this is the Calle de Almagro?'

An odd question, thought Adela. They were in the Calle Miguel Angel, nowhere near Almagro, and it seemed strange for someone to get out of a taxi without knowing where they were. So instead of answering, she adopted a polite smile and murmured: 'May I?'

She was determined to get into that taxi as soon as she could.

'Don't go today, madam,' said the slipper. 'Go another day. Tomorrow, maybe. That would be a better idea. What you had planned for today, leave for tomorrow. It's starting to rain, haven't you noticed?'

It *is* raining, you mad old bat, thought Adela, but before she could say anything, the exotic slipper added: 'Anyway, do you really know where you're going? Do you know how to get to the Calle de Ayala?'

‘Easy,’ interrupted the taxi driver, who had been quiet up to this point, but was no doubt exasperated by his passengers’ conversation. ‘The quickest way from here is to go across the Plaza de Rubén Darío, down the Calle de Almagro and then—’

‘It’s going to rain. Come back another day and go a different way,’ insisted the slippered woman. ‘You wouldn’t want your fur coat to be ruined, would you? It’s so beautiful,’ she said. Only it came out: ‘Ish so beautiful,’ with a Brazilian accent. ‘Ish going to rain . . . Anosser day.’ But in the end, she did get out of the taxi and allow Adela to take her place. The whole thing was absurd and yet . . .

Once she was in the taxi, Adela did not turn around. She would never know what that woman looked like from a distance, or how that voluminous head of blond hair stood up in the rain, or whether, to step over the spreading puddles, she had to hitch up her green tunic and reveal her silk slippers. By the time Adela finally settled into the taxi she had reconsidered her destination.

Before heading off, the driver asked her: ‘So you want to go to the Calle de Ayala?’

She shook her head. ‘No,’ she said without looking back, not even a glance, ‘take me to the Palace Hotel.’ And then she added: ‘You don’t have to go along Almagro to get there, do you?’

To which the taxi driver, who was by nature talkative and a stickler for detail, replied: ‘No, it’s easy’ (apparently everything was easy for him) ‘from here, if you prefer, we can go down to Castellana, across Colón, and then straight on until we get to the hotel.’

‘Perfect – my husband is waiting for me, you see,’ said Adela, as if the driver needed this detail.

She didn't look out of the window again until they reached the fountain of Neptune. That mad old bat was right, she could go to Mulberry & Mistletoe tomorrow, that way she'd be setting out from a completely different part of Madrid. It was raining, after all.

Even though Adela Teldi always liked coming back to Madrid, the city of her birth, there were certain streets she carefully avoided. Like the Calle de Almagro, for example, with its plane trees with leaves that made you sneeze, and its pavements, which had hardly changed since her childhood. So little had they changed, in fact, that if for some unimaginable reason she had found herself walking down that street, it would have been hard for her not to fall back into the silly games of her childhood: avoiding the cracks in the paving stones or playing a kind of mental hopscotch. But there was no reason for Adela to go to that part of the city. Her Madrid had shifted, and the shops, the hairdressers, and the restaurants she frequented, even her friends' houses, were all a long way from that block, once so familiar. Luckily. So the following day, around four in the afternoon, Adela set out from the Palace Hotel and had no trouble getting to the Calle de Ayala, where the catering company had its premises. And when she arrived, a young man showed her into a pleasant waiting room.

'I'll be with you in a moment, madam,' he said to her. 'My boss isn't in. He's almost always here, but something came up and he had to go out. It's just unlucky, but don't worry, I can help you. I'll just go and get something to write with, Mrs . . . ?'

Carlos left the sentence hanging for Adela to complete.

'Mrs Teldi, with a T for Teresa,' she replied. 'And what is your name?'

'Carlos Garcia, at your service, madam. I'm sure we'll be able to meet your needs. I'll be right back.'

While he was in the other room looking for the list of menus, pulling out the albums with photographs of buffets and sumptuous tables adorned with flowers and still-life arrangements, he could see Mrs Teldi through the gap between the curtains: she was walking around the waiting room, surveying the portraits hanging on the walls. He saw her smile at some of the personalities in the photos as if she knew them, occasionally tilting her head to read a dedication. There's not a lot people can do while they're waiting. Some light a cigarette, others walk up and down as if taking possession of the space by measuring it out. Some settle down, taking off their coats, undoing a button or two.

One more album, thought Carlos, mustn't forget to show her the fruit arrangements, and he glanced guiltily at Adela: it's not good to keep clients waiting. But she had made herself comfortable on the sofa, having shifted a South American poncho that must have been bothering her. Now her coat seemed to be bothering her too, though it wasn't all that hot in the waiting room. Suddenly, impatiently, she removed first her coat and then the scarf that was covering her throat. Mrs Teldi's movements were so hasty that, for a fraction of a second, the slight hollow at the base of her very white and fragile neck was exposed.

What a pity, thought Carlos, still peeping at the stranger. That neck must have been quite unforgettable once. Then he went back into the waiting room with the papers and the albums.

Two or three days later, when the door of room 505 at the Phoenix Hotel shut behind them, the rest of the world ceased to exist for Carlos and Adela. The piped music could have been 'Love Me Tender' or a flamenco song: it wouldn't have made any difference. When they paused in their love-making they could have drunk Fanta or Bailey's without ice, it could have been light outside, or not, cold or oppressively hot. None of that mattered: the only thing they sensed was love. It was the typical chance meeting between a mature woman and a young man: they began by talking business, how the party would be organized and so on, then they had sandwiches at the Embassy, got drunk together in the bar of the Phoenix, and ended up in bed. A casual encounter, and predictable enough. But they saw each other again the next day, and the day after, and the one after that, and when the door of the hotel room shut behind them, off came the shirt with the Mulberry & Mistletoe logo, the Armani skirt, the red bow tie and the sky-blue blouse, all in perfect silence, kisses guiding their way to nakedness. And, still without a word, they set about exploring their naked flesh inch by inch, with passionate attention to detail. The piped music brought them the voice of Wilfrido Vargas singing, 'There's nowhere left I haven't kissed,' but neither was interested in what their ears might register. Carlos and Adela heard, saw, smelt and felt through the skin – 'every inch a source of bliss' – and bliss it was for Adela to run her smelling, seeing, hearing hands over that young skin, so young that, kiss after kiss, what it inspired was not so much desire as tenderness. How lucky, how lucky you are, Adela, she said to herself. Kiss him while you can, no questions asked, no past, no future. Make love the way castaways do, or the terminally ill, the way only old women like you can make love. Stroke his thighs, tangle your fingers in his hair, don't let a morsel of that beautiful body go to waste. You're a lucky woman. And what's he thinking? . . . Just as well nature hasn't given us the facility to read other people's thoughts. So kiss him, taste him, love him, Adela, she told herself. And afterwards, forget. Don't forget to forget, for heaven's sake. Forgetting is essential, because the world is still there waiting outside the door of room 505.

This adventure had taken Carlos by surprise and swept him away, but not once did he look back. Falling in love is like the flight from Sodom and Gomorrah: if you stop to look back you may find yourself turning into a pillar of salt, a sterile, impotent statue, sensibly (all too sensibly) wondering: What the hell are you getting yourself into here, spending three afternoons in a row with a woman who could be your mother? Have you even taken a proper look at her?

No. Carlos hadn't taken a proper look at her, because in the microcosm of room 505 the laws of perspective had been suspended, so it was impossible to view anything more extensive than the curve of a neck or the lobe of an ear. When you're under the sway of an all-consuming passion, love in its purest state, all you can see are millimetres of skin electrified by desire, and ever-new paths opening before you. Carlos set off to explore without a compass. 'I want to take the longest way from your hips down to your feet . . .' He was not a great reader of poetry and had no special interest in Neruda, but the ways of love for poets and waiters are the same. Sooner or later, both are faced with the same obstacles on their amorous voyage: peninsular fingers, hill-like knees, the deep dale between the thighs. The path is long and it may take the explorer some time to reach the Mount of Venus. And when he got there, for the first time, Carlos lost control of his tongue – it had developed a mind of its own.

The role of explorer was not unfamiliar to him, but it had always been just that: a role. 'This is what women want, or this . . .' The exploration was perhaps more clinical than passionate, but it always seemed to work. He considered himself an accomplished actor, yet until he stepped into room 505, his amorous experiences (which included a hopeless search for a woman in a painting) had always felt rather like sitting an entrance exam. Was he worthy of admission to the club for hot lovers? Or the club of tender lovers, the ones who hug girls afterwards when all they really want is to leave – all right, I'll cuddle her a bit, a little kiss here, an I-love-you there, but stick to the script They freak out if you start ad-libbing.

In room 505, however, there was no script, no map, no compass. And there was no need to work himself up by imagining that the line of an unfamiliar neck might fit the perfect curve of a woman in a portrait he had discovered in a wardrobe all those years ago. With other women it had always been deceptively easy: all he had to do was shut his eyes and Lola, Laura, Marta, Mirtha, Nilda, Norma . . . and so on, through to the end of his neat and not-so-little black book, he could imagine them all with the neck of the woman in the painting.

But that skin . . . Adela's skin (he hardly dared to say her name: it was superstitious, like the fear of looking back and turning into a pillar of salt), Adela's skin did not extend beyond the minute path marked out by his kisses. Love has such feeble eyes it does not see wrinkles or imperfections, a short-sighted lover will admire a freckle simply because it's *hers*.

* * *

Adela was not short-sighted. And she had long since quit the club of obliging lovers, which has different statutes for its male and female members. Women have to know how to sigh convincingly and how to turn up the heat by talking dirty at the appropriate moment: those are the golden rules. The language of passion is a delicate balancing act: you might, just might, get away with *cunt* in certain circumstances, but *fanny*, well, no, and *cock* is OK, but *knob* . . . excuse me! There are strict rules about these things, and sometimes role-play is more convincing than sincerity, but you have to know how to pull it off, when to say what, how to soften or raise your voice, because obscenities are like exotic food: there are aphrodisiacs and purgatives.

Adela knew all this, of course, but none of it mattered to her any more. She had given up employing those skills in her affairs years ago, and she certainly wasn't going to start again with this boy. Yet although she felt that her long years of play-acting had earned her the right to concentrate on actual pleasure without bothering to pretend, somehow the paths her kisses traced on Carlos's skin didn't seem entirely new. It was as if once, many years ago, her hands had explored this territory. It was a silly, absurd idea, but for the first time in a while, she felt she had lost control of what was happening to her. She of all people, after so many lovers, so many affairs, so many attempts to cauterize her solitude.

Her sister's name – Soledad, solitude – had slipped unexpectedly into her thoughts, giving her a start.

'What's wrong? Are you all right?'

'Fine. Don't stop kissing.'

But it was too late for any kisses to blot out that name, part of a long story she would have preferred to forget. And so holding Carlos tightly, Adela resorted to a method that had served her well over the years. She had applied it successfully since the day her sister died: the best way to forget guilty caresses is to smother them with thousands more, because nothing diminishes guilt like the tireless repetition of the sin, which then strips it of meaning. And that is what Adela had been doing all those years, trying to forget one particular body by loving so many others.

For a moment the trick seemed to be working. Adela smiled: the danger had been averted once again, and she was feeling rather pleased with herself, until she noticed that strange but familiar sensation in her thumbs.

By the pricking of my thumbs, something wicked this way comes. I've done all this before, she thought. I'm sure I've loved this body, this skin . . . But then she tried to shake herself out of it: Come on, Adela, the only wicked thing going on here is that you're falling in love with a twenty-one-year-old boy. Don't let yourself. Just keep quiet and enjoy it. You'll be able to love him again tomorrow, and Friday too, and maybe a fourth or a fifth time after that, but don't think any further ahead. As you know only too well, my dear, dreams do exist, oh yes, but only so long as you don't try to make them come true. Room 505 is paradise for as long as it lasts: two, three, four days, maybe even quite a bit longer, think of that; you might be able to enjoy *months* of love just so long as . . .

Just so long as you're sensible about it, she told herself sternly. As soon as he walks out that door, ring up Mulberry & Mistletoe and cancel all the arrangements for the party, promise you'll do that.

As soon as he's gone, you're going to pick up that phone and change your plans. The idea of spending a weekend with a house full of guests plus *him* is just bonkers. Out of the question. This is where your passion belongs, between these four walls, and only a hopeless dreamer would attempt to live it out in public. *Carpe diem*, kiss, don't think. Love and forget, Adela. Dreams melt away at the touch of reality. Enjoy yourself now and pay later by giving up on seeing him outside this room. Make sure you call that chef.

Two hours later, when Carlos had left the room at the Phoenix Hotel and love had given way to practicalities, Adela sat down on the unmade bed to ring the number just as she had promised.

'Hello, is that Mulberry & Mistletoe? Could I please speak to Mr Chaffinch? It's Mrs Teldi here . . . Aha, pleased to meet you, so to speak . . . Yes, that's right, exactly, Teldi, with a T for Teresa. I dropped in the other day to arrange some catering, and since you were out, I talked with your assistant. Did he tell you what we needed? Well, I'm ringing now because I've changed my mind . . .' Adela stroked the sheets and closed her eyes tight, although what she was really trying to do was shut off other, more obstinate senses, for the scent of Carlos's skin was still clinging to the treacherous sheets and was even more delicious than when he had been there in person – and more dangerous too. (Oh God, the scent of absence!)

Adela wanted to light a cigarette so as not to smell that perfume, but something stopped her.

'Pardon? Yes, sorry, I'm still here, Mr Chaffinch. I wanted to tell you that . . .' Her hand ventured further afield now and discovered forgotten patches of warmth. (Careful, Adela, many stupid things have been done on account of an empty hollow in a warm bed . . . but only by naïve, romantic women who don't know any better.)

‘Can you hear me, Mr Chaffinch? I’m so sorry, I was thinking . . . You see, I rang you because . . .’ (Don’t do it, Adela, don’t do it.) ‘Actually, I rang to confirm the arrangements,’ she said, crumpling, because the sheets still held the shape of Carlos’s body. He hadn’t been gone ten minutes, and she could still feel the kiss he had left on her lips, saying, ‘Till tomorrow, my love . . .’ She could also feel that inexplicable tingling in her thumbs, warning her that something wicked was on the way.

‘Yes, yes, that’s right, it’s all going ahead . . . except that instead of a whole weekend, we’ll just do the dinner on Saturday night.’ (What a coward you are! As if that were any kind of solution.) ‘Is that all right then? I’ll ring tomorrow and we’ll go over the details, what do you think?’ (Game over: you lose, just like all those women you’ve always laughed at.)

‘That’s right, all settled then. Tell me, Mr Chaffinch, you and your assistants, how will you be getting there? . . . Excellent, I’ll send you a cheque. So it’ll just be the one day then, but a very special day it will be.’

5

The Fifth Day

Little Indiscretions
Part Three: Sorbets and Other Frozen Desserts

Madrid, 25th of March . . .

Dear Antonio,

I told you, I told you! The Teldis have turned up, just as I predicted. You won't believe this, but the very same day I wrote my last letter to you, Adela Teldi paid us a visit here in person at Mulberry & Mistletoe. She wants me to cater for a party at this house they've got in the south called The Lilies. At first it was going to be a weekend, with lots of guests staying over, breakfast, lunch and dinner and so on, the whole deal, but in the end it'll just be one big dinner on Saturday night. It doesn't matter, it'll be less money, but the amazing thing is that my hunch was right.

So what does it all mean? Well, for a start it means I can help you get in touch with them, like you asked me to. The Madrid address is easy: they're staying at the Palace Hotel, and I'll give you their address at The Lilies too, in case you'd prefer to write to them there. And now let's get down to business – we mustn't let all these strange coincidences distract us from serious culinary matters.

Have I got a treat in store for you this time! My secret tips for making sorbets, the aristocracy of cold desserts. But before I launch into my little indiscretions, a request.

It makes sense for me to keep writing, since I'm sending you these recipes, but from now on I think it would be simpler for you to ring me. Reverse the charges of course, it goes without saying. I hope you won't be offended, but I can barely read your writing. And what with the green ink you always use, it's like . . . well, like a row of tatty parrots perched on a wire. There are whole sections I can't for the life of me make out, like the paragraph where you're telling me about Teldi, something about the disappearance of political prisoners in Argentina, if I've understood it properly, and God knows what else. In any case, that part of the letter is practically illegible, though I'll try and decipher it properly tomorrow on the way down south. But whatever it is you want to say to Teldi, I would strongly advise you to make an effort with your handwriting: no-one's got the patience to read three or four pages of green scribble. He'll give up straight away. It's the curse of our times, Antonio: no-one has any patience any more, everyone gets bored so easily.

Except for me, of course. Here are my plans, then: I'm off to Málaga to do this big dinner the Teldis are throwing for a group of collectors, God knows why. I'll keep you posted. I'm sure it'll be interesting. I love big parties with lots of house guests, something unexpected always happens. I'm taking Chloe along to help (the girl I told you about in my first letter: she's not a bad waitress), along with Karel Pligh and Carlos Garcia. They've both done the country-house thing before, so I'll be able to concentrate on the food and my beloved desserts. I'm even planning to invent one specially for the occasion, a sorbet surprise worthy of the Teldis: cold, expensive and very showy. What do you think?

Speaking of desserts: here are this week's secret tips, this time they're for making sorbets and gelati. But do remember what I said, Antonio: make an effort with your handwriting . . . You wouldn't be planning to blackmail Teldi, would you now? You have to be very careful with that sort of thing. Pardon my indiscretion, but I'm curious to know what you've got in mind. We are old friends, after all.

All right. Here they are then, finally: this week's two little indiscretions.

A trick used by le maître Paul Bocuse
to improve the consistency of a mango sorbet

To maintain the consistency of a fruit sorbet, especially if it's made with mango, you need to keep a sprig of marigolds handy, or better still, two sprigs. What you do is . . .

6

The Sixth Day: Ernesto Teldi and Miss Ramos

The rotunda of the Palace Hotel has featured in countless photographs as the calm, discreet backdrop for interviews with a whole host of celebrities and stars. Its carpet, woven on Royal Looms, has muffled the cat-like tread of writers like Julian Barnes making his way towards an armchair perfectly situated for him to sit and pose with his expensive pair of French moccasins on display. The Kentia palm trees in the lobby were an inspiration for Latoyah Jackson's new look when she first peered through their branches to reveal her oval Versace-Medusa face. Famous athletes and celebrated actors, left-wing intellectuals and right-wing politicians (moderately right-wing, of course): all of them have at some point come to rest in this cosy yet well-lit space, unique in all Madrid, and not just because the photos turn out so well, but because it is one of those places with its own special aura. It sends out the sort of message that says: I, ladies and gentlemen, am someone who appreciates quality but disdains ostentation, who only seeks comfort when it comes with a touch of artful decadence. I honour the life of the mind, but artistic sensibility is incomplete without a certain – how shall I put it? – deft, almost imperceptible touch of sophistication.

The unique ambience of the rotunda at the Palace says all that, or at least that is what Ernesto Teldi imagined it to say, which is why he had chosen it as the setting for his appointment with the journalist and photographer from *Patron of the Arts*, a magazine with around 350,000 subscribers throughout Europe. This prestigious publication had been trying to set up an interview with Teldi for months – 'A professional piece, of course, very classy, but with a human slant: the personal life of the high-flyer, in the style of *Tatler*, you know the sort of thing.'

Teldi had been waiting for Miss Ramos and her photographer for some time. On the table in front of him, the remains of a frugal breakfast were arranged as if for effect: grapefruit juice, a cup of tea, crumbs (presumably from a slice of toast), while the lord of this little domain flipped through the pages of *The Financial Times* (the arts pages, naturally).

'Good morning, Miss Ramos. Agustina Ramos, isn't it?' A kiss for her, a firm handshake and a slap on the back for the photographer. 'Allow me to introduce myself: Ernesto Teldi,' he added, his manner poised between familiarity and reserve. He had discovered that this worked well on the better sort of journalist, and especially on the likes of Miss Ramos: usually very well educated, sometimes left-handed and occasionally cross-eyed (a trait that may add a touch of originality to an otherwise nondescript appearance). Often, remarkably often in fact, these journalists were also the daughters, nieces or close relatives of some unknown or unjustly forgotten painter, a painter of enormous talent (what a barbaric world we live in) and for these reasons Miss Ramos and her ilk considered themselves hard done by. They were acutely aware that working for a glossy but pseudo-intellectual magazine like *Patron of the Arts* was a miserable waste of their intelligence, but what really peeved them was having to endure the company of Chema or someone like him.

Chema was the photographer. He was much younger than Miss Ramos, had the unforgivable habit of chewing gum and dressed with an absolute disregard for aesthetics: a dire combination of stripy Nikes and checked trousers, say, proof positive of his bad taste, which didn't stop him taking good photographs, so good, in fact, that they tended to overshadow the impeccable prose of Miss Ramos. This time, however, she was determined not to be overshadowed, which was why she had prepared a battery of penetrating questions for Ernesto Teldi. Some were hard-hitting, even impertinent, all were backed up by careful research: intellect and gossip, blended 50-50, a foolproof recipe, mused Miss Ramos. She was going to show her ignorant bosses at *Patron of the Arts* what a top-class interview should be.

'Good morning, Mr Teldi.'

Miss Agustina Ramos had almost disappeared from view into an enormous sofa with claret upholstery – it was no doubt very comfortable, but far too voluminous for someone of her modest dimensions. Nevertheless, she got her tape-recorder going.

'One, two, three, testing,' she said, adding, by way of a label: 'Interview with Ernesto Teldi, Spanish-Argentine art dealer and collector—'

'I would just say Spanish,' interjected Teldi with a marked South American accent. 'Many people think I'm Argentine because I lived for a long time in Buenos Aires and my surname sounds vaguely Italian, but I assure you I'm Spanish through and through.'

Miss Ramos didn't like to be interrupted. What a drag, now she would have to stop and rewind the tape. And, besides, there was absolutely no need for him to butt in. She had prepared the interview thoroughly; she knew perfectly well Teldi had started out as a young man in Madrid with ambition to spare but not much money, and that, at the end of the sixties, ignoring everyone's advice, he had decided to give up a steady job and try his luck in Argentina. It was hardly an ideal time to make the move – the country's glory days were well and truly over, and yet against all the odds Teldi had managed to make a fortune, especially in the seventies and eighties, buying up paintings in bulk at absurdly low prices (compared with what they'd fetch in Europe): Sorolla, Gutiérrez Solana, Ruisiñol, Zuloaga, even occasionally minor works by Monet, Bonnard or Renoir, gems that had come to Buenos Aires at the beginning of the century. Thanks to these good deals, Teldi was now a successful businessman, a highly respected professional, and he had recently become a generous patron of the arts. All this made him an ideal subject for the magazine Miss Ramos had the misfortune to work for, which was only interested in the rich and in artists who were famous because of the price a bunch of philistines were willing to pay for their work. Nevertheless, there are dark corners in the life of every eminent man, and Teldi was no exception. Miss Ramos was determined to seek them out, even if it meant opposing the directives of her insufferably stupid bosses. She would show them what a real arts journalist can do. But before going for the jugular . . .

'Tell me, Mr Teldi, for you, is art business or pleasure?' she asked, because this fundamental question was an obligatory part of any interview with *Patron of the Arts*.

Same old drivel, thought Teldi, silently cursing Mr Janeiro, the entrepreneur who owned this magazine that humiliated serious minds like Miss Ramos by forcing them to ask hackneyed questions: business or pleasure?

Teldi leant back in his armchair. Privately, he agreed with Miss Ramos about the stupidity of the question: everyone knows that art these days is a business first and foremost. Nevertheless, he trotted out an appropriate reply.

'Well, of course, it's neither one nor the other. Art is a source of aesthetic experience, part of the common heritage of humanity. It is what distinguishes us from the animals and brings us closer to the gods.'

Right, thought Miss Ramos. Now that she had discharged her obligation, she could get down to business. She pulled out a little notebook in which she had patiently summarized the key facts and dates from Teldi's CV. Are you ready, Mr Teldi? she said to herself. Brace yourself; here comes the first cruise missile. And she launched into her first penetrating question, cleverly laced with vitriol, but before she could get to the end of it, she was distracted by two strange sounds. One was emanating from the jaws of the photographer, who was chewing gum in time with another sound: click, click, click, CLICK, went the shutter as Chema dodged around Teldi, taking shot after shot. This always drove Miss Ramos up the wall, but there was no point complaining: the editor of *Patron of the Arts* believed in having the photos taken during the interview. 'They've got more life and authenticity that way, Ramos. You don't get it, do you? You still haven't realized we're living in a visual culture. A gesture's worth a thousand words. Do us a favour and stop whining.'

So Agustina Ramos didn't whine, not even when Chema thrust himself between her and Teldi to immortalize the way the dealer stroked his chin as he replied to the tricky question the young lady had left dangling.

'No, no. I'm afraid you're mistaken, my dear. It was easy to buy paintings back then, but I can assure you it had nothing whatever to do with Argentina's political problems or the repression and the horrendous crimes committed by the military. The art boom had begun before all that. You realize of course that I've been a member of the UNIC for years' (IC for Investigating Committee, of course). 'As I said, I'm a member of a body set up precisely to investigate human rights violations; so I'm hardly likely to have taken advantage of those unfortunate circumstances to . . .'

'To get rich by ripping off families that, as well as being torn apart, also had their property devalued during the dictatorship—'

'Quite, my dear,' broke in Teldi, who knew that the best way to handle this sort of virago was to confront her directly and to get the upper hand as soon as possible. 'That's precisely why we set up the PFVST, the Philanthropic Fund for the Victims of State Terrorism; and it's a well-known fact that I was one of the founders of the fund, at considerable personal risk, believe me. Remember we're talking about the period from seventy-six to eighty-three – not the best time to go playing the hero, I can assure you.'

He was looking at her. His suave philanthropist's gaze seemed to settle tenderly on Miss Ramos's ankles, which were the most attractive part of her anatomy. Nice ankles, he seemed to be saying with his eyes, and Miss Ramos almost smiled, because she wasn't completely immune to a man's gaze, especially the gaze of a *connoisseur*. Nevertheless, like a true professional, she managed to hold onto her aggressive manner.

'Yes, yes, perhaps it wasn't a good time for heroism, but curiously, with everything that was going on, it seems to have been a good time for making a great deal of money. As you mentioned yourself, those were the years of state terrorism. So what's your secret?'

'There is no secret,' Teldi replied (his gaze sliding down from Miss Ramos's ankles to her shoes, which she suddenly felt like hiding, lest those gallant eyes discover that her expensive-looking footwear was fake). 'You see, Agustina' (such a pretty name, the way he said it), 'in the period we're talking about, there was only one way to succeed: a good deal of hard work and contempt for the military. But we're here to talk about art, not politics, aren't we, my dear? So perhaps we should alter the focus of our conversation.'

At this point, Chema took advantage of Teldi's emphatic pause on the word 'focus' to capture an image of him making his point with an expression of such grandeur that a lady having breakfast two tables away let out a stifled 'oh', and elbowed her husband in the ribs.

'Look Alfredo, it's someone famous!' she said. 'Look, over there, on the left. Isn't it Agnelli, the owner of Maserati? He looks just like a Florentine cardinal!'

And the husband, apparently up on such things, informed her that Agnelli had nothing to do with Maserati; he was the owner of Olivetti, the multinational, didn't she know anything? Meanwhile Chema went on flashing his camera and Miss Ramos made a valiant effort to back Teldi into a corner with her penetrating questions.

'All right, it's true that no-one has ever been able to link you with the military, and that's very much to your credit, because surely, if a link were discovered, well, the stain would be indelible. So let's leave all that aside and talk about art, but even where art is concerned, there have, I'm afraid, been a number of rumours about your highly profitable deals. Is it true, for example, that you once bought a magnificent Monet for a ridiculously small sum, then sold it for twenty times its value, while the former owner of the painting, unable to pay his debts, ended up committing suicide?'

'Well, it's true about the transactions,' said Teldi with a charming smile, 'but the rest of the story is a little fanciful. The former owner of the Monet is not only alive and well, he's also a good friend of mine and now one of the richest men in South America. I like to help people out and expect them to do the same for me. Is there something reprehensible about that, Agustina?'

Mr Teldi was coming to seem less reprehensible to Miss Ramos. Especially when their eyes met, which didn't happen very often, just often enough to make her want more. In fact, Miss Ramos, who prided herself on being an infallible judge of character, had to admire the way he was handling her aggressive questioning: smiling calmly, even once (just once alas!) stretching out his right hand towards the sofa where she was sitting, although he didn't go so far as to actually touch her. The perfect gentleman, naturally. His gaze settled on her again. Miss Ramos felt as if she were melting, and would soon be no more than a puddle on the claret-coloured sofa. My God, his aura! No camera could ever capture it, the aura of this exquisite philanthropist and patron of the arts. Besides, she thought, however hard I try to do my duty as an aggressive interviewer, the facts speak for themselves: as he says, hard work and a passion for art, that's how he earned his money; and you have to consider what he's done with it too.

'Setting up two schools for abandoned children, my dear,' (two little words that were music to her ears) 'and scholarships to nurture talent, not just for painters but for musicians and writers too. We can never do enough for the arts. After all life has given me, I feel I should give something back, you see.'

Of course she does: Miss Ramos can see clearly now. This man is so sensitive, so perfectly straightforward, and what he says is so true.

'I've got it,' said the wife of the man named Alfredo, sitting two tables away. 'It's not Agnelli. He's an actor, that guy. What's his name . . . ? Sean Connery? No, I don't know, that moustache and the grey hair . . . But I'm sure I've seen him in a film. They never stop acting, even in real life, but it always seems so natural, doesn't it, Alfredo?'

Alfredo had no opinion on the matter. He couldn't have cared less. Distinguished-looking men with grey hair may fascinate a good many wives, but husbands will obviously not be so susceptible especially husbands who happen to be bald. Besides which, Alfredo couldn't hear what they were saying, although he was certain of two things: it wasn't Sean Connery, and that poor girl, the journalist, was falling into the same hypnotic trance as his wife. If you ask me, he's a small-time con-artist, thought Alfredo. But all he said was: 'Let's go, Matilde.'

Meanwhile, Teldi was saying to Miss Ramos: 'Yes, yes, but let's not restrict ourselves to Art with a capital A. It's all very well to talk about Monet and congratulate oneself on being the lucky owner of so many wonderful works, but there are other things in life that give me much more pleasure, things I feel I can talk about with someone like you. I'll let you into a secret, my dear. But perhaps if you switch off the tape recorder first . . . You see, it's not the sort of thing that would interest a magazine like *Patron of the Arts*, with its three hundred and fifty thousand subscribers among the . . . they really should call it *Art Shark*, don't you think?'

Miss Ramos couldn't have agreed more. She switched off her tape recorder. Then she looked at Chema to see if he was going to butt in and spoil things as usual. But Chema, who had finished taking photos, was standing ten yards away, chewing gum and inspecting his exposure metre.

'Perhaps it's rather frivolous, but it's the sort of thing I really enjoy, and I know you'll find it amusing. The philanthropists you interview are probably always telling you how they hob-nob with other famous patrons of the arts, getting together to talk about the pieces they're planning to buy, or throwing parties just to show off their latest acquisitions to friends and rivals – a Byzantine virgin, say, bought from some dealer who specializes in extracting such objects from Eastern Europe. You know the type, swindlers the lot of them. Not that I don't occasionally participate in that sort of pantomime myself. I do – I go along to their cocktail parties and do business with them, but the people I really like are the ones who are passionate about Art with a capital A, my dear, and by that I don't mean things that cost a fortune, but things that are truly unique. Just to give you an idea, let me tell you what I'm organizing for next week . . .'

You can tell me anything, Ernesto Teldi, thought Miss Ramos. What do I care about my art-shark bosses, and hard-hitting interviews and all the stupid, unscrupulous people who try to fling mud at you? There are always slanderous rumours about anyone who really stands out. If only I could . . . if only I knew . . . While all these thoughts were running through Miss Ramos's mind, she maintained the outward appearance of a dispassionate journalist, thanks to her professional reflexes. Resist, Agustina, she said to herself, as if her scruples were the walls of a besieged city. Keep on resisting. But Agustina's gunpowder was damp.

'Look, I'm organizing a little get-together in a few days' time, you really must come,' said Teldi, as if the idea had just occurred to him and it wasn't a devious way to side-track Miss Motor-mouth, with her artistic pretensions and her dangerous questions about his past in Argentina. 'I come from a humble background and I like to mix with simple people. I should explain: I've invited some collectors to my country house. Not big collectors, mind you, the kind with more money than sense, who hoard Picassos or collect Folio editions of Shakespeare and never read past the first page of *Hamlet* – they're always quoting "To be or not to be," without knowing the rest of the speech, which is better still, don't you think? – "Who would fardels bear, To grunt and sweat under a weary life . . ." and so on. You know what I mean: the kind of people who love possessions rather than art. No, the guests I've invited are not like that at all.'

Ernesto Teldi then proceeded to seduce Miss Ramos (and, incidentally, the magazine's 350,000 subscribers, including all the major players in the international art game) with one of his original ideas.

'Naturally, I wouldn't want you to mention this in

Patron of the Arts. You can keep the sharks happy with the politically correct side of my activities, if you see what I mean. You can tell them about the artists I sponsor, my efforts to bring art to a wider public, my scholarships to foster young talent – that'll do for them. They don't have the sensitivity to appreciate this sort of thing. So it's just between you and me, OK?'

And as if to drive his point home, he went on to explain that he would be delighted if she could join them the following weekend in the south. It would be an opportunity to meet some truly eccentric collectors: tin soldier fanatics, seekers after exotic daggers and stiletti, not to mention beer-mug and stuffed-animal fanciers, or connoisseurs of saucepans, porcelain dolls and antiquarian books of ghost stories. 'People who really appreciate the objects for their own sake. The way they fall for those sublime bits and pieces, it's so pure, and that, for me, is how all art should be appreciated.'

Ernesto Teldi prudently avoided mentioning that by gathering eccentrics such as these (and plying them with the contents of his cellar) he was often able to pick up very rare pieces for a song before they came onto the market. Miss Ramos didn't need to know such petty details. What someone of her aesthetic sensibility couldn't help but recognize, however, was the generous spirit of his initiative: bringing together a varied group of real experts, in the most tasteful and refined of settings, free of snobbery and greed.

'You're more than welcome to come, if you'd like,' he insisted.

Life is so unfair, thought Miss Agustina Ramos. She was still half buried in the claret-coloured sofa, and for a second the enveloping warmth of the cushions helped her to imagine what the gathering might be like, with all those interesting people. No famous, insufferable painters, no filthy-rich philistines incapable of telling a Monet from a Manet, none of the usual *Patron of the Arts* pond-life. Just genuine aesthetic sensibility, she thought, looking at Ernesto Teldi's handsome hands, which had once again advanced towards the armrest of the sofa. He was watching her.

'Well, Agustina? Hmm, my dear?'

It was so unfair. Agustina my dear would have given anything to be able to say yes, but, just her luck, that weekend she had to be on the other side of the world, interviewing a Japanese collector who owned a Van Gogh suspected by many of being a fake. Now *there* was an art shark who had better watch out. She'd be storing up her nastiest questions for him. A boring assignment in Japan instead of a party at Teldi's house. Typical, she thought, I never have any luck, never.

'That's such a pity, such a pity,' said Teldi, who had chosen this psychologically crucial moment to bring the interview to a close. 'I do wish you could come. But don't forget, my dear, not a word about our little secret. People are so narrow-minded,' he added. 'It's really quite sad: all they want to know is how much I give to young artists and how much I spend on sponsorships. Money, money, money, it's all they can think about. But we may as well give them what they're after, don't you think, my dear?'

Agustina took her leave. He kissed her hand, the hand that wrote for *Patron of the Arts* and would compose an extremely dull and conventional but glowingly positive profile of Ernesto Teldi, a man who, in the space of a few short years, had risen to become a philanthropist of international standing.

'You're a truly remarkable person, Mr Teldi,' she said

to him, as he bid her farewell with a wink of complicity almost as intimate as a kiss.

'Goodbye, Agustina. We'll be seeing each other.'

And as Miss Ramos walked towards the door with a voice in her head crying When? When? and Ernesto Teldi sat down again with a sigh of relief, like someone catching his breath after an obstacle race, two things happened almost simultaneously.

'Now I remember who that man is. It's the actor who played the cannibal in *The Silence of the Lambs*,' exclaimed the woman two tables away. 'Alfredo, do you think he'd mind if I asked for an autograph?'

'Mr Teldi,' said a bellboy who had appeared from nowhere, as bellboys should, 'a letter has come for you. It's just been delivered.'

Alfredo's wife was approaching Teldi. Soon she would be able to hear his voice. So would her husband.

'Shit!' he exclaimed, standing up abruptly when he saw the envelope in the bellboy's hand: it was the second such letter he had received in twenty-four hours. Both had been written in a crabbed hand using green ink: the letters looked like a row of parrots on a wire.

'Did you hear that, Matilde?' said the gentleman named Alfredo to his wife. 'You see? I told you he wasn't some foreign actor.'

Ernesto Teldi couldn't decipher the signature at the bottom of the page, but part of the text, written in capital letters, was clear enough for him to make out five words that had figured in the previous letter: 'Colonel Minelli . . . Don Torcuato Airport.' And then, in a tangled scribble that almost seemed like a burst of laughter: 'Remember, Teldi?'

Part Three

The Night Before the Departure

Others apart sat on a hill retired
In thoughts more elevate, and reasoned high
Of providence, foreknowledge, will, and fate,
Fixed fate, free will, foreknowledge absolute,
And found no end, in wand'ring mazes lost.

Milton, *Paradise Lost*, Book II

Editor's Note: The recipe that follows is the last one sent by Nestor Chaffinch to his friend Antonio Reig. He had presumed that after his trip to the Teldis' country house, their correspondence would continue. As we know, this was not to be. Destiny had decided that Nestor's work should remain unfinished and unfinishable. The chapter devoted to *petits fours* is dated 27 March. It must, therefore, have been written the day before his departure. As usual, Nestor occasionally interrupts his culinary notes to pass on news.

LITTLE INDISCRETIONS
PART FOUR: PETITS FOURS AND OTHER AFTER-DINNER DELICACIES

One of the high points of a good meal is the arrival of the little after-dinner treats that are usually served with coffee. Chocolate truffles, caramelized cherries, biscotti with or without almonds, millefeuilles with glacé oranges . . . There's no better way to round off a menu than with these delicious morsels, and, as we shall see in a moment, they too have their little secrets, jealously guarded by the professionals. For example Lucas Carton's tiny soufflés. The recipe is as follows:

[. . .] but first, dear Antonio, let me digress for a moment, I promise it won't take long. Remember in my last letter I was telling you I had this strange feeling that the various parts of my life were coming together to form a peculiar puzzle of coincidences? (A disconcerting feeling, to say the least, I'd even say creepy if I wasn't half Italian and worried about bringing bad luck on myself: gettatore, gettatore*). Anyway, it seems to have stopped. A spanner got into the works of fate, and at least one of Madame Longstaffe's supposedly infallible predictions has turned out to be wrong. It*

had to do with the love life of my assistant Carlos Garcia, the one who's responsible for getting me mixed up with this fortune-teller in the first place. You may remember we went to see her to get a love potion that was meant to help Carlos find the living image of his ideal woman. Well, to my great surprise, and relief, not only has my young friend lost interest in love potions (before finishing the bottle) he's also lost interest in his ideal woman (the one in the painting). He told me he's fallen in love with a real woman – a flesh-and-blood, living, breathing woman – and forgotten all those fantasies he used to have. I don't know her, and although I've tried to draw him out, so far he's refused to tell me her name. My guess is she's a bit older. Maybe some thirty-year-old divorcee, who knows? It wouldn't surprise me, they can be quite attractive . . . Anyway, if you're interested, I should be able to give you more details in my next letter, because I may well meet her tonight. You see, Carlos urgently needs to sell the flat he inherited from his grandmother so he's asked me to help him. I put him in touch with an acquaintance who works in property, and we're going round in a bit to take a look at the place. So today I'll get to see the flat and the portrait and most likely the girlfriend too. She'll probably be there to give him moral support at such a crucial time, don't you think?

Anyway, I'm wittering on like I always do in my letters. You don't need all these details. The important thing is that the spell has been broken and I don't feel like I'm being driven along a path any more. It was like a sort of determinism. I think that's what it's called when your destiny is fixed in advance. But that's all over now. Madame Longstaffe's potion didn't work and the boy has fallen in love with another woman who has nothing to do with any predictions, so you see I feel free. It's such a relief to realize that no-one can know or determine your destiny, not even some crafty old witch. That's why I'm feeling so good today, dear Antonio. In fact, I feel so good that before I give you Lucas Carton's recipe, I'll slip in another one that's even better. This is my most precious indiscretion. Here goes:

In 1911, the chef at the Waldorf Astoria in New York discovered an infallible secret method for making a cold soufflé that looks exactly like a hot one. These days one of the most interesting petits fours being made is a cold pistachio soufflé. Because it is so small it is perfect for . . .

1

Nestor and the Woman in the Painting

'Small but perfectly formed: ideal for the client I have in mind,' said Juan Solis, the real estate agent, with an admiring little whistle. 'What a *find*, Nestor!'

Nestor Chaffinch and Carlos looked at each other, and then at Solis, who was opening and closing drawers, inspecting the contents of biscuit tins, expertly pacing out the distances, walking around and weighing things up, as if making a complete inventory. He had broken a personal rule in coming to Number 38 Calle de Almagro with Nestor and Carlos. In twenty years as a real estate agent he had never agreed to see a property on a Saturday night – absolutely out of the question – he spent his Saturdays practising t'ai chi. It was the only way he could maintain his emotional balance in such a stressful profession. But the sacrifice had turned out to be worthwhile. Solis felt he had discovered a pearl, and didn't mind saying so, over and over again. He was full of praise for Number 38: the height of the ceilings, the ideal orientation of the windows, the quality of the woodwork, and kept repeating with great emphasis the part about it being 'small but perfectly formed', and therefore just right for his client.

Nestor was not particularly curious about this client who apparently considered a 250-square-metre flat 'small' (and in the Calle de Almagro, no less). But as he walked away, leaving them to it, he heard Solis mention, in a discreet but intentionally sonorous whisper, somebody by the name of Baggerscheit.

'A kid who sings heavy metal,' added the whisperer, by way of explanation. 'He's huge, a real phenomenon.'

No doubt he is, thought Nestor before slipping away through a door on his left. He was disappointed. Carlos had come on his own, without his new girlfriend, so he would have to wait to satisfy his curiosity. Now he had a choice: either he could follow Carlos and Solis from room to room, admiring the flat and making the appropriate noises, or he could entertain himself. Off you go, Juan, he thought, discover the unexploited potential of Number 38. In the meantime, I think I'll sit down and wait here in this little room . . . I can note down a few things I mustn't forget for tomorrow's trip.

Switching on the light, Nestor realized that there was nowhere to sit. Sheets covered all the furniture in the room, and the looming shape of what seemed to be a large armchair, underneath the dustiest of them all, seemed more like a relic from a bygone age than an inviting place to sit. He looked around and discovered that he had stepped into a semi-circular room with walls that must once have been yellow. At the far end was a fireplace and there, sitting in the hearth, like a woman looking out at the world through a window-frame, was the portrait of a lady.

Nestor approached, examining her features curiously.

This must have been the young woman he had heard so much about, the woman in the wardrobe . . . Because of Carlos's straitened circumstances, the room was lit by a single bulb that dispensed such a feeble glow that the cook had to open the door wide so that the light from the corridor would illuminate the portrait at the far end of the room.

'Baggerscheit's going to love this purple vestibule,' said Solis's voice. 'It is purple, isn't it, son? You can't see a damn thing in here.'

And it was true. Even with the door wide open, Nestor couldn't see a damn thing. He rifled through his pockets. Chefs, even if they don't smoke, often carry a lighter, or matches at least, and sure enough, Nestor found a small box of Mulberry & Mistletoe matches in the pocket of his waistcoat decorated with the company insignia, a motif at once floral and magical: the mulberry tree, favoured food of silkworms, and mistletoe, a talisman for finding hidden treasures. It was most appropriate. Anyone else would have seen the portent in those symbols, anyone but Nestor, who innocently lit a match.

'Listen, son, my client will want to know how much of the furniture's coming with the flat, and remember he's keen to buy the lot if he can. He's about your age, actually, but he's absolutely loaded. Have you heard his latest hit. "Kill me with the Lawnmower"? Great stuff.'

Solis kept calling Carlos 'son', and his insistent voice began to work its way into the small yellow sitting room. Nestor could hear every word of the agent's patter, which went on and on as if to provide an odd counterpoint to his own silent activity. He had lit a match and, with the uncertain precision of someone who doesn't yet know that he is on the point of making a strange discovery, he moved the flame up and down in front of the picture.

First the halo of light illuminated a woman's forehead, then her platinum blond hair, then it hovered a little too long in front of a pair of blue eyes so that by the time it moved on, the flame was nearly out. Nestor tried to use the fading glow to reveal another of the girl's features, her mouth at least, but the flame receded and died, as if it were trying to preserve a secret. Too late: the secret was out. While Nestor was looking for another match, he could have sworn that under cover of darkness those mocking lips were saying, in a faintly familiar voice: 'Ah so it's you, Nestor, back again?' or more simply: 'Good evening, Nestor.'

The flame of the second match opened a breach in the darkness of the yellow sitting room and the voice fell silent immediately, dispelled by the light, like all enchantments. But when he examined the woman's lips up close, it seemed to Nestor that they were slightly open, as if she had just been speaking.

'What's in that room, son, the one with the door open?'

It was the voice of Solis, the pioneer, discoverer of unknown lands. But Carlos diverted him with a request.

'Hang on, Mr Solis, let's leave that room till last. First I'd like to show you this one here on the right. It's a dressing room. Your client may want to use it as a gym. I think there might even be an old massage table in there.'

'Excellent! You're in luck, because Baggerscheit wants to buy the whole lot. Everything. Let's take a look.'

So Nestor had a while longer to make absolutely sure, not that he needed to: the blonde woman in the painting was Adela Teldi, the woman he had met in Buenos Aires when she was in her thirties, the perpetrator of that little indiscretion he had told his staff about one afternoon to stop them asking prying questions about his moleskin notebook of culinary secrets. Nestor no longer needed confirmation, but with the third match, he verified, one by one, the presence of Adela's defining features. Life's experiences had yet to bring them out, but they were in a latent state in that smooth fresh face, with the somewhat absent expression in the blue eyes he had seen staring at Soledad's lifeless body. Even now, by the flickering light of the match-flame, he could detect a hint of incredulity in those eyes, just as he had when the broken, lifeless body of her sister was found sprawled on the paving stones of the patio three floors below, three floors closer to hell. Nestor, Adela and all the other witnesses could see Soledad's head, tiny and black like a full stop, while her twisted body lay in the shape of an absurd question mark. That's Mrs Teldi's younger sister, all the eyes confirmed, while down below the question mark was spreading a dark stain. It was the beginning of Soledad's slow revenge on two of the onlookers: her unfaithful husband and Adela. The bloodstains left by suicide are so stubborn. They never wash away completely.

Piecing together these coincidences, Nestor turned his thoughts to Soledad: for Carlos, her son, she remained faceless. And now, of course, it all made sense: the flat at Number 38 Calle de Almagro, where Carlos's father was not welcome; Teresa's frostiness; the stoney silences . . . and this portrait, that Teresa had consigned to the back of a wardrobe no doubt in an effort to forget both of her daughters – it was too painful to remember Soledad, and it was better to banish Adela from her mind than to hate her.

The match went out again. Nestor lit a fourth, and this time his gaze slid down over the young woman's shoulders to her hands. What was that round green object she was holding in her fingers? It looked like a jewel, or perhaps a cameo . . . But rather than lingering over it, he moved the flame back up to her eyes and, as it flickered out, the last pieces of the puzzle fell into place. What surprised him most was Carlos's blindness. In the picture, Adela couldn't have been more than seventeen or eighteen years old. Nestor had recognized her instantly, but of course he had the advantage of having known her when she was still quite young. That day at Mulberry & Mistletoe, Carlos had met Adela properly, but amazingly he hadn't made the connection. She was the one he had been searching for everywhere, constantly seeing her eyes or her neck in those of other women, so how could he not have recognized her? Three days earlier, at Madame Longstaffe's house, he had said: 'I never see whole people, Nestor, only parts. I only notice the smaller details that make them unique . . .' Like a man lighting his way in the dark with a match, thought Nestor, without realizing that this was exactly how he had discovered Adela.

He who sees life in fragments will not take in the whole picture, as Madame Longstaffe might have put it.

'Of course, "Kill me with the Lawnmower" isn't my client's only hit. "Shitless in Gaza" was huge too. What? You're telling me you've never heard of it. You're kidding. You've got to get out more, son. It's only sold two million. And just think, he'll be writing his next hit right here in this room,' said Solis. 'Your flat and everything in it will be his.'

Yes. Let's hope he does take the whole lot, that Baggerscheit fellow. It would be for the best, thought Nestor as he stroked the frame of the picture, which seemed not to have gathered any dust, unlike the rest of the objects in the room. Sell the house and everything in it, all in one go. It's odd how some places seem to attract coincidences, like Number 38 Calle de Almagro. Soledad's body must have been taken from this flat to a grave that Carlos had never visited. But now that Number 38 had opened its doors to Nestor, revealing secrets within secrets: a story of adultery between brother- and sister-in-law, the tragedy of Soledad . . . You might have thought that would be enough bad luck to last a lifetime, but years later, the gods had seen fit to add a few more twists.

Nestor's hand was still resting on the frame, as if on a window-ledge, and it struck him that he and the woman in the picture were an odd couple: she on her side of the mirror, he on his, she looking out at him, seeing nothing, while he could see all too clearly and he didn't much like what he saw. Destiny likes to arrange coincidences, he thought. Life is full of them, when you think about it. It must happen all the time that two people who share a common history walk past one another in the street without realizing . . . Or two brothers separated at birth sit next to each other one day on a bus . . . Their paths might cross, or they might not, he thought . . . So many coincidences, most of which go unnoticed. Perhaps it's better that way.

By the time Nestor joined Carlos and Solis, who were about to inspect a room at the end of the hallway, he had made up his mind what he was going to do.

'This is one of my favourite rooms in the whole flat, Mr Solis,' said Carlos. 'I know it's not much to look at, but see that wardrobe? I used to play in there as a kid. It was full of junk – still is. When I inherited this place, the only thing I salvaged from in there was a painting I'm very fond of, the portrait of a woman.'

And that wardrobe is where you belong, Adela Teldi, or at least where your story belongs, thought Nestor. It was clear to him now that chance occurrences, however uncanny, didn't become coincidences unless a witness was there to point them out. He had always considered discretion as the wisest policy for someone in his position, with intimate knowledge of so many private lives. Most of the tricks destiny plays on us pass unnoticed, he thought, and so will this one. Your story will remain here in this flat, Adela Teldi. Right here is where you will stay for ever, my dear, locked up in that wardrobe, you and your adulterous little indiscretion with its unforeseen consequences, your home-made Greek tragedy and your soap-opera scandal. Because that's how I want it to be. We'll go to your house, we'll serve your guests, I'll prepare my finest desserts . . . and no-one will ever know of the furtive connection between a respectable client and a staff member of Mulberry & Mistletoe Catering Company.

'Carlos, are you there?'

'Hang on, Nestor, I'll be with you in a minute. I just have to see what Mr Solis wants.'

'I'm interested in this copper washbowl, son, and that old lamp too, but what I'd really like to see is that portrait you found in the wardrobe.'

Nestor wasn't listening to any of this. No doubt Carlos and Juan Solis were making good progress in their negotiations, but all the chef could think about was his discovery, and how it wasn't so hard to cheat destiny. If the gods can play tricks, so can I, he concluded, with a certain satisfaction. And then, using an elaborate gastronomic image that came so easily to him, he vowed his own little indiscretion would never be divulged, because coincidences, he thought, are like soufflés: they come to nothing unless someone takes the trouble to beat, stir or otherwise shake up the egg-whites.

From where Nestor was standing, he could see Solis, who was still measuring and estimating the value of the place, like the shrewd estate agent that he was. He even went over and measured the painting of the woman. It's not as if the secret's bound to come out, thought Nestor, seeing the agent so interested in the portrait. This house will be sold, and soon it will all be forgotten. Luckily Carlos seems to have found himself a new woman, so he's forgotten all about the one in the painting. What a blessing, because now he can never find out who he's really been in love with all along . . .

'A very nice picture, son, but it's not worth much. I'd advise you to sell it along with the flat. You're in luck, because Baggerscheit loves blondes. You don't want to hang on to any of the other furniture or fittings, do you?'

'Just the picture,' said Carlos. 'It has sentimental value. It's part of my childhood—'

'Oh do grow up,' said Nestor, butting in. 'I thought we'd agreed you were going to stop fantasizing about ghosts.'

'Oh, there you are, Nestor,' said Carlos with a start. 'Where have you been?'

'I've seen her, Carlos,' Nestor said, ignoring the question, 'and she belongs in that yellow room. The picture should not be moved. It should be left exactly where it is.'

Carlos didn't understand. He didn't understand at all. He even found his friend's reaction funny. 'Hang on, what's happening? Don't tell me you've fallen in love with her too.'

'Come on, she's not that gorgeous,' said Solis. 'How much do you want for her?'

'The thing is, I don't think I want to sell her. I've already told you, the picture is part of my childhood. You just don't sell things like that, even if they don't mean as much as they used to . . .'

But both Solis and Nestor seemed determined to make an issue of it:

'Come on, son, get rid of it while you can. Don't be silly. Where else are you going to find a buyer like this?'

'Think about it, *cazzo* Carlitos. You don't even know who the woman is, and you're being offered a nice sum of money. What difference does it make to you now? It was just some fantasy you had.'

'He's right,' said the agent. 'If you're smart, you won't let a chance like this go by, because Baggerscheit' – stressing each syllable of his millionaire client's name – 'he'll take the lot, childhood memories and all. At a fair price, of course.'

2

Chloe Trias and the Ghosts

The night before leaving for the Teldis' house, Chloe thought it wouldn't be a bad idea to pack some clothes. Maybe she wouldn't get a chance to wear her bikini, but she might as well take it, just in case. Everybody is hungry for sun in March, even apathetic girls like Chloe Trias. But then she suddenly realized that when she'd walked out of her parents' house and slammed the door behind her two or three months earlier, she'd left her bikini behind. She'd have to sneak back for it. Just so long as she didn't run into her old folks – what a fucking drag that'd be.

Chloe examined the house from outside. There were lights on in five of the downstairs windows, so there must have been something special going on. Upstairs, however, two dark balconies laden with dim, forgotten objects revealed that the Triases had become 'a childless couple' as they wryly liked to say. Since Chloe's departure, they had rearranged the house in response to the new situation, so the large ground-floor rooms were full of people while the windows upstairs were shuttered. It was one way of dealing with the emptiness.

Chloe knew this. She understood. The gravel near the front door crunched under her feet, but luckily that sound, so evocative of childhood, no longer reminded her of the games she used to play there as a girl with her brother Eddie. All things fade with time. Pain can be anaesthetized by carefully covering it up with layer after layer of insignificant memories. Many years had passed since the day Eddie left, so Chloe felt no nostalgia as she walked up the path and heard the gravel crunch. There was only one part of the house that was dangerously charged with memories, and she had no intention of going there. She looked up. The darkness of the windows was reassuring.

The bedrooms of dead children are shrines to their spirits, but also a refuge for the cowardice of the living. Few have the courage to live with their memories and weave them into the present. Only the strongest parents can keep a photograph of a dead child in the sitting room, fielding questions from people who don't know, living with the sight of a perpetually fresh smile, indifferent to the passage of the years. The rest of us grow old while they, by contrast, seem to grow younger, filling us with guilt for not having made the most of their brief time among us, for not having guessed that they would disappear, leaving everything unfinished, not just their lives and their dreams, but also, more wrenchingly, the things that happened on the day of their death: a silly argument, say, that will never be resolved, an argument about nothing, really. And all we can remember are a few hurtful words that can never be taken back now: 'If only I hadn't said this or that . . . If only, if only . . .' But nothing can bring the dead back to life or fulfil their destinies.

Without actually betraying them, most of those who remain prefer to forget those who have gone. They shift the departed out of their daily lives, while keeping them present in some remote part of the house: a guilty but comforting shrine, like Eddie's bedroom.

Just as deep wounds heal, leaving a layer of hard, insensitive scar tissue, when children die or run away, so too does loss fade into nothingness. While the photos of Eddie, his books and belongings, and Chloe's things too, had gradually been removed from the rest of the house, their bedrooms had been preserved intact, beds made and clothes in the wardrobe, as if they were still children and might come home from school at any minute. They were at once absent and present. Not a bad way to deal with it, really. After all, you have to go on living.

Chloe crept past the door of the sitting room on tiptoe, so as not to have to say hello to anyone. She knew exactly what was going on beyond that inch of wood: the holy ritual of her parents' canasta night. There would be two card tables covered in green cloth, one on either side of the window. Her mother would be presiding over the noisier table while her father directed proceedings at the other – the perfect couple, an advertiser's dream, as Karel Pligh had described them one day. And he couldn't have put it better. They were the perfect example of a successful couple. She was good looking and so was he. Both were moderately unfaithful, moderately unhappy and moderately prone to insomnia.

As she crept up the staircase, Chloe couldn't help stopping for a few moments in front of one of the wooden banisters, the fifth to be precise, which was darker than the rest. This was an old ritual – as a child she was convinced she could see the face of a gnome in its grain and by scrutinizing his expression she could tell how the day would turn out. He's laughing! Fantastic: I'll pass my maths test. He's frowning: better not tempt fate . . . As she came to the banister, Chloe realized she was now too grown up to read the grain, yet prompted by an old superstition she stroked it fondly, like a talisman that had lost its power. One more step, and another, and another, and Chloe had reached the top of the staircase without the old wood creaking to give her away. She crossed the landing and, without stopping, passed on quickly to her parents' bedroom. Hers was further along and she was thinking about the clothes she wanted to take to the Teldis', just a bikini and a pair of T-shirts. It would only take a couple of minutes to grab what she needed and get out of there. Cool. Everything would be in its place, clean and ironed, because her pretty plastic TV mother made sure it stayed that way: 'This is Chloe's room, these are Chloe's teddy bears, those are Chloe's nice clothes – everything's just as it was, nothing has changed.'

But before she reached the door of her bedroom, Chloe hesitated. The voices of the canasta players drifted up from the sitting room, amplified by the stairwell: an indistinct murmur from which a more strident voice rang out now and then. There's always one especially raucous chicken in the coop.

'Bunch of arseholes,' she said, 'just as well I don't have to see their ugly faces.'

At which point an ugly and all too familiar face appeared in a doorway downstairs. Spying between the banisters, Chloe could see Amalia Rossi, her mother's old Italian friend, coming out into the hall. She must have had more to drink than usual because she was saying: 'Let me go, Maria, I'm practically one of the family, after all. Why shouldn't I go upstairs? What's the problem? Is it my fault if your *carosposo* has been in the little room for over an hour? Do you want me to pee on the carpet? Come on; don't be silly! I know where it is. I'll just pop into Clo-clo's room.'

And up she came, the bitch. Chloe could hear her footsteps on the stairs, passing by the silent gnome and coming ever closer. There was no alternative: Chloe had to go back to the door at the end of the corridor, a door she never opened (when it came to memories, she wasn't brave either) and try to hide against the jamb. She might not be visible, but there wasn't much space. Carosposo would have to be completely drunk not to see her shoulders protruding. So when the heavy breathing drew nearer, all she could do was open the door. Fucking hell, it's Eddie's old room. That stupid bitch! Now what? Well, what else could she do, now that she was inside, but shut the door and switch on the light . . . ? It had been such a long time, fucking ages.

Can someone's smell survive for seven years after their death? It can. Shrines to dead children never smell of must or mothballs, however long they have stood empty. Even their most inaccessible corners remain free of mildew, and the air stays fresh, with no whiff of neglect. Or that was how it was in Eddie's room, at least. It is no simple feat to create the illusion that such a room is still inhabited. All the talents of a brilliant set designer had been deployed, and Chloe was drawn in, captivated by the lifelike effect created partly by the curtains and the bedspread with its ink-stain which seemed to say: Come in and see for yourselves, ladies and gentlemen, nothing has changed – smell, touch, look. You can quite easily imagine that the occupant of this room had just slipped out for a beer with his friends. And yet on closer inspection, the permanence of death was subtly apparent in certain details, particularly the excessive tidiness. Everything was precisely in its place: Eddie's bookshelves, from which he would often choose a fabulous story to read aloud to her; his collection of model cars, lined up with morbid precision on the shelves; and, next to them, his sporting trophies, entwined with a scarf. And there was something artificial about the objects laid out on what had once been Eddie's desk: the papers and folders neatly piled up, the pen and pencil strewn at romantic angles, yet not quite offsetting the overall theatrical effect.

What struck her most on entering her brother's bedroom was neither the deceptive smell of life nor this excessive neatness, but the *size* of everything. The years had gone by, but Eddie's room had been frozen in time, creating the curious illusion that all the objects in it had shrunk, as Chloe discovered to her amazement: the bed, the bedside table, and the sofa where Eddie used to lie with his legs up on the backrest, everything was so much smaller than she remembered. And like a bewildered Alice in Wonderland, Chloe discovered that a bedroom remembered from childhood can produce the same distorting effect on a girl as a mysterious little cake that says EAT ME. She must have grown too big, that must be it. She must have become enormous because it wasn't like this before. Before, her brother was big and she was small, but now the room as a whole seemed the right size for her, she thought, sitting down on the tiny chair where she always used to sit. Gathering her courage, she began to explore, opening a wardrobe to find Eddie's clothes: his little shirts and shoes, all so small by contrast with her oversize memories. The clothes were neatly folded under their plastic wraps, but apart from that, it wasn't funereal. Small, yes, but not dead, because the smell of Eddie was still clinging to the fabric. It was so real that Chloe recoiled in silent shock causing her to bump into her brother's old desk.

And as with the rest of his things, the desk at which she had so often seen him writing no longer seemed so huge but was just right for her. Feeling like Alice, she sat down on the chair, her feet resting comfortably on the ground, so she could reach out and touch Eddie's notebooks, which he had never allowed her to read. She opened one, and, for the first time, started leafing through his drafts: twenty pages written in a tight, childlike hand, followed by a passage with so much crossing-out it was illegible. The part that was so difficult to decipher must have been something secret, perhaps the pages he didn't want to show her the day he died. 'Please, please, Eddie,' she had implored him so many times, 'tell me what you're writing. I bet it's a story with adventures and romance and crime and stuff, isn't it . . . ?' But her brother's reply was always the same: 'No, Clo-clo, not yet. One day I'll let you read what I've written, I promise you. But this is nothing, nothing important.' And now, trying to read her brother's notebooks, all Chloe could make out was a handful of disconnected ideas, sketches of plots and reams of isolated, unfinished sentences that didn't make any sense. 'Nah, this is rubbish, Clo-clo. I guess before I can make up a good story I'll have to live fast, have loads of experiences, get drunk, fuck hundreds of girls, kill someone or something . . .' And hearing her brother's voice in her memory, Chloe tried to smother it, because she didn't want to remember the last things he said before leaving for ever. That's right: I don't want to, I don't fucking want to remember. Fuck you, Eddie. If you hadn't had that stupid idea of going off on a motorbike at 200 kilometres an hour looking for experiences, you'd be with me now. I *hate* you. You had no right to go away like that . . . Chloe reached out towards her brother's bookshelf and the pile of folders. Like a spoilt child who was not getting her way, she swiped at the papers and knocked them off the table, mixing up all Eddie's scribbles, his efforts to bring together beautiful words, his incoherent notes full of clumsy sentences . . . all those futile attempts that, as Chloe saw it, had cost him his life.

'Hey, Maria,' said an indiscreet voice, the kind that carries through doors, in this case the door of Eddie's shrine. 'I don't believe it. It can't be true. I almost died of fright when I saw her . . .'

There was a murmur, then someone interrupted the voice with a question that Chloe couldn't quite catch. And then: 'Yes, dear, I mean the photo of your daughter Clo-clo I just saw in her bedroom, the one on the table. A lovely photo and it's a recent one, too, isn't it? I have to say it gave me a start. It's amazing what's in the genes, don't you think, my dear? If I hadn't seen it with my own eyes I wouldn't have believed it. Chloe has become the spitting image of her brother Eddie. She *has*, my dear. Don't look at me like that. The eyes are different, true – Eddie's eyes were very dark – but apart from that, I swear, even with that pasty look she has, like a half-starved Hare Krishna, if she took out all those rings she insists on putting through her lips she'd look exactly like your son, *poveretto mio*, God rest his soul.'

'God rest his soul,' said Carosposo's grating voice once again, coming from somewhere near the bottom of the staircase. Despite the distance, Chloe could hear her distinctly through the closed door of the bedroom-shrine that seemed to have shrunk down to her size. '. . . and what if it turns out you don't like getting drunk, Eddie? What if you don't get to fuck hundreds of girls or you don't have loads of experiences worth writing about?' Now the memory of their last conversation distracted her from Carosposo's chatter. Chloe could hear the voice of the little girl she was back then, questioning her brother and, as if the magic shrinking room had assumed Eddie's role and transcribed his reply, Chloe's gaze fell on one of the scribbled sheets where, in the midst of a great mess of crossing-out, she saw a legible sentence of fourteen words, written in her brother's unmistakable hand: 'Well then, Clo-clo, I'll just have to steal someone else's story, won't I?'

'Just like her brother,' someone said, but Chloe could no longer tell apart the voices of the guests downstairs from those that inhabited her brother's old room.

'Chloe's going to be twenty-two soon, isn't she? The same age as Eddie. I don't know about you, Maria, but for me that girl, wherever she is now, however punk or grunge or whatever she tries to be with all that piercing everywhere, she's the reincarnation of her brother, may he rest in peace.'

3

Serafin Tous and the Pizza

On the night before leaving for the Teldis' house, two of the characters in this story were feeling lonely. One was Karel Pligh, whom Chloe had left behind in a bar, promising to be back in a few minutes, but she still hadn't returned.

The other was Serafin Tous.

It's just as well no-one can see how people behave when they are alone, in private, because otherwise even the most sensible individuals would appear to be totally mad. If a window cleaner, for example, or a nosy neighbour, had looked through the windows of Serafin Tous's flat, he would have seen a middle-aged gentleman with a three-day growth, clad only in a very dirty pyjama top and unlaced shoes, sitting in front of a grand piano and staring at a telephone, as if he had been there for months. On closer inspection, the window cleaner or prying neighbour would have noticed that the man was not as naked as he appeared at first. Now and then he jiggled his leg in time with some inaudible tune, revealing (thankfully) a pair of stripy shorts beneath his filthy pyjama top. The sense of relief would have been short-lived, however, for the observer would also have discovered that, rather than sitting on a stool, the gentleman was balanced awkwardly on a pile of art books, his elbows resting on the lid of the piano, and that he was clasping a box containing a half-eaten smoked-salmon pizza, details that added a rather greasy and sordid touch to the picture. And what with the character's glassy eyes, his sloping shoulders and hair slicked down with sweat, the scene was a sad one indeed. In short, Serafin Tous, with his catatonic hands and his eyes glued to the telephone, looked like the archetypal victim of anxiety and unrelenting insomnia. And there was nothing deceptive about his appearance: it was nine o'clock at night, he hadn't slept for three nights and it looked very much like this would be the fourth.

Observant people know that there are two ways of looking at a telephone anxiously. There's the edgy look of the person who's hoping it will ring, desperately awaiting the tones of a beloved voice, or perhaps a long-awaited job offer. Serafin Tous, however, was fixing the phone with the other sort of anxious look: as if it were a diabolical device, a malevolent magnet luring people to it against their will. Get thee behind me, Satan, or, if you prefer: My Father, let this cup of damnation pass from me.

While the pizza was still warm in its box, it had been relatively easy for Serafin to stop himself from dialling a number that was firmly lodged in his memory. It was an absurd but effective method: he took a bite of pizza, stuck melted cheese all over his fingers, spilt the tomato . . . then took another slice, and another . . . and so he kept temptation at bay. It was as if he were poised between two contradictory impulses: he really did hate pizza, yet here he was wolfing it down when what he wanted most in the world was to dial that number, and he wasn't going to let himself.

How long had he been sitting there like that in front of a piano he was trying not to play, eating food he detested and stopping himself from picking up the phone? Quite a while. This was the sordid culmination of night after night spent trying to be sensible only to find his good intentions undermined by the image of a red door with a name-plate on which the word 'Freshman's' was inscribed in gothic lettering. He swallowed another mouthful of pizza. The taste of the fish was truly disgusting yet somehow pleasant too. Now he knew how it could happen, the descent into squalor and degradation you see in certain American films, those characters who won't get dressed or go out for days on end, holed up in their evil-smelling apartments surrounded by overflowing ashtrays, empty bourbon bottles and take-away food containers (Chinese or pizza as a rule). Those apartments are the celluloid image of the pit into which even the most respectable person can fall at any moment. Once you're on the slippery slope . . . and to judge by Serafin Tous's apartment, he was slipping dangerously. Luckily, he neither drank nor smoked, so at least he was spared those aspects of the squalor: the acrid reek of a thousand cigarettes, bottle after empty bottle feverishly drained without ever quenching the thirst. But all the other signs were there: he was descending into hell.

When night fell, Serafin didn't switch on the lamp; he stayed put, in the same position, enveloped in darkness, illuminated only by the lights from the street. It was better that way; neither he nor anyone else could see his unsightly stubble or the glassy look in his eyes. How patently ridiculous. The best thing for him to do at this point would surely have been to dial the damned number and be done with it. The only way to get the better of temptation is to yield to it, said someone who no doubt knew what they were talking about. So why not do it? It's really very easy, just pick up the receiver and key in the number you know so well. Then all you have to do is say, with a firm and impersonal voice, 'Good afternoon. Is that Freshman's? Listen it's . . .' But there Serafin hesitated: even making an imaginary phone call, he couldn't bring himself to give his own name. 'It's . . . a client. I'd like to speak with one of your young men. His name is Julian. Is he there?'

Yes, it would have been perfectly easy, and he wanted to do it, but Serafin's hand did not reach for the phone. Instead, he gripped the pizza box like a shipwrecked sailor grasping at a raft. He opened the box and ripped off a piece of cold pizza. It stuck in his throat. The dough seemed to be swelling; the cheese was rubbery and the tomato had an acid after-taste . . . His gorge was rising. He felt sick enough to throw it all up. If only I could, he thought, at least it'd get all that bloody filth out of my gut.

Shocked by the vulgarity of this expression, which was most uncharacteristic, he sat up straight and, with the air of a guilty child, looked around for the portrait of his wife. It wasn't on the piano, where it had been a few days before, nor was it on the mantelpiece, where it had lived for so many years. Nora, my dear, where are you? And just at this point the telephone rang.

The sound was so unexpected that Serafin jumped, as if Nora herself were making a trunk call from heaven. He wiped his hand on his pyjama top, and was about to answer when an insane thought occurred in his mind: What if it was *him*? Fat chance. Lovely Julian with the blond crew cut was the last person who'd be calling him. Meanwhile, the phone carried on ringing. He'd have to answer it eventually. He reached out and picked up the receiver.

'Hello.'

At first he didn't recognize Adela Teldi's voice. And he couldn't make out what she was saying. Sorry, what was what? She was chattering on in the quick, flat voice people use when talking to old friends – a torrent of words from which Serafin gradually managed to extract some sense. Finally he grasped what was she was talking about: she was, in effect, proposing an escape plan. She wanted him to come along to a small party her husband was throwing for a group of art dealers at their house down on the coast. 'And I won't take no for an answer, my dear. It's exactly what you need. You can stay two or three days, soak up a bit of sun and rest. You really haven't been looking well recently. Life goes on, you know. It's about time you began to forget your dear Nora.'

It wasn't his wife that Serafin couldn't forget, but the invitation was like a life-line away from his misery all the same.

'Yes, of course, I'd love to,' he said, amazed that he could still muster the will to escape.

'We're planning to leave tomorrow morning. Would you like me to come round and help you pack?'

Serafin trembled at the thought of Adela or anyone else entering his squalid pigsty.

'Absolutely not, my dear, everything's perfectly in order. You'd be amazed,' he said, and after listening to a few more details about the party he hung up abruptly, as if he were afraid that she might notice the foul smell over the telephone.

For a moment he sat clasping the receiver like the consoling arm of a friend. Then he reflected that the invitation had come just in time, miraculously. He had to get away. It didn't matter where. The only problem was that the plan involved Ernesto Teldi, and he had never warmed to Adela's husband.

Sitting in the same position, still unable to detach himself from the telephone and move away from the piano, Serafin asked himself why he felt that way about Ernesto Teldi. Everyone else seemed to admire him, but Serafin remembered several occasions on which Teldi's conduct had struck him as less than wholly admirable. Perhaps I envy him, he thought – who wouldn't? And really, should I be sitting in judgement, when only a moment ago, before destiny threw me a life-line, I was all at sea myself?

God bless Adela, he thought. May God bless her and keep her safe from that awful husband of hers.

Spite and disdain are effective antidotes to a variety of passionate emotions. To his great surprise, Serafin realized that during the few minutes he had spent thinking about Teldi, he had actually started to feel better. He looked at the pizza box and thought: I must tidy up. He stroked the top of the piano, even opened the lid, and for once the sight of the keyboard did not remind him of his visit to Freshman's or that cherubic boy who had turned his life upside down. Strange how uncharitable thoughts can suppress desire – and as if to test his new method, Serafin decided to go on being spiteful. He sat up straight on his makeshift seat, let his legs swing back and forth and thought about what a first-rate snob Adela's husband was. And once again, miraculously, he managed to forget what had been obsessing him until then, and to forget it so completely that his hand came to rest calmly on the piano keys, without the usual shiver running down his spine. It was all right. The descent into hell had come to an end. And, as if to prove it, his fingers touched the keys and began to play a few unrelated chords – reminders not of a shameful past but delicious promises for the future. He would probably be bored out of his mind at the Teldis' house, but there are times when boredom is a godsend. Serafin was hardly aware of it, but his fingers had begun to gain confidence, improvising in a style as orthodox and monotonal as the Teldis' party would probably turn out to be. There wouldn't be any boys of course, just a group of dull art experts, droning on about paintings and sculptures and so forth. Perfect, perfect, he thought, although (and for a moment his fingers froze) from what he remembered of Adela's hasty explanation on the phone, if he had understood correctly, the guests might be slightly more colourful on this occasion. 'Eccentric collectors,' was the expression she had used, before adding that they were also potential clients for Teldi. Potential suckers, thought Serafin. He might be long in the tooth, but he's as sly as ever. And now Serafin's fingers were playing a few bars in harmony with his opinion of Ernesto Teldi; it sounded very like a particular horn trio. It was Prokofiev's *Peter and the Wolf*, the stealthy tread of the wolf in the snow. It had come to him quite unconsciously.

For ten long minutes of respite, the boy with the crew cut was absent from his thoughts. And that was by far the longest stretch of peace he had enjoyed since the day it had occurred to him to visit Freshman's. The pang returned, of course, but by then Serafin had discovered how spite can provide temporary but effective relief from an unhealthy passion. Who would have thought it? In any case it had been more effective than a visit to Madame Longstaffe. She had promised to investigate his case, but he'd heard no word from her. I wonder what the old charlatan is up to now, thought Serafin.

4

KAREL AND MADAME LONGSTAFFE SING *RANCHERAS*

At Number 29 Calle Corderitos, on the edge of the lively but rather seedy area of Malasaña, there's a little bar called Juanita Banana, a favourite with tropical music fans. The afternoon and evening crowds are rather more enthusiastic than discriminating: they love anything Latin and are keen to try out the merengue and conga steps they've just learnt at one of the many local dance schools. Up until this crowd leave, around three in the morning, there are soft red cushions on the seats to make them comfortable for cuddling. The waiting staff are good-looking Latin Americans with not a great deal of experience in hospitality. The music is catchy and popular. The playlist features the Santo Domingan singer Juan Luis Guerra, Anạ Gabriel's Mexican *rancheras*, and Gloria Estefan's Cuban-American *sones*, which always get everyone singing along. While they dance and chat with their friends, the clients put away a good number of *mojitos* with Bacardi or shots of tequila with salt, gulped down to insistent cries of 'Get that down ya'. They emerge in high spirits: that Latin music is *fan*-tastic, that was *so* wicked.

Yet, as the last of these converted latin music lovers wander off singing, *vacilón, qué rico vacilón/cha-cha-chá, que rico cha-cha-chá*, their voices dying away and the stragglers disappearing, an altogether different club springs to life as if by magic on the premises of the Juanita Banana: a secret club, to which only the initiated have access. The Juanita Banana seems to withdraw into itself. The red cuddle-cushions vanish from the seats to expose bare wood, and in no time at all the place fills up with a sort of fog, as if someone behind the curtains were blowing out clouds of cigar smoke, while the young, attractive waiting staff are replaced by a new shift. The first to arrive is René, a Cuban with a snub nose in the middle of his broad, dark face. René is the barman, a master with the daiquiri, and an inventor of numerous unusual Congolese concoctions made with plants like *kolelé batama pimpí* (sesame, to the uninitiated), which, as everyone knows, has an aphrodisiac effect when mixed with caffeine and can also be a highly effective treatment for asthma.

Another key figure in the exclusive late set is Gladys, who waits on tables with as much agility as her ninety-seven kilos of ample Colombian flesh will allow (though she is as light on her feet as any young girl when she dances to a *son* by the maestro Escalona). The third staff member – or members, rather – are the identical and inseparable Gutiérrez twins, a pair of virtuoso musicians who between them can play any instrument from Cuban drums and bongos to the peasant accordion, including, of course, the guitar, Mexican trumpets and even the reed flute, not that there's much call for Andean instruments at the Juanita Banana, where the music is predominantly Afro-Caribbean.

One night, as it happened, two individuals were making their separate ways towards this extraordinary establishment, both hoping to relax and forget all worries with a little sing-song, accompanied by the Gutiérrez brothers. One was strolling on the left side of the street, hands in pockets, whistling a tune as if anticipating a special pleasure. The other was walking along the right side, protected from curious looks with a huge overcoat. They reached the door at the same time . . . After you. No please, madam, after you, I insist. Madame Longstaffe stepped inside, followed by Karel Pligh, who was determined to make a night of it before heading off to the Teldis' country house. Their little exchange was marked by the cool and deferential politeness of complete strangers who have realized they belong to the same sect or secret society.

Having taken up positions at opposite ends of the bar and ordered drinks (caipirinha for Madame, a daiquiri for Karel), each settled in for a night of pleasure. There was no-one else in the club, a situation that tends to break down barriers between staff and clients. Three caipirinhas later, René had come out from behind the bar to sit with Madame Longstaffe, while Gladys and Karel were improvising a duet on the dance floor. They had chosen one of the classic Cuban songstress Bola de Nieve's songs, which, with the Gutiérrez brothers' instrumental accompaniment, had a lilting, Santiago-de-Cuba feel that delighted the clairvoyant. After this performance, Madame Longstaffe asked Karel his name, and invited him to try a drink from her Brazilian homeland.

'It's called *cachaça*. Try it. Does wonders for your musical interpretation.'

So Karel gave it a try. Minutes later all the staff were watching and listening as Karel cleared his throat in preparation for a big song from the heart, with Madame Longstaffe perched beside him on a bar stool.

If Nestor Chaffinch had been able to observe this scene, he would no doubt have found further confirmation of his theory that chance encounters only become coincidences if a witness is there to piece things together. Karel and Madame Longstaffe spent a pleasurably intense evening together singing *Aurora, Yo tenía que perder. En eso llegó Fidel*, and even *The Girl from Ipanema* in Portuguese, but since they were complete strangers, it never crossed their minds that they might have friends or acquaintances in common. Despite her formidable paranormal powers, Madame Longstaffe failed to make the connection. It should have been simple for such a renowned clairvoyant to give some indication of the events that were to take place the following day at the Teldis'. Like the Weird Sisters before her, she could easily have foreshadowed Nestor's imminent death. She could also have warned Karel about the curious circumstances in which the death was to occur. At the very least, she could have repeated the prophecy she had already pronounced for Nestor and Carlos that afternoon when they had gone to see her: Nestor has nothing to fear until four Ts conspire against him. She could have revealed all this to Karel Pligh as well as explain how events would flow from the combination of a series of little indiscretions and some strange forces brewing in the ether. But Madame Longstaffe made no mention of these things, perhaps because she was too busy teaching young Karel yet another sensual little number – this time by the

Mexican Paquita la del Barrio – which made such a perfect duet.

* * *

And yet perhaps, in her own crooked and darkly humorous way, she *was* trying to tell him something. The question still hangs in the air at the Juanita Banana, like the lyric of the song they sang together, propping each other up, their voices hoarse from the *cachaça*, accompanied by the Gutiérrez brothers on guitar and piano, after Marlene Longstaffe had made Karel Pligh practise the chorus three times. It wasn't a Cuban or a Brazilian song but a Mexican *ranchera* made famous by Paquita la del Barrio, and it went:

> *I cheated on you once, I cheated on you twice, I cheated on you three times, and after three times, I never want to see you again . . .*

5

Ernesto and Adela in the Lift

The night before they set off for their country house, The Lilies, Ernesto and Adela Teldi went over their arrangements for the party.

'If we count Mr and Mrs Stephanopolous, that makes a total of thirty-three. I've never liked that number,' said Ernesto Teldi.

'Why? Because that's how old Jesus was when he died? And Alexander the Great, and Evita Perón too, no?' said Adela. 'I really don't think you should worry about it. You're not usually superstitious, not about that sort of thing anyway.'

They were talking on the phone. The couple were staying at the Palace Hotel, occupying adjoining rooms with a communicating door, though neither had yet found a use for this discreet facility so thoughtfully provided by the management. So many secret lovers must have blessed that door, safeguarding their respectability, allowing them to make their separate exits without fear after an assignation. In this case, however, the door had precisely the opposite function: in appearance it joined the rooms, but in fact it was never opened, because the Teldis led parallel lives like two lines travelling through time, one beside the other, never the twain to meet. Or perhaps they wouldn't have to go quite that far: social convention would no doubt unite them in one tomb, since that is the ineluctable destination for any well-matched couple, even if in life neither could care less about the other.

'Did I tell you about the problem with Mr Algobranghini, Adela? He hates Stephanopolous. I think they had a fight once over a Persian scimitar. Very touchy, the pair of them. Just make sure they don't end up at the same table and spoil our evening.'

Stephanopolous and Algobranghini figured alongside dozens of other exotic names on the guest list Adela was consulting as she spoke with her husband. Next to each name, a note in Ernesto's business-like hand indicated the collector's area of interest: there were two knife collectors, three 'Dickensiana fetishists' (so he had written), three with a passion for Greek icons (so long as they featured St George), a 'Rapanui statuette fan' (A what? wondered Adela for a moment), while the remainder consisted of collectors with less outmodish tastes: letters from famous people, tin soldiers, antiquarian ghost stories, or Fabergé eggs. Adela went through the list to see if she could recognize anyone, but none of the big names from the art world were there. She smiled, wondering which of the guests was Ernesto's prey. Algobranghini, the knife and sword collector? The ghost-story specialist, Miss Liau Chi? Or perhaps the chosen one was the only guest whose name was not accompanied by a note, a certain Monsieur Pitou. Adela shrugged her shoulders. After many years of observing her husband exercise his dealer's flair –

making a mint from the resale of treasures picked up for a song – she had begun to find the game amusing. Especially in the last few years. Teldi was now rich enough to forget about profit occasionally and set off in pursuit of a rarity. Acquiring unique pieces was the culmination of a lifetime devoted to art. There could only be one reason for a party with such a guest list: the capture of a piece that was presently in the possession of an eccentric collector whose reluctance to sell would soon be overcome by her husband's sweet-talking flattery.

'I don't want fixed seating arrangements, Adela. It should all seem casual, but I'm counting on you to make sure Stephanopolous and Monsieur Pitou sit with us: Pitou on my right and Stephanopolous on yours.'

Monsieur Pitou. Adela ran her eye down the name on the guest list. But what could his specialist interest be? Whatever it was, Adela was sure this mysterious gentleman was the prey, because Ernesto always made sure that the guest he had a particular interest in was sitting to his right. But what was he hoping to acquire at a bargain price after the party? A rare Turkish dagger? A *billet doux*, perhaps?

'Anyway, don't worry, we can talk about the details later. Leave it, Adela, there's no time now,' said Teldi. 'How long will it take you to finish getting dressed? Can we leave at nine? It takes over an hour to get to the Suarez's place.'

That night, Ernesto and Adela Teldi had been invited to dinner by some friends who were not involved in the art world. It was a quarter past eight. Adela was sitting on the bed, she still hadn't put her face on, but she was an expert at quick make-up jobs.

‘Let’s meet in front of the lift and go down together,’ she said to her husband.

And they met precisely at the appointed time: punctuality was the only virtue they had in common. As they stepped into the lift, Adela took the opportunity to examine herself in the mirror. Three floors, she thought. She had three floors of delicious descent during which to ascertain that she really was looking beautiful – naturally, since she had dressed for *him*. Carlos Garcia had not, of course, been invited to the Suarez’s dinner, but a woman in love (no, not in love, Adela, don’t even say that in jest, better say a woman still under the illusion of love) always dresses for her lover, even if he can’t see her. Which is why, like a bride dressing up for her groom, she had drenched herself with perfume and emerged from her room radiant and fresh, bright-eyed and glossy-lipped, exuding such a powerful aura that even her husband couldn’t help noticing.

‘You’re looking particularly beautiful tonight, Adela. You have the glow of youth,’ he said, and she accepted the compliment with a smile because she knew it was true: whatever lies the cosmetics companies come up with, love (or the illusion of love) is the one and only fountain of eternal youth.

The lift went down past another floor, the last before reaching the lobby: a few seconds left, thought Adela, in which to savour her happiness. Tomorrow, tomorrow, we will be together for a day, for a few hours, in my kingdom for a few hours. The lift came to a sudden halt. The lights flickered, looked as if they would go out, but finally stayed on dimly, bathing them in the sickly half-light of emergency rooms.

‘Christ almighty,’ said Teldi, looking for the telephone.

He soon found it and rang reception to ask what was going on.

'A blackout, sir, we're very sorry. It's not the hotel, it's the local supply. The whole block is blacked out. Is there something I can do for you?'

Crossly, Teldi asked her to ring and inform the Suarez household that they might be delayed, before adding: 'And do me a favour, ring the electricity company or the council or whoever, and keep me informed. We're not in the Third World here. In Madrid they should be able to fix this sort of thing straight away.'

'Yes, sir, of course. I'll let you know as soon as we have any information.'

The Teldis looked at each other in the yellowish light. Ernesto shrugged helplessly while Adela studied the walls and the door. Would they have enough air to breathe? Would the temperature rise sharply and ruin her make-up? What a disaster that would be! Even faces rejuvenated by happiness can crumple in absurd situations. And this situation was absurd. To say the least.

'If only there were a little seat, like in the old lifts,' said Ernesto. 'It's easier to be patient sitting down, isn't it? But the worst that can happen is that we'll be late to dinner. And that doesn't really matter; they're pretty dull people anyway.' Ernesto sighed and loosened the knot of his tie. It was more a reflex action than a reaction to the heat.

Trapped with her husband, Adela found herself thinking about Carlos, while Ernesto was thinking about a love letter. Used to dealing with the unexpected, Ernesto remained unruffled and made use of this unforeseen hold-up to go over in his mind every word of a delicate love letter he was planning to buy the following day from one of his guests. 'I want you, I trust you, I am coming to you': so began the document, in the hand of Oscar Wilde, no less. It wasn't an extract from the original manuscript of *An Ideal Husband*, as one might be forgiven for thinking, but a plea written three years earlier in a letter addressed to a mysterious and unidentified Bertie. Who could the person with such an eminently Victorian name have been? Teldi had come up with a fascinating and scandalous hypothesis, but he wouldn't be able to verify it until the letter was in his possession. I want you, I trust you, I am coming to you, he repeated to himself, savouring the words with a collector's glee, entertaining the possibility of keeping this find for himself and declining all offers to sell it, although for such a document any offers would be very considerable. More and more, however, Teldi preferred possession to profit. A beautiful love letter, he thought, deeply moved, an exquisite love letter.

Love and tenderness were far from Adela's thoughts. She had become suddenly, intensely conscious of her husband's physical proximity. They had not been so close to one another for a long time. There had been no friction between them in all the years of their convenient matrimonial arrangement (I won't interfere with your life, and you don't interfere with mine). Parallel lives meet only at infinity or in the grave, and at that point nothing matters any more. Adela pondered this idea for a moment: 'Together for all eternity.' It sounded like a punishment. She had never been able to understand why people worried so much about where their mortal remains would end up and the company they would keep: lovers' ashes scattered over the sea or a field of daisies . . . so romantic, even sublime, but ashes are just ashes, and dead bodies are dead for good. Adela was not so arrogant as to believe that her remains would go on loving or longing for anyone.

Life, however, would go on administering its doses of desire, pain, love or agony, the life she was living in the here and now would put her through all that and more . . . Suddenly she was physically aware of the distance separating her from Carlos's body, while her husband's, which had never bothered her particularly until then, felt far too close. And for a moment Adela considered what happens when two strangers end up in a lift together: they move to opposite corners so that their bodies don't touch, they look at the roof so that their eyes don't meet. They fidget uncomfortably, pretend to whistle or consult their watches, willing the door to open, come *on*, open, because having your personal space invaded by a stranger is unbearable.

Teldi was leaning against the wall in one of the corners. He wasn't bothered by the proximity of Adela's body. Why should he have been? She was part of him, part of his identity, after all. Since they had made their implicit pact to lead parallel lives all those years ago, Adela had been as much a part of him as his hands, his legs, his skin or the clothing covering his body. And he loved her, naturally, the way we love something we have always looked on as an extension of ourselves.

Adela had felt the same way about their marriage until now. She had taken lovers to make her feel alive, and sometimes she had even loved them and considered leaving her husband. But in the end she had stayed. Why leave when she could already do just as she liked, when their parallel lives were functioning perfectly and their shared territory was large enough for them not to get in each other's way: two beds in separate rooms, two bathrooms, two doors to come and go through as they pleased? One of the major and often overlooked advantages of having money is being able to dispose of a large amount of space.

In the lift, however, unable to distance herself from her husband, who had just undone two buttons of his shirt and was now proceeding to remove his shoes, Adela was overcome by something like nausea. As she looked at Teldi's moustache, in which droplets of sweat were gathering, and the mass of artificial hair beginning to stick to his scalp with the heat, the memory of Carlos came back to her, and he seemed all the more handsome by contrast. She gasped as if she were running out of air, and all her muscles ached with the desire to get out of there, to flee into other arms, not Teldi's, arms that didn't smell of old flesh. Once again, Adela felt frightened: had she let herself go too far this time? Remember, dear, she said to herself (trying to remain aloof and detached), love is eternal, so long as it lasts. I will always love you until eight-thirty. That was the prudent strategy she had used with her other lovers. She had learnt early on that the verb 'to love' should only be conjugated in the present tense. Adela repeated these precepts to herself, while trying not to look at Teldi, trying not to see how his shirt was sticking to his body. The only way to make passion last is to ration it out in small doses and never to consume it all, so there's always something left to desire . . . In the past she had followed these sensible rules.

It had become unbearably hot and sticky. They were breathing each other's air. Ernesto rang the concierge again, and in addition to his grating shouts and complaints, Adela had to put up with his physical presence: the rancid smell of his sweat and his slippery hand, which had fallen inadvertently onto her right arm.

The contact sent an electric pulse down her spine, sharp and stunning as a revelation. She realized that she had been able to live with this old body, with a husband whose hair stuck to his scalp when he sweated, simply because she didn't usually notice all the details she was seeing now, in the forced proximity of the lift. They had always been independent of each other, turning a blind eye, travelling a good deal, keeping out of each other's way, respecting each other's space and expecting the same in return. But that freedom will shrink with time, thought Adela suddenly. One day, inevitably, her role as a socialite, and the only thing that made her life bearable, would come to an end, and she would be reduced to sharing her solitude with *him*. No more friends, no more travelling, just more of *him*, more aches and pains, more illness. God, that's what old age is: losing all of your personal space.

Fifteen minutes. Adela would never have imagined that being confined in a lift with her future for just fifteen minutes could turn her world upside down and overturn the convictions of a lifetime. When the lift lurched into action, the movement made her feel so dizzy it was as if she were dropping down through the lobby into hell itself. And during the brief descent, with the lucidity of those who are about to die, Adela saw her entire love life flash before her in the mirror. She saw the young Adela Teldi, beautiful and remote, whose only desire was to collect lovers who would make her feel still more beautiful and more remote.

Then a twinge she had been trying to ignore for years made her linger over the image of a faceless man, which melted into the image of her sister Soledad's blood, spilt on the patio of her house in Buenos Aires. Fortunately the vision didn't stop there, but rushed on to show other trivial affairs intended to blot out the memory of that blood. A long string of inconsequential adventures culminating with the appearance of Carlos's beautiful body in the mirror, as if he were physically there.

Then the lift reached the ground floor and the door opened.

'At last, about time,' said Teldi, gathering his things. He looked around for his tie which had ended up in a corner, and then for his shoes.

'Where's the left one? How can I possibly have lost it in such a tiny space? We've almost melted in here.'

Adela bent down. She was about to pick up the shoe and give it back to him without further ado, when a perverse impulse stopped her and she froze in that servile posture. She looked at Teldi and, as if needing to confirm with a gesture what she had discovered in the last fifteen minutes, she said to him: 'Let me help you, Ernesto.'

Kneeling before him, she made herself hold his foot and slide his shoe on.

'What are you doing, Adela? Have you gone mad?'

But Adela hadn't gone mad, she wanted to smell that old flesh again, she wanted to plunge to the very pit of all misery to be sure that when she got out of the lift, the resuming of a daily routine wouldn't let her forget what she had felt in the last fifteen minutes, that foretaste of what the future held for her. Old age means losing all your personal space, she repeated, and by the time it comes I won't have the strength to run away or any reason to change my life, because my life will have shrunk so much there will be nowhere to go, and no-one to go there with. The heat had made Ernesto Teldi's foot swell; she had to force his heel into the shoe, and the stiffener broke.

'Leave it, will you. What the hell are you doing? Come

on, get up,' said Teldi, and when he saw her face, he added: 'You look terrible, Adela. You should get changed, and so should I.'

'Yes,' she said, 'but this time I think I'll take the stairs.'

Adela didn't look back. She didn't know if her husband had stayed in the lift to go back up to the room, or what he had done. All she knew was that she had three flights of stairs to climb while thinking about Carlos and trying to sort out her emotions. It's too late to cancel the dinner now, she told herself. I'll go ahead with life as planned for the next few days, but then it's goodbye Ernesto. Adela didn't feel out of breath. She felt as light as a child climbing those three flights of stairs, because she had just sworn that for once in her life she was *not* going to do the sensible thing. She was going to give love a chance.

Part Four

The Mirror Game

'There has been in this incident,' he said, 'a twisted, ugly, complex quality that does not belong to the straight bolts either of heaven or hell. As one knows the crooked track of a snail, I know the crooked track of a man.'

G. K. Chesterton, *The Innocence of Father Brown*

'This trick is done with mirrors, isn't it?'

Agatha Christie

1

Arrival at The Lilies

Houses in which a sudden death is about to take place do not differ noticeably from more innocent dwellings. Their wooden stairs do not groan like crows cawing, nor do their walls stand guard like melancholy sentinels. And Westinghouse cool rooms where the doors are destined to click definitively shut behind someone in a few hours time do not purr invitingly, tempting the reckless to step inside. All that is sheer fantasy, and yet, there on the doormat of The Lilies was an enormous cockroach, plain for all to see. Cockroaches are unpleasant creatures, with an obstinate team spirit. Often, as soon as you dispose of one, another will appear from nowhere to replace it, a second offender just as fat and shiny as the first, imitating its behaviour with a sort of stoic exactitude, like the countless little cockroaches found on the doormat by the characters in this story as they were arriving at The Lilies.

If this renewed presence was some kind of portent or sign, it was a sign that everyone could see, sitting there, bold as ever, wiggling its antennae. And each guest, noticing this insect on arrival, did what people normally do when they see a cockroach: step on it.

Ernesto and Adela Teldi were the first to arrive at the house and set eyes on that ugly insect. It gave them something to say to each other. They hadn't spoken in the plane from Madrid and had exchanged barely a word during the trip from Malaga airport to their home, near Coín on the Costa del Sol. It was a rambling old house largely covered with wisteria, often mistaken by people who knew nothing about plants as the lilies that gave the place its name.

'I told you those caretakers you took on were hopeless,' said Ernesto Teldi. 'You don't often see a cockroach in the garden. I hate to think what it's like inside.'

As he pushed the key into the lock he glanced around. The rest of the garden seemed to be in reasonable shape: there were blue hydrangeas on either side of the front door and the flowerbeds were looking good too. A few leaves could be seen swirling in a corner of the otherwise neatly raked lawn, that stretched away to a small fountain with lilies and, beyond that, a box hedge.

'At least the gardener seems to be doing his job,' said Teldi. 'But the caretakers are a lazy pair, they're not even here to let us in. Where on earth can they have got to?' he added as he turned the door handle.

Stepping in, Ernesto Teldi squashed the cockroach, making it crunch under the sole of his shoe. 'Shit,' he said, wiping the remains of its carcass onto the doormat. Inside The Lilies, Ernesto and Adela were confronted with another domestic setback. They found the caretakers in a state of high anxiety: a very serious family problem had come up and they had to leave urgently for Conil de la Frontera in Cadiz. 'It's a very serious matter, madam,' they said. 'We're awfully sorry, such a tough time right now.'

'Well go then, immediately, and don't bother to come back,' said Teldi, not looking at his employees but at Adela, as if she were the one who should have been awfully sorry.

But Adela poured oil on troubled waters and convinced them to stay until the team from Mulberry & Mistletoe arrived, so that they could explain all the ins and outs of the house. Teldi then deigned to address the caretakers directly with the tone of offended authority generally reserved for deserters: 'One last thing: do me a favour and remove that dead cockroach. Then I never want to see the pair of you again.'

'Yuck! A cockroach!' said Chloe two hours later when she found an identical creature on the doormat, but very much alive, waving its antennae to welcome her. 'It's dis*gus*ting; someone's got to get rid of it. I'm not into killing animals, but this is really vile.'

Nestor and Carlos stopped to examine the insect. As a chef, Nestor found cockroaches deeply repugnant, as he told the caretakers when they came to open the door.

'I don't know where it can have come from,' said the woman. 'We just got rid of another one like it. Mr Teldi must have brought it in on the sole of his shoe, because there are no vermin in this house. The kitchen is clean as a whistle, I swear. Come in, come in and have a look.'

Nestor went in with the caretakers.

'And what about that bloody cockroach?' asked Chloe. 'You kill it, Carlos.'

So Carlos, who had no problems with that sort of thing, squashed the insect just as Ernesto Teldi had done.

'Done,' he said. 'Come on, Chloe, take that stuff to the

kitchen while Karel parks the van. I'll go help unload the rest of the gear.'

Oh yuck, a disgusting *šváb*! thought Karel Pligh, seeing a third cockroach on the doormat, as glossy and slimy-looking as its cousins. Now how the hell do you translate *šváb*? He hesitated for a moment without realizing that, thanks to his comprehensive knowledge of Latin music, he had on many occasions sung a famous Mexican song named after the insect in question. But just at that moment Karel didn't have time for further entomological or musical reflections – he was carrying a basket full of pots, pans and other kitchen utensils that Nestor needed to prepare the meal at The Lilies that night – so Karel squashed the *šváb* with all the force of his Nikes and continued on his way to the kitchen: there was a lot to do before the guests arrived.

The Teldis and the staff of Mulberry & Mistletoe spent the whole of the morning and a good part of the afternoon getting ready, each in his or her own particular domain. Ernesto shut himself in the library to make a series of phone calls. He wanted to be sure that none of his guests would be prevented from attending by a last-minute hitch. As for Adela, she had a lengthy discussion with Nestor about the details of the menu. (How odd, she was certain she had seen his face somewhere before, but where? Where had she seen that moustache? It would probably come back to her in a minute but in the meantime it was best to pretend she hadn't recognized him.) Then Adela told him she would prefer not to have to deal with his staff directly.

'If you could look after everything, Mr Chaffinch, including the flower arrangements – you can take what you need from the garden. I have a few things to sort out with my husband upstairs and as soon as I'm free I'll come down and we can discuss any changes of plan.'

Nestor put her mind at ease: that was what he was paid for, after all, to take care of everything so that the hosts could relax. She needn't worry about the food or getting the house ready (in spite of the caretakers' desertion). 'We're a small but efficient team,' he said, 'and we get on well together. That's the main thing. It's almost like a family business. The young ones are like children to me, as you'll see, my dear, especially Carlos.'

After this declaration, culminating with that surprisingly familiar 'my dear' – He must say that to everyone, thought Adela, it doesn't necessarily mean anything – she watched Nestor slip away discreetly like a true hospitality professional.

From that moment onwards, Mulberry & Mistletoe took possession of The Lilies.

The Teldis handed the reins over to Karel, Chloe, Carlos and Nestor, who proceeded to organize everything, setting tables, arranging flowers, moving furniture. 'Do whatever you think is best,' Mrs Teldi had said, and, having catered for many similar parties, they knew just what needed to be done. Soon they were coming and going as if they'd known the place for years. Each employee worked without supervision, at his or her own pace, and so each came to discover a different facet of The Lilies. Some say the personality of a house is completely subjective: the same house can be charming or menacing, beautiful or ugly, inviting or hostile depending on the eye and state of mind of the beholder. Some say that no two visitors will ever see the place in the same way, and it may well be true. The

Lilies certainly made a different impression on each member of the Mulberry & Mistletoe team. Nestor, for one, got a fright when he entered the sitting room, intending to give it a quick dust. An uncomfortable little chill ran down his spine, but it wasn't so much the style of the decor that disagreed with him as one object in particular: the letter tray.

'What are you looking at?' asked Ernesto Teldi, who had come in to get the paper.

Nestor started flicking the feather duster with a dexterous wrist action, and moved away, intently scrutinizing the walls and sundry insignificant objects while raising a protective cloud of dust.

'Lovely room, beautifully decorated,' he said. 'With a bit of dusting and some flowers from the garden it'll look splendid,' he added, turning his back so Teldi couldn't see what had caught his attention.

Ernesto then picked up the only thing on the letter tray: a thick envelope addressed unsteadily in green ink.

Shit, he thought, before disappearing with the envelope.

Shit, thought Nestor, flicking the feather duster even more vigorously, as if the house were suddenly full of invisible cobwebs.

For Carlos Garcia, however, The Lilies was a calm, light-filled house that reminded him strongly of his childhood. While trying to keep his mind on the job, he found pretexts for visiting one room after another, haunted by the impression that he was at Number 38 Calle de Almagro – not the run-down, neglected property that he was about to sell, but the mysterious flat full of nooks and crannies that he had known as a child, the domain of his Grandma Teresa. For Carlos, The Lilies and Number 38 were like mother and daughter. He even noticed that the choice of colours was identical. The entrance hall was painted red, the sitting room yellow, and what colours would the bedrooms be? For a moment Carlos forgot that this house belonged not only to his lover from the Palace Hotel, but also to her husband, and, like a curious child, he decided to investigate each of the bedrooms, hoping perhaps to find a lavender-hued dressing room or a secret chamber with a wardrobe in it.

'Might I enquire what you're doing up here?' said a voice that, luckily, did not belong to the owner of the house but to Nestor Chaffinch, who was standing in the doorway. 'What on earth are you doing opening wardrobes?'

'Nothing, Nelly. Nothing, I swear,' said Carlos.

Nestor looked at him quizzically. His expression was quite different from Nelly's when she scolded him for looking in the wardrobe, but the situation was the same.

'Aren't you going to say anything?' asked Carlos. He would have preferred a reprimand to this inscrutable silence. 'Aren't you going to tell me to get back to work, to stop ferreting around in other people's wardrobes? Aren't you going to ask me why, Nestor?'

But Nestor, who was already leaving the room, turned back and said: '*Cazzo* Carlitos, one day you'll learn that in life there are times when it's best not to ask questions. Especially when you suspect you'd be better off not knowing the answers.' And then he added, in a different tone of voice: 'Come on, let's go down to the kitchen. I need you and Chloe to help me prepare the dinner.'

*   *   *

For Karel Pligh, The Lilies wasn't warm, or yellow, or full of nooks and crannies. Nor did it revive childhood memories. To him it seemed like the sort of place you only read about in books, a fairytale mansion full of bathrooms, more than one per person he calculated, and all that wasted space, at least fifteen families could have lived in it. He was walking around the dining room positioning the chairs around the five tables, on each of which he had placed a candelabrum and a floral arrangement. He was amusing himself, setting the scene with meticulous attention to detail. In the West, he thought, you always feel like you're living on a film set. It was a feeling Karel enjoyed. In the course of the evening he would no doubt learn a good deal about sophisticated gatherings of this sort, and if he was observant and did his job well, who knows, maybe one day he would be a guest at a dinner like this or even have a house like The Lilies. It was just a question of hard work and good fortune.

Chloe would be proud of me then, he thought. Or maybe not. Karel wasn't so sure. Who knows what goes on in the mind of such an adorable, capricious young girl, with her pierced lip and her hair shaved up the back? Stumped again, all he could do was to count it among the inscrutable mysteries of the West.

Chloe was in the kitchen with Nestor and Carlos, peeling tomatoes. Hundreds of tomatoes, mountains of them, which left her no time to wonder about the house. She would no doubt have found it every bit as awful as her parents' place, a showpiece rather than a home. Its welcoming appearance was fake, the inviting warmth of the entrance hall a lie, the homeliness of the open fire a sham. No genuine feeling anywhere in this shit-hole, Chloe would have concluded, if she hadn't been so busy peeling tomatoes.

But she soon tired of this repetitive task and said to Nestor: 'This is such a drag. When me and my brother were kids, we used to hang around in the kitchen and they'd always come up with a story to tell us. Have you got your book of little indiscretions there, Nestor? Why don't you read us something to pass the time? Come on, read us something.'

'Forty-four, forty-five. Just concentrate on the tomatoes for now and forget about stories, we need exactly sixty-six skins to make the decorative flowers, two per dish. I'll be watching to see how yours turn out, Miss Trias,' said Nestor firmly.

For a few minutes the conversation lapsed into silence as they went on working methodically. The Lilies was abuzz with the noise of different activities. From where he was standing, Nestor could hear sounds emanating from various places: Carlos breaking ice in the kitchen sink, Karel laying the table in the dining room next door . . . And Ernesto and Adela, what were they up to? Nestor imagined them far away, up in their rooms, although Adela would have to come down to the kitchen soon. It was getting late.

'Come on, Nestor, this is a real pain in the arse . . . Why don't you tell Carlos and me another one of those stories you've got hidden away in your notebook? I love stories,' she insisted, 'not just for the gossip, though. Everyone's always getting the wrong idea about me. I know you think all I want to do is have a good time, but I'm interested in other things too, like literature for example. I bet you wouldn't have guessed that. It's 'cause of my brother Eddie, he wanted to be a writer too, . . .'

Chloe chattering on in her usual silly way, thought Nestor. A chef with a dinner to prepare for a large group of distinguished guests has no time to lose, so he didn't pay much attention to what she was saying. He missed the bit about her dead brother, and the bit about how he had wanted to be a writer, but he did catch the 'like you, Nestor' at the end.

Like me? he wondered, then burst out laughing. 'So I'm a writer now, am I?' But then he had to attend to a pan of bechamel sauce that was boiling over.

It was always the same: when Nestor was busy at his work, he forgot about everything else. All he could think about were his saucepans, or, in this case, the tomato flowers that would be used to decorate the plates for the warm lobster salad. Had he not been such a conscientious and meticulous chef, he might have been alarmed by what happened next.

Chloe went on talking louder and louder in a vain attempt to provoke some reaction from Nestor or Carlos. 'Come on, Nestor, relax,' she said. 'Just one story. It doesn't matter if you've already told it. Tell us the one about the woman whose sister topped herself in Buenos Aires. You know, the girl who threw herself out the window, that was a cool story.'

Nestor was so utterly focused on his bechamel sauce that he didn't notice the door opening. Chloe didn't notice anything either. Only Carlos realized that Adela had her hand on the door and was about to step into the room, but when she heard what Chloe was saying, she froze.

'Yeah it was like a horror movie,' Chloe went on. 'Tell us that one again.'

The door closed again just as it had opened, and Carlos

went on breaking ice while Chloe chattered away as if nothing had happened. Just as well, thought Carlos. Adela obviously decided to come back later, and that's just the thing to do. It's better if no-one's around when we meet for the first time here. If she'd come in just then, unprepared, Nestor would have been able to read something in our faces.

'Fucking hell, Nestor. And you too, Carlos,' said Chloe. 'You could at least *say* something to me. I don't see why work has to be so incompatible with a bit of communication between human beings.'

But neither Nestor nor Carlos was listening. One was thinking about sauces, the other about love, and Chloe got bored and let her gaze wander until it came to rest on the door of a large cool room on the other side of the kitchen. 'Westinghouse 401 Extra-Cold,' she read distractedly before noticing her reflection in the stainless-steel door. Her face was distorted and enlarged, as in a trick mirror. Chloe amused herself readjusting her hair and checking how cool all her studs and rings looked, especially the one in her lip. This mutating, fairground mirror-image made her laugh and she stopped thinking about Carlos and shameful secrets and Nestor's little moleskin notebook.

Twenty tomatoes later, when all the flowers had been carefully placed on the plates, Chloe asked Nestor what else he wanted her to do. After consulting his watch, Nestor said he didn't need any more help in the kitchen, so she could go upstairs and get changed. 'It's still early, but you need to make sure your uniform isn't crushed and your apron is spotless. Off you go. Carlos and I will finish this. You go and give your uniform a good iron, all right? And after that, you know what you have to do, don't you, my dear? All those rings and studs and other bits of metal you're wearing are coming out, aren't they? You can pack them away in that enormous backpack of yours. I can't imagine what you've got in there. Anyone would think you were heading off for two weeks in the desert.

'Ah . . . women,' Nestor added with a smile. He was in very high spirits: everything was going exactly according to plan.

A Pearl Jam CD was playing in the room that Chloe Trias and Karel Pligh had been given to share. Chloe had already taken a shower and, with her wet hair wrapped in a towel, she was rummaging through her backpack in search of her maid's uniform, a severe grey smock with a white collar and cuffs, a white organdie apron, and one of those small lacy caps that prestigious catering companies like Mulberry & Mistletoe have rescued from oblivion and use to give their services that extra touch of class.

'Where the fuck is that maid's get-up?' she said, pulling the clothes out of her backpack, all the clothes she had picked up at her parents' house the day before. There were far too many things: shirts, a bikini, a pair of Bermuda shorts made in China (just perfect for strolling around the garden at The Lilies), everything except the uniform. As she continued rummaging, Chloe started to get worried. 'Jesus, don't tell me I left the fucking thing at the old folks' place – what a fuck-up! I was in such a rush I don't know what I grabbed in the end. It's definitely not here. Nestor won't exactly throw a tantrum, but he's ain't gonna be happy.'

It was seven-thirty. Early still, but not early enough to solve the major problem of having left her uniform in Madrid. Shit, shit, shit! Chloe paced up and down in her room. Suddenly she had a life-saving idea. It was her only chance.

She looked in the wardrobe. Karel had brought two waiter's uniforms. Yes! Such an organized young man! You could count on Karel to bring a spare set of work clothes. In the hospitality business you have to be prepared for all eventualities, and luckily, Karel was. So now Chloe knew what she had to do.

'It'll be fun dressing as a guy,' she said.

An hour later the front doorbell rang. It was still too early for the guests to be arriving so rather than opening the door, Karel Pligh stuck his head out the window. He saw an affable-looking gentleman with a crew cut standing in front of the main door holding a small suitcase.

'Good afternoon. I am Serafin Tous,' said the man.

'And you're here for the party?' asked Karel from the window, unsure as to what the protocol was in such cases.

Serafin smiled. He was in good spirits, all the more so when he realized that Karel's handsome face, like a portrait in the window-frame, had not provoked any of those distressing urges that had been plaguing him recently.

'I have been invited for the party, and to spend the night. Ask Mrs Teldi if you like.'

Serafin waited a few seconds while Karel came around to the door.

'Good afternoon, sir,' he said.

And behind Karel, Serafin could see the serene interior of The Lilies. Such a peaceful house, he thought. Perfect, perfect. As I always say to Adela, it reminds me of a spa, a place where all anxieties are cured.

'May I take your suitcase, sir?'

As Karel Pligh picked up the case and headed off ('Follow me, sir, I'll show you the way'), Serafin Tous noticed a large, shiny, wet-looking cockroach waiting on the doormat to greet him. But he was short-sighted and in good spirits, so he misidentified the insect. Oh, a sweet little dung-beetle, he thought, giving it a gentle nudge with his shoe. Ah, nature! The country life! It was just what he needed: a haven safe from people who might know about his secret.

'Off you go, off you go,' he said, very gently, to what he thought was a beetle. 'Off you go and roll some balls.'

Not long afterwards, Serafin Tous had completely changed his mind about The Lilies. If the incident with the cockroach had occurred two hours later, he would certainly not have mistaken it for a beetle. The Lilies, so blessedly peaceful when he arrived, now struck him as an old pile full of junk, the house of a collector with far more money than taste. Yes, that's what Serafin thought, sitting on the terrace with a newspaper in one trembling hand and a glass of sherry in the other, thoroughly shaken by what had just happened. As he settled down to read the paper and sip his sherry Nestor's unmistakable pointy moustache had appeared at one of the windows opening onto the terrace – the moustache he had encountered at Freshman's and again at Madame Longstaffe's.

'Good evening,' said the moustache. 'I'll just leave these here, if you don't mind. They're for decorating the terrace.'

As Nestor put the candles on the table, he smiled, and that smile was so disturbing that Serafin couldn't help himself: he spilt the sherry on his trousers. A suspicious-looking stain began to spread across his crotch.

Dear God, he thought. Nora, darling, isn't there something you can do to save me from this terrible coincidence?

2

EVERYONE WANTS TO KILL NESTOR

If Madame Longstaffe, the famous Bahian fortune-teller (and keen collector of taxidermic specimens), had been invited to this party for collectors of rare objects, no doubt she would have sensed the shadow of a crime hovering over The Lilies. Or perhaps not, since even if she had been among the guests, none of them was present when that sinister, negative energy took possession of the house.

The collectors had not yet arrived and would still be a while coming; the only people in the house were the characters who have already figured in this story, each of whom was getting dressed for dinner. As they performed this routine task their thoughts wandered freely, unconsciously, and it so happened that four of them were thinking the same thought simultaneously: they all wanted to kill Nestor. Or at least they were all wishing, fervently and hopelessly like tormented souls that they had never set eyes on the chef who knew too much.

Why did he have to turn up tonight of all nights? It's

completely stupid, stupid and unfair, thought Ernesto Teldi as he took a pair of cufflinks from a little box. A curious pair they were, in the form of gaucho spurs: not a good choice, for the sight of them spurred his memory back to a region of the past he had tried to leave behind. It had been a long while since he'd left Argentina and for more than twenty years now his respectable and impressive CV had gone unchallenged. The only thing he had left out were his early days as a smuggler, but was that really so terrible? Hadn't other respectable types started off in a similar way?

And now, years later, this character has the nerve to turn up in my house thinking I'm not going to recognize him. I come to my country house, I open the door and there he is flicking at my furniture and my art works with a feather duster, pretending to be one of the caterers. It's completely outrageous! I never ever forget a name or a face, though I was very careful not to show recognition when we ran into each other. 'There's no doubt about it, this man is Antonio Reig, our old cook from Buenos Aires,' muttered Teldi.

Sitting brazenly on his bedside table were three letters written in green ink. He had received the first just over a week earlier. The signature was no doubt deliberately illegible and the writing was difficult to decipher, but the general content was only too familiar: the roaring airplanes and the screams that filled his nightmares. The one name he was able to make out was clearly linked to an episode he had considered long forgotten. That name was Minelli. Other scribbled paragraphs reminded him of the young men's cries, the dark sheen of the Río de la Plata, the one-way trip, and his smuggler's light plane, employed for criminal purposes. And what was the intention of these wavering lines accusing him anonymously from the bedside table? What was it they were asking for?

Why money, of course.

So unfair, said Teldi to himself, looking at his little silver spurs, the symbol of everything he had achieved in life through all his hard work: money, success, respect. He had earned it all, and it was rightly his because the only shameful thing in his past was that one night when Minelli had asked to borrow his light plane and Teldi had lent it to him, no questions asked. 'Not something to be proud of,' said the green lines. All right, it wasn't something to be proud of, but it wasn't really that terrible either, and he had paid dearly for it already. Ever since then, his sleep had been inhabited by nightmares and screams, repeated over and over, hour after hour. People think that men like me don't feel or suffer at all, but what do they know? What does anyone know, really? Teldi looked back over the years and convinced himself that he had spent half his life getting rich and the other half apologizing for being so successful. All that work: his generous patronage of the arts, the vast sums of money he had donated to worthy causes, setting up charitable organizations . . . for what? In the end, none of those good works had redeemed him in the eyes of others. People think that men like me give money away out of vanity or to buy forgiveness, when really it's the winner's pathetic tribute to the loser. Look at me, we beg, I need you too. I need you to accept me, to admire me, to love me.

And now, thought Teldi as he fastened his right cufflink (which is always harder to do), now all that hard work is at risk. 'You and I know what happened in 1976,' said the last of those knotty lines in green ink, which looked like a row of parrots on a wire. Teldi was convinced that if the author of those lines were to tell the plain truth, no-one would believe him. Who would believe that the only thing Ernesto Teldi had done wrong was to lend his light plane to Colonel Minelli? Lending a plane to an army officer, just the once, without questioning what for, is hardly an offence; the truth would have to be embroidered a little. It would be so easy to cross the fine line between telling it the way it was and claiming that he had collaborated in the Dirty War. A blackmailer can twist the truth however he likes – all he needs is a single detail, a subtle nuance. 'Be careful, Teldi. Remember how easy it would be for me to go to the papers with your story,' said the letter. 'You think about it. I'm not going to write to you any more. I'll get in touch with you directly so we can sort out this little misunderstanding . . . Perhaps by telephone, or perhaps . . .' Here the green writing became completely illegible, but Teldi could tell where the blackmailer was heading. So I suppose he decided to turn up at my house, he thought, bold as brass. And here he is, under my roof. How dare he!

I suppose he thinks he's untouchable, thought Ernesto. Having finally secured his cufflinks, he was now putting on his jacket. He doesn't realize I've remembered who he is and he's waiting for a moment to catch me off guard in order to screw money out of me. And the worst thing is, I'll end up paying what he asks, however much it is, just to be rid of him, the dirty little leech.

Ernesto Teldi was about to leave his room. I'll work it out later, he thought, after the party, how much I'm prepared to pay him. Life goes on, I've got other things to worry about. At least I've got wealth. And it comes in useful when leeches like Reig need to be disposed of.

As he reached for the door handle, the silver spurs knocked against it with a little *ting*. The sound was almost imperceptible but it rang like an alarm in his head. He realized his mistake: money wasn't the solution, it would only make the leech fatter and greedier. You spend your whole life achieving respectability, then someone comes along and destroys your reputation just like that. The only good leech is a dead leech, he thought, surprising himself. He had always been a firm and efficient man but he preferred to avoid conflict. Sometimes, however . . .

Was it better to fatten a leech with money (since he did have enough to tolerate a bit of bleeding) or should he find another way to get rid of it? The question would keep needling him all through the evening.

Meanwhile, Serafin Tous was in the grip of a similar anxiety, and wondering what magic he could call on to eliminate Nestor. Not a magic spell, the sort Madame Longstaffe might have pronounced, or her ancestors the Weird Sisters. No, while Ernesto was pondering leech control, Serafin was toying with the sort of home-made magic remedies we have all fantasized about at some stage. If only I could press a button and make him disappear, I'd do it without a second thought, mused the inoffensive Mr Tous. Oh God, if only there were some secret device I could activate to make him vanish, with a simple click. I can't let him wander about. If I could just seal him away hermetically, like bacteria in cold storage or the patients in a hospital for tropical diseases, isolated for the public good.

Serafin Tous was sitting on the lid of the lavatory. In outward appearance, he was a respectable judge, with his close-cropped grey hair, his legs crossed tightly and his clasped hands resting on his thighs as if in prayer. The party would be starting soon. How on earth was he going to get through it, while maintaining the serene composure expected of a judge? Three, four, maybe even *five* hours of social interaction awaited him: participating in banal banter, smiling, admiring the works of art in Ernesto Teldi's collection. Would he, in short, be able to perform the familiar routine of social gymnastics in such a fragile state of mind? With a mechanical gesture, Serafin tore off a piece of lavatory paper as lengthy as the night ahead and used it to mop his brow.

But the party was just the beginning, he thought, and there would be more testing moments to come. Nestor would be so busy with the catering he wouldn't really have time to indulge in malicious gossip; in fact, he probably would not even get the chance to tell anyone where he had first encountered the venerable judge. Thanks to the party, his secret would be safe, at least for tonight. But it would only be a momentary respite. Now the fellow knew his name and his profession. He also knew who his friends were, and it would be simple for him to make sure everyone found out about Freshman's. The real danger would begin in the days ahead. It was impossible to predict just when he would strike: tomorrow perhaps, or the next day, or the following week . . . Such was the exquisite torture he would be put through: the waiting and the uncertainty, until one day a caustic smile or a subtle sign from a friend would confirm that everything was lost, and that his one small slip had become public knowledge. Serafin pressed his knees together, keeping his legs crossed in a tight X, as he reflected on how swiftly malicious rumours could spread. Often, ironically, it's frivolity rather than malice that sets it off, he thought. He had seen it happen so many times. It's terrible to think that the most shameful secrets are often revealed simply for the pleasure of sharing a little indiscreet gossip among friends: You'll never guess where I met Serafin Tous the other day . . . you know, that judge, a pillar of the community. Did you know he was a queer, a poof, a paedophile? Didn't you know? A few remarks like that and everyone pricks up their ears. Really? Do tell . . .

I've seen it happen, thought Serafin, still sitting on top of the lavatory. Careers cut short, lives ruined. And the most extraordinary thing is that people don't do it because they're evil or unthinking, or even because they're jealous. It's all down to vanity. All they want is to be the centre of attention for a few minutes. Honestly!

From where he was sitting, Serafin could not see his face in the bathroom mirror, just his hairline and his wrinkled forehead. A whole life spent trying to flee, trying to forget that delicate boy with whom he had played the piano all those years ago, only to end up giving himself away like this. He winced and the lines on his forehead deepened. Behind them was a crowd of jostling thoughts, but the most insistent was that silly, childish wish: If only I could push a button; if it were that easy to get rid of the pest, I'd do it without a second thought. And Serafin Tous, who normally wouldn't have dared hurt a fly, swivelled around to examine the flusher, wishing he could use it to free himself of Nestor and flush away all his fears and anxieties. He pushed the button and a thundering roar made the little room tremble as if the plumbing were about to burst. Good Lord, thought Serafin, you can tell the hosts don't come here often: nothing works properly. But summer homes are always like that. So many things can go wrong:

flooding, cracks in the walls, even dangerous short-circuits. Serafin stood up, and, as if a household spirit had been waiting to confirm his theory about the dangers of holiday houses, when he tried to switch on the light over the mirror there was a huge flash. The bulb had blown. Just as well he had good reflexes and was able to jump out of the way, otherwise he might have got a shock. This place is so dangerous, he thought. I'll have to tell Adela. Someone could have a nasty accident in here. Or maybe, thought Serafin, falling back into his childish wishful thinking, maybe it would be better to say nothing. After all, sometimes you do happen to be at the right place at the right time. You might witness an accident, for instance, and do nothing to help the victim. You might hear him shouting and know that you should reach out and give him a hand but stand there instead, unmoved, and do nothing – or worse, you could even give destiny a little nudge. Serafin examined the light bulb, which was now giving off a delicious burnt smell. Accidents can happen so easily, he thought. You don't actually have to do anything, just be ready to give bad luck a helping hand, and that can be as simple and easy as pressing a button. Yes, thought Serafin, emerging from the bathroom with a more positive outlook and a few new ideas, all sorts of unexpected things can happen in the course of an evening. You never know, do you?

While enjoying the delicious meal organized by Adela and talking with the guests at his table, Serafin Tous would toy with the idea of provoking an accident. It would give him something interesting to think about for the next couple of hours.

* * *

The third person who would have liked Nestor to disappear was Adela Teldi. But she was not yet laying plans. Instead she was thinking: Careful, remember what he said. Carlos is like a son to him. Don't forget that.

As she was getting dressed for the party that evening, Adela tried not to look at herself in the mirror. She was scared of what she might find in her eyes: the anxiety caused by two discoveries she had made quite by chance that afternoon. First she had recognized Nestor and remembered that he was a friend of Antonio Reig, who used to be their cook back in Buenos Aires. Then she had discovered something even more disturbing. Like a doubting Thomas, she wouldn't have believed it possible unless she had seen it with her own eyes and heard it with her own astonished ears; there were simply too many coincidences, and none of them good. Not only did the caterer happen to be someone who knew about her past, but as she was entering the kitchen unannounced, she had been lucky (or unlucky?) enough to overhear him talking with his staff, and from what she heard, she was sure he had told them everything that had happened back in Argentina, including the death of her sister.

Trying to repress that memory, as she had done so often in the past, Adela inspected her body, searching for the paths traced by Carlos's hands, hoping they would help her to forget. But this time, instead of giving her pleasure, the inspection was painful, so painful that she almost expected to see physical wounds on her arms and shoulders. There were no wounds, but the pain persisted and Adela expressed it in mathematical terms, the summation of her anxiety. One, this man has recognized me. Two, he has already told his employees what he knows about my life. And three, he said that Carlos was like a son to him. You don't have to be very smart to put these three things together and realize that, given how fond he is of Carlos, he's bound to warn him not to get mixed up with the likes of me. But of course he wouldn't even think of doing that unless he knew about our relationship, and he doesn't, not yet, of that at least I'm certain.

This gave her some relief. The pain ebbed, but only for a moment, because she soon realized that it was only a matter of time before Nestor found out about her and Carlos. Love, she thought sadly, flaunts itself, as you well know, my dear. Love can't help giving itself away: a beatific smile, a slight trembling, a special tone of voice, a glance . . . at some point Nestor would surely discern one of these symptoms in one or other of them. And then the game would be up.

She was afraid her eyes in the mirror would betray all this – the fear, the danger, the impending end of her love affair – so she turned away. But it isn't easy to get dressed without looking at yourself. Adela had chosen a reliable, plain, black gown. In a woman's wardrobe there are always some things that require the use of a mirror and others that don't. There are temperamental dresses that call for a considerable amount of testing, tweaking and adjusting. Others are less capricious and can be relied upon to do the job. It was one of these Adela had selected from the wardrobe. She slipped it on quickly, without thinking, but then she faced the problem of how to fix her make-up and hair without looking in the mirror. She would have to look at herself, just briefly, so as not to let the other, left-handed Adela who lived on the dark side of the moon tell her something she didn't want to hear, something along the lines of: 'You see? I told you. It had to happen. You should have listened to your thumbs, they've always warned you when something unpleasant is about to happen. And omens and portents aside, what did you expect, you silly old thing? Did you think you'd be able to get Love with a capital L for free? It was only to be expected; something was bound to go wrong. Face it, twenty-five years of marriage and a long string of lovers take their toll, to say nothing of that painful secret you've been trying to hide even from yourself. You were so brave yesterday when you decided to make a clean break, promising that when the party was over you would risk it all to allow love a chance. Perhaps you thought you were paying a high price. Well that was nothing. Yes, you'll have to endure insecurity and the fear of losing him, but that isn't all. The past always comes back to collect its dues, Adela: your sister, the affair that led to her death, the guilt . . . it's true those memories are only ghosts, but ghosts have a nasty habit of coming back to haunt the living. They come back when you least expect them, in the most unlikely forms, and the ghost of what happened in Buenos Aires is here now in the form of a chef with a pointy moustache.'

The mirror could not tell Adela any of this, because she would not look at it. As she had done so often in her life, she simply stopped herself from thinking. If you prevent ideas from forming, they don't exist, or at least they can't hurt you. But that was just a trick. Whether she looked at the mirror or not, whether she thought about it or not, Adela knew that she would have to do something to prevent Nestor from putting an end to her new-found happiness. The best thing would be to get in first, talk to Carlos and tell him the truth, because in the end, thought Adela, why would he care about an old story, something that happened years ago, in another country, to people who meant nothing to him? An error of youth, a silly fling that ended badly, true, but who hasn't committed a little indiscretion at some point in their life?

By the pricking of my thumbs, something wicked this way comes. As she tried to zip up her dress, Adela's fingers brushed against her bare skin, and she could feel her thumbs pricking. A strange presentiment made her fingers retract as she was struck by the similarity between the feel of two bodies and the form of two names, one fresh in her mind, the other buried deep in her memory: Carlos Garcia and Ricardo Garcia. She imagined them side by side, like father and son. The strange sensation persisted, prompting the realization: the same skin, that same touch, and the same surname. But where do you get these mad ideas from, Adela? That's ridiculous! As if two men with the same surname had to be related! Garcia, for God's sake, it's one of the most common names in Spain. You really are losing your marbles, my dear. Why don't you stop being silly and have a proper look in the mirror? It's no good trying to do it like this, you'll go out looking a fright, like a witch on a bad-hair day.

But Adela didn't dare. She was too scared of what she might see in the background: another coincidence, too awful even to imagine. What if Carlos Garcia *were* the son of Soledad and Ricardo? What then? A one in a thousand chance, and the odds against that gossip-monger of a chef putting two and two together must be a million to one, but then, what if . . . ?

What if it were true and he knew? thought Adela, looking directly into the mirror now for the first time, unafraid. I'd just have to silence him for good. But fortunately that won't be necessary. There couldn't be that many coincidences. So stop worrying and get dressed, you're going to be late.

Then Adela did something she hadn't done for years: from her jewel box she took the green cameo that her mother, Teresa, had given her for her fifteenth birthday. She couldn't remember ever having used it as a brooch, but that old jade disc with its gold setting went well with the austere black dress she had decided to wear. And now stop being silly, she told herself as she headed for the door. She opened it, and then shut it behind her. She looked around the landing, at all the things she would soon abandon forever, and she smiled. A small price to pay, really, for what the future holds, as long as nothing goes wrong. And nothing will go wrong. I'll make quite sure of that.

Adela went down the stairs. She was going to play the role of Mrs Teldi the model hostess one last time, and tomorrow . . . whatever happened, tomorrow would be the first day of the rest of her life.

As Adela went downstairs, Chloe was thinking, Nestor! I could strangle him. Only he could have come up with waiter's uniform like this. It's like a Mao suit or something. It's so tight I'm going to fry like a chicken.

Nestor had not been amused to discover that Chloe had left her waitress's uniform at her parents' house. It always gave Mulberry & Mistletoe's catering a nice touch of class, he felt, to have a girl waiting in a dark smock, a little cap and a white organdie apron. 'But I suppose if you've left it all behind in Madrid, there's nothing else we can do. All right then, Chloe, go and put on Karel's spare uniform. But if you're going to dress as a man,' he warned her, 'do us all a favour and play the part convincingly. Walk like a man, lower your voice so as not to give the guests a fright, comb your hair back, and above all, for God's sake, remove those rings and studs and things, will you?'

In the room over the garage, which she was sharing with Karel Pligh, Chloe had put on the trousers and the severe-looking jacket, which buttoned right up to the neck like a biker's leathers, and she was standing in front of the mirror, removing her rings and studs, gently, so as not to hurt herself, reciting the origins of each piece of metal: this came from my mate Hassem for Christmas; this I bought in a cheap junk shop; and this one Karel gave me . . . he's so sweet, and gorgeous with it. As she removed them, one by one, she realized it had been ages since she had seen her face unembellished, and faces change, it's fucking amazing how they change. She decided to comb her hair before removing the ring in her bottom lip, because she knew it was going to hurt. She looked in Karel's sponge bag and found a comb and a tube of gel, then turned on the tap. She was starting to get into this cross-dressing thing. She began to imitate the way she'd seen any number of men, from Karel Pligh to her brother Eddie, comb their hair. The Travolta method: the right hand wields the comb, while the left follows, stroking. Hey, this is fucking cool. It looks good, I look like . . . and her hands acquired a life of their own, combing away, stroke after stroke, slicking all her hair back until she looked like a boy, a young man of twenty-two. That was how old she would be next month.

'What the hell are you doing in there, Chloe? Hurry up, for God's sake. Nestor will be furious.'

Off in her own world, Chloe vaguely heard Karel Pligh's words through the bathroom door and her hand froze.

'What? What is it? Who's that?'

'It's Karel, who else? We're really late, open the door or I'm going down without you.'

Instead of acceding to this demand, Chloe kept looking for the eyes she thought she had seen in the mirror. Without turning around, she said: 'You do that, K. Go down and stop scaring the shit out of me.'

And as she spoke, she realized that the eyes looking back from the mirror were not blue like hers, but black and stern and they seemed to be saying: Don't talk like that, Clo-clo. You never used to talk like that.

'Is that you, Eddie?'

The face in the mirror looked like Eddie's, but it wasn't. It was hers: the hard and quite possibly unhygienic ring in her lower lip was a give-away. Not Eddie's style at all.

'Hang on, Eddie, just a minute, I'll take it out for you. I promise I'll never wear it again.' And, very carefully, she removed the last ring from her lip so that her brother's reflection could smile back unimpeded from the mirror. 'There, that's better, now let me touch you.'

The whole scene lasted no more than a minute. Chloe was back in the world of her dreams, playing with her brother, but then she reached towards the reflection to caress his eyes, so different from hers, and as her fingers touched the glass she realized that the spell had been broken, and the face looking out from the cold surface of the mirror was a girl's face, her own.

'I'm not going to warn you again, Chloe. Nestor has called us three times.'

All the mirror showed now was a girl dressed as a boy. She looked like Eddie, true. She had the same hairstyle, and the uniform she had put on was even reminiscent of the leathers he had worn that last afternoon, but the eyes were different. Once again those dark eyes had abandoned her.

That night, as she waited on the tables and attended to the guests, Chloe would keep trying to meet them again in every mirror in the house.

'Are you playing hide-and-seek with me, Eddie?'

3

The Dinner at The Lilies

Ernesto Teldi raised his glass and said: 'It's a great privilege for Adela and me to be able to gather thirty-three of the world's most original and important art collectors, and to welcome you all to The Lilies tonight.'

From their appearance, there was no way of telling that the thirty-three people seated around the dining room at The Lilies, their gazes converging on Ernesto Teldi, were all specialist collectors, each one an expert in a particular field of art or antiquities. Most trades and professions have some kind of distinguishing characteristic, a way of dressing or talking, a particular form of pedantry or snobbery, but collectors of rare objects have nothing in common except their idiosyncrasy; each one is a unique specimen, in the most literal sense. Take Mr Stephanopolous and Mr Algobranghini, for instance. Both knew all there was to know about knives and swords, but apart from that the only thing they had in common was an immoderate fondness for tawny port. When the Teldis charged their guests' glasses for a toast, both Algobranghini and Stephanopolous rejected the *cava*, opting instead for a slim red glass of '59 vintage Royal Port. In all other respects, their personalities could not have been more different. Despite his Greek name, Stephanopolous was a pure product of the British establishment: Eton, Oxford, a life in the country, surrounded by dogs, cats and horses. Algobranghini on the other hand looked like an old-style tango singer. Karel Pligh was captivated by his pinstripe suit, the carnation in his buttonhole and his slicked-back hair. Every inch the Buenos Aires wide-boy, he thought as he refilled the collector's tiny glass for the tenth time. The reincarnation of the tango master, Carlos Gardel, I swear.

A curious observer would have been struck by the bewildering diversity of styles on display that evening. It was an odd assembly to say the least. Despite her name, Miss Liau Chi, the famous collector of ghost stories, seemed to have stepped out of a novel by Wilkie Collins (rather than a plane from Hong Kong). The three 'Dickensiana fetishists' looked respectively like an overweight boxer, a severe Breton matron (in the mould of Becassine, from the old French comic books) and, more appropriately, the living image of Mr Squeers, the mean-minded teacher from *Nicholas Nickelby*.

Also present were the icon collectors (a young woman who looked like a model, an Orthodox priest, and a young man with a smooth, angelic face, who appeared to be much younger than his passport said he was). On seeing this youth, Serafin Tous couldn't help thinking, What an exquisite creature. But immediately his gaze slid from the cherub to the kitchen door, behind which Nestor was no doubt lurking among his pots and pans. I hope he burns his hand and has to be taken to hospital, thought the judge. Was it really so terrible to wish a little domestic incident on someone, a little time off work . . .

or maybe a serious accident that would dispose of him for good, and leave Serafin and his friends in peace?

But leaving these bad wishes aside (the air at The Lilies was thick with them that night, and all were meant for Nestor), let us resume the description of the guests. The rest of the line-up was composed of conventional-looking ladies and gentlemen, with two exceptions: the 'Rapanui statuette fan', who looked like the reincarnation of Humboldt the naturalist, and Monsieur Pitou, the guest of honour, an eminent expert on the love letters of the famous. All through the evening Monsieur Pitou had been the object of Ernesto Teldi's subtly seductive attentions. He was a tiny man, less than four and a half feet tall. He had exquisite hands and his limbs and trunk were perfectly proportioned, but his face . . . The owner of the world's most beautiful love letters was spectacularly ugly and his body was shrunken, as if a love spell in reverse had turned him from a prince into a frog.

Having sat down again after his ritualized words of welcome, Teldi said: 'Now, dear Emile, before we go into the library, I'd like to thank you for having given me one of the most moving experiences of my life.'

With a conspiratorial gesture, he opened his jacket to reveal the white corner of a love letter that Pitou had sold him before dinner. The sale had gone smoothly. There had been no need to bring out the heavy artillery of his bargaining skills. An odd fellow, Monsieur Pitou. There was something alarming about the way his froggy mouth was smiling back at him now, displaying a magnificent set of teeth. It had been a bit too easy to acquire that curious love letter signed Oscar Wilde. And the price was very low. Could his guest have cheated him? 'I want you, I trust you, I am coming to you . . .' The handwriting was indubitably Wilde's, and the date proved that it had been written three years before the author had used the very same sentence in one of his most famous plays. It was really quite a discovery, as long as it wasn't a fake, of course. But I'm being paranoid. No-one's going to try to cheat a dealer of my reputation . . . my *current* reputation, that is, he thought uneasily, remembering the letter scribbled in green ink sitting on his bedside table. Then he thought about how in the hard world of art dealers a little scandal, a little indiscretion, was enough to label you as one more shady businessman. Imagining the worst, Ernesto Teldi saw himself transformed overnight into one of those pathetic individuals, those ridiculous has-beens stripped of all respect, fair game for any scam. Perhaps it was happening already. Pitou was an intuitive dealer with a gift for anticipating the market. Had he guessed somehow that Ernesto Teldi's reputation was not so unimpeachable after all?

Monsieur Pitou was sitting there in front of him with his toad-like eyes, smiling. What Teldi saw as he looked at him, however, was not an amphibian but a more insidious and harmful creature. Filthy leech! If my reputation is ruined, it will be your fault, he said to himself, thinking of Nestor, not for the first time that evening. Again and again as he chatted with his guests and played the charming host, a question kept nagging at him: What the hell am I going to do about that vile leech? The toad stuck out a very long tongue, as if he were trying to catch a fly, then pulled it back in with a smile.

'Are you feeling all right, Teldi? You're looking thoughtful.'

And Teldi, putting the unexpectedly well-priced love letter in his breast pocket, where it was safe and warm, close to his heart, told himself there was no way he could allow that blackmailer, that leech in the kitchen, to ruin his career or in any way tarnish his hostly charms. I should just squash him and be done with it, stop him from interfering with my life. But how? *How?* Maybe there's a way . . . yes, I think I can see a way . . . but for now it can wait.

'This way, this way please, Monsieur Pitou,' said Teldi to the collector of love letters, taking him by the arm. 'Let's go to the library and have a glass of cognac. I want to introduce you to Mr Stephanopolous.'

Ernesto Teldi's library is so renowned that it hardly needs to be described. Anyone who reads *House & Garden*, *Country Living* or other such lifestyle magazine is bound to have seen a photograph of it: a room that testifies to its owner's exquisite taste and passion for unique pieces. The whole is perfectly harmonious, not dominated by one or two features that clamour for attention. Often, in collectors' houses, objects are piled up like a Turkish bazaar. Not so in the library at The Lilies. The visitor is never overwhelmed. There is a certain artlessness to the arrangement, as if, over many years, the objects had made themselves at home, each in its place. On the right, for example, a small Manet hangs on the wall, watching over the entrance: it is the same model whose naked figure in *Le déjeuner sur l'herbe* caused such a scandal. Here, however, elegantly blending in with the other paintings, she could easily be overlooked by all but the finest of eyes. Across the room, an art deco statuette of a faun keeps watch over Manet's model, by happy chance it might seem, yet the symmetry is deliberate. And so it is with the other magnificent pieces, none of which is ostentatiously displayed, while a variety of comfortable chairs – a chesterfield, a pouf, a sofa – invite the happy guests to make themselves at home and enjoy this feast for the senses. The discreet harmony of the whole is not disturbed by the glass case containing a small and intriguing collection of tin soldiers or by the panoply of knives, daggers and *stiletti*.

'I sold that dagger with the red handle to your husband last year, Mrs Teldi,' said Gerassimos Stephanopolous to Adela. 'Since then, its value has tripled. And do you know why, my dear? Because last month *Time* magazine published a photo of Attaturk, or perhaps I should say Mustapha Kemal, wearing the very same dagger in his belt. What a stroke of luck! He has such good business sense, your husband, but I don't mind him getting the better of me, truly. I'm a great admirer of your husband . . . and of his taste,' said the Greek, looking at Adela as if he were mentally valuing some exquisite artefact.

But Adela was immune to flattery that night. She had spent the whole dinner being mechanically pleasant, a skill she had acquired over many years of tedious social obligations and could now exercise without mobilizing a single neuron: Yes . . . No . . . Really? But how extraordinary! Adela was expert at keeping a conversation going on auto-pilot with these rudimentary but effective interjections, and pursuing her own train of thought while her face and gestures gave the impression that she was totally engaged by her guests.

'Really, Mr Stephanopolous? Do tell me more! I'd love to hear all about Mustapha Kemal and his red dagger.'

The collector was only too happy to launch into a long monologue, during which in Adela's mind the founder of modern Turkey and his youthful exploits mingled with thoughts of quite a different nature.

'As I'm sure you know, in 1912, when Mustapha was still a boy . . .'

(Where was *her* boy, Carlos? Where could he be? wondered Adela. During the dinner he had served the tables furthest from hers and she hadn't been able to catch his eye at all. But the time for *digestifs* had come, and watching Karel and Chloe move among the guests, offering them *cava*, armagnac and malt whisky, brushing against them as they went back and forth, Adela hoped she could exploit the mingling to touch Carlos surreptitiously too. She wanted to brush her hand against his arm as if by accident, caress the back that she would later on be kissing, when the dinner was over, when all these people were gone, when there were no more faces to smile at or conversations to pay attention to.)

'But that's incredible! Is that really how it happened, Mr Stephanopolous? How fascinating!'

'Exactly as I told you, my dear, and I'm delighted you appreciate the irony of it. If not for that incident, Mustapha Kemal would never have come to be called Attaturk.'

(Where are you? Where are you, my love? Come closer, I want to smell you, I want our bodies to touch in front of all these people, Teldi and his friends. A sweet foretaste of tomorrow, when I will be through with this life and we won't have to steal glances across a crowded room.)

'Metaphorically speaking, one might say our hero belonged to the tribe of dreamers,' Stephanopolous was saying, encouraged by a 'You don't say!' that Adela had thrown in to keep the conversation moving along. 'But whether or not he was a dreamer, the fact is the young Mustapha played his cards so well that he was able to bring Turkey into the twentieth century. Although it did mean giving up certain things, traditional customs and so on . . .'

'How fascinating,' Adela remarked adroitly, which was all the encouragement he needed to go on for another three minutes, allowing Adela to focus on finding Carlos among the heads of her guests wreathed in smoke. He wasn't there. For a moment she imagined him in the kitchen, hearing what she most feared Nestor would tell him. The thought made her wince with pain.

'Awful, isn't it?' said Stephanopolous, noting Mrs Teldi's reaction to his account of one of the bloodier episodes in Turkish history.

(No, Adela, you needn't worry about that. The chef isn't likely to tell him tonight. And by tomorrow you will have talked with Carlos and told him everything he needs to know about your past. But . . . wouldn't it be better to silence that interfering chef for good?)

'And that, my dear, is where the dagger with the red handle comes in. As I'm sure you'll appreciate, a dangerous situation like that called for expeditious, one might even say sanguinary, measures.'

'Indeed, quite, absolutely, Mr Stephanopolous,' said Adela on auto-pilot, while the non-mechanical part of her mind thrilled at the sight of Carlos over near the door, threading his way across the crowded room towards her with a tray full of tall glasses. She smiled inwardly.

What took you so long, my love?

Meanwhile, Carlos was thinking: There's Adela, at last I can be near her. And he made his way across the room, drawn as if by gravity, longing to touch her in the midst of the crowd, in front of everyone, as platonic lovers touch, as secret lovers thrill to the merest hint of a caress. Maybe I could even kiss her shoulder when I offer her a glass, he thought.

'Excuse me, madam, I didn't mean to . . .'

She smiled. She was so beautiful.

'Is this champagne or *cava*?'

'*Cava*, madam, may I?'

And as he leant forward, drawing closer still, his waiter's eye, accustomed to picking out singular features by which to identify people, noticed a green jade cameo that Adela was wearing as a brooch.

'Attaturk's objective was to show that Turkey was ready to enter the modern world, like any Western nation, but of course . . .'

(The gold setting, the green stone . . . My God, it's the cameo from the painting, the one the girl is holding. And, as if he were seeing Adela for the first time, Carlos searched for an explanation in her face.)

'Of course daggers have come back into fashion now, and not just there, but right through the Muslim world. A remarkable development, as I'm sure you appreciate. And who could have predicted it? I certainly didn't. Did you?'

(It's her; it has to be. The *cava* in the glasses began a weird dance to the rhythm of Carlos Garcia's trembling hand. The bubbles rose to the surface and burst, each exclaiming: My God, how is it possible? How can I have kissed her a thousand times and loved every inch of that body without realizing that she was the woman I had been searching for all along?)

Now Carlos couldn't stop looking at the stone, and the cameo's green gleam recalled other childhood memories: the silhouette of his Grandma Teresa playing solitaire in the yellow sitting room ('You're mistaken, young man, there's no woman in a wardrobe here. I don't know where you got that idea from'); himself as a child, his finger caressing the delicate curve along which, twenty or so years later, he would plant his kisses.

'No! No! The worst of all, my dear, was not the discovery in itself, however terrible it may seem, but the fact that, ironically, we have never really seen their faces. We look, but we don't see. It's absurd, but that's the way it is, you know, all the more so with Turkish women, who are obliged to wear a veil, however beautiful they are . . .'

(That was why it all seemed so familiar: The Lilies, which was so like Number 38, the platinum blond hair of the woman in the picture, just like Adela's hair, despite the difference in age . . .)

'Are you listening, my dear? You look tired.'

'Not at all, Mr Stephanopolous. Do go on, please.'

The brooch on Adela's dress glowed, prompting a thousand questions. Yet, urgent as those questions were, they would have to wait until the party was over. Then I'll be able to get it all straightened out, thought Carlos while the rocking glasses, like a drunken oracle, reminded him of something Nestor had said earlier that afternoon: '*Cazzo* Carlitos, one day you'll learn that there are times in life when it's best not to ask questions. Especially when you suspect you'd be better off not knowing the answers.'

'And what, might I ask, is your problem, young man?'

Mr Stephanopolous had interrupted his historical disquisition, surprised by the way Carlos was standing there, so close to Adela, as if he were participating in the conversation, a waiter with a tray full of glasses brazenly listening in on the guests.

'We have our drinks, young man, and no doubt you have other guests to attend to. So off you go.'

At the sound of Stephanopolous's voice, Carlos snapped out of his reverie. He hardly dared look at Adela, as if he were frightened the others would guess his secret. Apologizing, he began to move away, but as he did, he noticed a miniature green scimitar in the knife collector's buttonhole, facing Adela's green cameo like a reflection in a pond. Of course it might not be the same cameo. What if it were just a coincidence, another one of old Madame Longstaffe's tricks? They say there's always a catch to her prophecies.

Carlos walked away, trying not to look back, but his incredulity got the better of him. He stole a glimpse of Adela still chatting with the knife collector, and even from a distance he could see the two pieces of jewellery, the cameo and the scimitar, face to face, precious and cold, like the insignia of an opulent world, which, for him, was so full of enigmas. You're such a hick, he said to himself. Maybe in the old days jewels were unique pieces, but now they're mass produced. You idealize these rich people because they live in a world that is alien to you, but there must be hundreds of green cameos, and hundreds of green scimitars like the one that stuck-up Greek is wearing.

Carlos swung around. The glasses clinking on his tray, some full, others half empty, put an end to his reassuring reflections. Don't be a fool. It's her; it has to be. The resemblance is too strong. But what's the link with Number 38? I wonder if she knew my grandmother. Or my father? Nestor will be amazed when I tell him. It's so weird, like destiny was winking at me or something . . .

At that very moment, Chloe was being subjected to a bit of winking too not by destiny, but by Liau Chi, the collector of ghost stories.

'Come over here for a minute, young man,' she said, steering Chloe into a corner of the sitting room.

'What's your name? How old are you? What's your star

sign? Aries? Or maybe Capricorn? Do you like ghost stories? Do you believe in reincarnation? Did you know that those who die young always find some way of coming back to earth and living out the part of their lives that destiny denied them?'

Uh oh, seriously off her rocker, thought Chloe, trying to slip away. She was feeling hot under the tight collar of the waiter's uniform and the madwoman from the East thought she was a guy and was trying to make a fucking pass at her, when all she wanted to do was find her brother.

All through the meal, as she was serving the guests, Chloe kept trying to find Eddie's eyes in the various mirrors at The Lilies, the eyes she thought she had glimpsed for a moment in the bathroom mirror while she was getting dressed. She searched unsuccessfully in the tall mirrors of the dining room, a round mirror in the entrance hall and any shiny surface she could find. Between dessert and coffee she even disappeared for a few minutes, bounding up the stairs to her room over the garage, hoping that she might be able to relive the experience of a few hours before.

Eddie, are you there?

The face looking back at her from all the mirrors was certainly similar to Eddie's, but the eyes were hers, as blue as ever.

What the fuck did you expect? You're losing it, girl. You're not going to find Eddie around here, so stop being a prat, she told herself. But on her way back to the party, she carried on looking in all the mirrors, and in every single one she was always alone.

In the library, Chloe stopped to stare into the mirror on the console beside the fireplace, trying to catch even the slightest glimpse of those dark eyes, but all she could see was the pale face of Liau Chi, expert in ghost-lore.

'Don't think I'm going to let you slip away this time, now that I've found you again, young man. Are you listening to me? I have something important to tell you, but before getting into astrology, I need another whisky. So bring me one straight away, will you?'

On the way to the kitchen Chloe continued her futile search, peering into still more mirrors. She begged the mirror in the entrance hall, Please, let me see something, just a shadow, even if it isn't real. She lingered in front of the dark window-panes, hoping their vague, deceptive reflections, so conducive to illusion, might grant her what the other mirrors had refused.

'Psst . . . psst, Miss Trias.'

Only one person in the world ever called her that. Still searching among the reflections, she recognized the face of Nestor Chaffinch, who was standing at the swinging kitchen door, gesturing.

The chef retreated, then reappeared a moment later, beckoning with an air of urgency. It isn't good form for a chef to leave the kitchen, except for the ritual greeting of guests and their compliments on the food. Nestor had just been through that formality, so now he had to stay at his post; but he still needed help.

'Come here. It'll only take a second, then you can go on with what you were doing.'

Chloe was happy to escape from the guests. A bunch of weirdos, it's like a madhouse here, she thought as she walked over to Nestor with her tray full of empty glasses.

'How can I help you, Nestor?'

They went into the kitchen together and Nestor pointed to the cool room, or rather to a very high shelf above its metal door.

'Some idiot had the bright idea of putting the detergent

up there. Can you see it? Bring a chair over and get it down for me, will you.'

Up she went. The metal door reflected the silhouette of a girl on a makeshift stepladder.

The unreachable shelf was filthy. Old rat-bait boxes, bottles of turpentine and various cleaning products were stacked there in disarray, under a dense mat of spiders' webs that anyone would have thought twice about disturbing. It looked like a hiding place for something sinister. Shifting a bottle, Chloe saw a scurrying multitude of those little black creatures she remembered from her childhood: when you touched them they would roll up into balls. Thousands of tiny legs, and round, moist-looking carapaces running for cover in some dark corner while one, blinded by the light, climbed boldly up Chloe's hand, heading for the darkness under her cuff. But none of this, neither the musty smell nor the cold tickle on her skin seemed to bother her, because on the way up to that shelf, when she glimpsed her reflection in the shiny surface of the Westinghouse cool room, for a fraction of a second Chloe thought she saw the dark flash of her brother's gaze. And she shut her eyes, trying to hold on to that vision.

'What *are* you doing, Chloe? Higher, just reach up and get it. Why are you stopping there, staring at yourself like an idiot? Come on, that's quite enough messing around. I haven't got all night.'

But Chloe didn't move or dare open her eyes, because she knew that when she did, Eddie would have disappeared again for ever, gone back to Neverland. The insect had climbed up to her shoulder now. The detergent Nestor wanted was just a few centimetres further along on that filthy, slimy shelf, but in spite of her boss's impatience and the voice of Miss Liau Chi, who had just come into the kitchen looking for her ('Come back here, young man, I have something to tell you, something you'll be very interested to hear, I promise you'), she remained perfectly still until, finally, that absurd pose became impossible to maintain and she reached out and grasped what she had been asked to fetch. When she looked at herself in the mirror-like door of the cool room on the way down, she was forced to admit once again that it had all been a fantasy: her eyes were hopelessly, unequivocally blue.

'Come here, young man, we must have a little chat, you and I,' insisted Miss Liau Chi.

4

A Door Shuts

Three-thirty in the morning and all the guests had finally gone home. Goodbye, Mr Stephanopolous, we'll catch up again soon . . . Thank you, Mr Teldi. Yes, see you soon. And thank you, Mrs Teldi, it's been a pleasure to talk with a woman of your intelligence. I did enjoy our little chat about Attaturk. Your remarks were so insightful . . . Goodbye, Monsieur Pitou, thank you for coming . . . Good night, Miss Liau Chi . . .

The voices had faded away, the lights had gone out, and, all alone in the kitchen, Nestor supposed he was the only person in the house still awake. He always liked to take a moment to savour his culinary triumphs in solitude, like an artist reliving his moments of glory or a lover indulgently recalling each detail of an amorous encounter, sometimes enjoying the memory more than the experience itself. The texture of my lobster salad was just perfect, thought Nestor, glowing with pleasure. Absolutely spot on: not too hot, not too cold; not too hard, not too soft. When I looked out from the kitchen and saw the smooth motion of Ernesto Teldi's moustache, I knew it was superlative.

Upstairs, at that very moment, beads of cold sweat were gathering in Teldi's moustache. Suddenly, he sat up in bed. It wasn't the usual nightmares. Lying there unable to get to sleep, he had just come to a decision. The time has come, he said to himself, it has to be tonight. It isn't sensible to let this sort of thing drag on; I'll go and have it out with him right now. Ernesto Teldi looked at his watch and guessed that the chef would be sleeping in his room up in the attic, a little room tucked away up there where no-one would hear anything. Just as well.

Oh, my sea bass with potato and dill soufflé, thought Nestor Chaffinch fondly, not up in his attic room but still down in the kitchen, with his elbows on the big formica table that had played its modest part in his success. When I went out to be congratulated by the guests, Adela Teldi declared that never in her life had she tasted a dish of such simple sophistication. What a splendid way of putting it!

At that very moment, Adela was gently touching her lips. Then she reached out and did the same to Carlos, sleeping next to her, as if she were trying to pass on a secret that she had not dared to put into words. She had sworn that as soon as they were alone together, she would tell him everything that had happened in Buenos Aires, so he would hear it from her rather than Nestor, and yet when the party was finally over and they were alone in Carlos's little attic room, neither of them said a word. A couple of times she had felt that Carlos was on the point of asking her something, but when two bodies are so hungry for each other, words are out of place.

I'll tell him tomorrow, tomorrow, I promise, thought Adela, between feverish kisses.

But when the fever had abated, and her well-preserved but middle-aged body lay still in Carlos's youthful embrace, Adela Teldi reconsidered. Love, she thought, is so complex, so delicate, this love at any rate . . . perhaps it would be better not to put it to the test with confessions and secrets. I have to talk with that chef, buy his silence if necessary, beg him if I have to . . . There's no alternative, my dear, she said smiling to herself. You have to make sure he keeps quiet, no matter the cost. At your age you can't afford to let anyone spoil this chance of happiness . . . The ship has gone down, and you're clinging to a plank, holding on for dear life. Adela kissed her lover's forehead. He was sleeping the deep sleep of the young, which was just as well. He would never hear what happened when she went down the corridor to Nestor's room.

And as for my mousseline sauce, thought Nestor in the kitchen, sighing with an artist's pleasure and a lover's devotion, only sensitive and melancholic souls like Serafin Tous can fully appreciate that smooth, rounded flavour, with just the slightest hint of lemon. During his little speech to the guests, Nestor had smiled knowingly at Serafin as he mentioned the mousseline and a look of tormented ecstasy had come over the judge's face. One needs to have a feminine sensibility to appreciate certain flavours, thought Nestor. I don't expect Mr Tous's friends are aware of that side of his personality, and they probably wouldn't care for it. But his little secret is absolutely safe with me. Not just because we met at Freshman's and it would be unprofessional to pass on information about a colleague's clients, but also because I won't hear a word against a man who knows his mousseline sauce.

03.47, click . . . 03.48. The phosphorescent numbers on Serafin Tous's alarm clock flipped over implacably, like the leaves of a calendar mercilessly marking the passage of time and the approach of a dreaded day. Unable to sleep, Serafin decided to get up. The night was black, conducive to melancholy but also to wild thoughts. I wonder where that miserable person is sleeping, he thought. That slanderer, that gossiping chef. Serafin didn't know the house, but he imagined that the rooms for the domestic staff would be up in the attic, so he headed that way. He didn't switch on the light. He groped his way in the darkness, so that when he passed the wardrobe mirror he was spared a surprising sight: in the eyes of this placid gentleman who wouldn't hurt a fly, there was a gleam as hard and sharp as a stiletto.

And what about my splendid chocolate truffles! thought Nestor, going over it all again, like a lover remembering and reliving every caress. Never have nuances of flavour been so masterfully blended, if I say so myself: vanilla, bitter chocolate, liqueur, a touch of ginger. That's the trick, the ginger is the secret ingredient that makes a really good chocolate truffle. Though of course only the cognoscenti can tell, the few who are capable of analysing such a magnificent symphony of flavours. That's why I got so cross with young Chloe when she put two truffles in her mouth at once. Two truffles! 'Let me tell you something. Miss Trias,' I said to her, 'only a person possessed of two souls could appreciate the full range of flavours in two of Nestor Chaffinch's truffles. Do you have any idea . . . ?' But she just said *fuck that* or *bollocks* or one of her other favourite expressions. With such a limited vocabulary, what kind of inner life can she have? That's the problem with the youth of today, thought Nestor sadly. I bet right now her dreams are full of heavy metal music or something equally brainless and vulgar.

But Nestor was mistaken, for as it happened, Chloe Trias was dreaming of her boss's chocolate truffles in the room she was sharing with Karel over the garage. And like a sensitive soul – or, rather, two sensitive souls – she was savouring the memory of that hint of ginger and the sweet vanilla, summoning up the delicious aroma of the liqueur. Yet this sophisticated gastronomical fantasy, which would have come as a great surprise to Nestor, did not last long. And in the throes of sleep, it was displaced in rapid succession by other dream fragments. A couple of Pearl Jam lyrics went through her mind, mixed with an erotic memory featuring the very tasty Karel Pligh, who was lying asleep beside her. Then, in the garden of The Lilies, she saw a cockroach on a doormat, reflected in a mirror, while Miss Liau Chi whispered in her ear: 'Do you believe in ghosts?' All this was quickly swept away by a rush of other equally incoherent images, but after a couple of minutes of turbulent dreaming, Chloe woke up and lay there, tossing and turning, unable to get back to sleep. Shit, she thought, now I'll probably be awake all night like a fucking owl. Periodically, light from one of the lamps shining on the façade of The Lilies burst into the room like the beam of a lighthouse. While the room was briefly lit up, Chloe looked sideways at Karel, then across at her pack, which was lying on a chair, spilling its contents like a torn rag doll. The room was plunged into darkness again, and Chloe remembered how she had panicked before the dinner when she couldn't find her maid's uniform. That was why her stuff was in such a mess: T-shirts, a bikini, underwear . . . everything except the case where she kept the framed photo of her brother. That red case had never left the bottom of her backpack, but the rest of her things lying scattered around the room looked like ghosts from one of Miss Liau Chi's books. Crazy old Chinese cow, thought Chloe, she's supposed to hang out with ghosts and see dead people and stuff and she couldn't even tell I was a girl. As if I looked like a fucking guy, she thought, before realizing that in a way she had fooled herself too: it was because she had dressed as a man that, for a few seconds, she thought she had seen Eddie's eyes in her reflection.

She tried to go back to sleep. Maybe tonight she'd be lucky and dream that her brother was coming to take her away to Neverland, like before. Come on, Eddie, come and play for a bit, she said like a little girl, but instead a pair of memories came to haunt her sleeplessness: the moleskin notebook Nestor always kept hidden in the pocket of his chef's jacket and the delicious flavour of his chocolate truffles. The truffles must have been put away in the Westinghouse cool room in the kitchen, she thought, the one that has a shiny metal door like in a house of mirrors.

Chloe kept tossing and turning, cursing her insomnia. She couldn't get to sleep, but each time she came close, pleasant thoughts began to stream through her mind, like the memory of Eddie's smile, the smile she thought she saw a few hours ago. And she could swear a voice was speaking to her, saying: Come on, Clo-clo, come down; here I am. But she was wary. She was afraid of going down to the kitchen and being disappointed again. This time her brother's eyes would not be looking back from the cool-room door. He was just playing games with her again. Like he used to when he was alive, and she would ask him: 'What are you writing, Eddie? It's a story with adventures and romance and crimes and stuff, isn't it? Can I read it?' And he would reply: 'Not now, Clo-clo. Later on, I promise.'

But he was lying. There was no 'later on', because her brother got it into his head that he had to live fast since he wanted to be a writer and nothing worth writing about had happened to him yet. And in pursuit of that stupid fantasy, he had gone away for ever and left her on her own.

Insomnia hatches strange ideas. Normally, Chloe wouldn't have thought of going down to the kitchen, much less looking for her brother's eyes in the cool-room door. Chloe was a sensible girl at heart, and she wouldn't normally have risked another disappointment: having to admit that her brother was playing hide-and-seek with her. But insomnia is not sensible. Come on, Chloe, it said to her, a chocolate truffle is just what you need. It's well known that chocolate helps you go to sleep. Come on, don't be frightened. If you're scared, all you have to do is not look at the door. It's a deceptive, distorting mirror, like the ones they have in amusement parks: it plays tricks on you, hurtful tricks sometimes, but you can just ignore it. Although, if you decide to be brave and look . . . who knows?

When the garden lamp shone into the room again, Chloe jumped to her feet. She was naked and two items of clothing lay strewn on the chair: 'Choose me,' said the T-shirt on which was written 'Pierce my tongue, not my heart'. 'No, choose *me,*' insisted the plain waiter's jacket, with its button-up collar, the jacket she had worn that night, pretending to be a boy. And, as if she were Alice in Wonderland again, Chloe hesitated, before finally deciding on the jacket.

Ah, what the fuck's it matter? she thought as she put it on. I'm just going down to get a chocolate truffle, I'm not going to be looking at myself in any mirrors.

It was four in the morning. That was the time on each of the characters' watches. The wall clock in the kitchen was running slightly slow and still hadn't chimed. That old Festina clock, clouded over with steam and smoke, looked down on Nestor, who, realizing how late it was, quickly roused himself from his pleasant reverie and, as if addressing an old friend, said: 'OK, mate, you've had a great day, and a pretty tiring one too, so it's time you toddled off to bed.'

Which is what he was about to do when something caught his eye.

'Oh sugar!' he exclaimed, suddenly realizing that he had forgotten to put the boxes of leftover chocolate truffles back in the cool room. That wasn't like him at all.

The kitchen clock struck four as Nestor opened the door of the Westinghouse cool room.

Ernesto Teldi's watch was very quiet, it didn't even tick. But it had a luminous face, which glowed in the dark as he climbed the stairs, heading for Nestor's attic room. Serafin Tous's Omega did not have this feature, so nothing, not even a phosphorescent dot, revealed his whereabouts as he tiptoed in the darkness, a beam from the lamp periodically sweeping across the façade of The Lilies, and shining in through one of the windows onto the stairs. Both Teldi and Serafin waited for the darkness to return so they could move without being seen.

* * *

It was 4 a.m. on Adela's watch too, but she had left it on Carlos's bedside table, beside the green cameo, so its luminous face hadn't witnessed her quick steps across the landing from Carlos's room to Nestor's. Nestor had been given the largest of the attic rooms: a very nice bedroom with two doors, one opening onto the stairs and the other leading to the rest of the servants' quarters. Adela Teldi came in through the second of these doors, a few minutes ahead of the other night visitors. She entered without knocking; in circumstances such as these, etiquette is inappropriate. What? she thought. No-one here? She took a few steps in the dark, then the lamp-beam shone into the room and revealed that it was empty, the bed untouched. Maybe he's in the bathroom, she thought, and sat down to wait. Two simultaneous noises made her start. It's him, he's coming, my God, what am I doing here? As Adela prepared herself, both doors opened at once and the silhouettes of two men entered stealthily. Yet neither shape was Nestor Chaffinch, so when the light shone through windows of the attic room again, three faces looked at each other in amazement, and like a startled and out-of-tune choir, the voices of Adela, Ernesto Teldi and Serafin Tous demanded in unison:

'What are *you* doing here?'

'What about you?'

'And you?'

Karel Pligh was not the only character in this story that was fond of a good tune. He was certainly not the only one who sang to express his state of mind. '*C'est trop beau*' is a lively song, and perhaps not an obvious choice, like a rollocking tarantella or an upbeat

Neapolitan folk song would have been, but when it came to choosing a tune to accompany a pleasant task, Nestor was no chauvinist. He didn't restrict himself to the repertoire of his beloved Italy. So the following scene unfolds to the tune of '*C'est trop beau*'. Nestor was about to put the boxes of truffles away in the cool room. He had stacked ten boxes on the table and he was going into the Westinghouse to put them against the wall at the back, where they wouldn't get in the way. '*C'est trop beau notre aventure/c'est trop beau pour être heureux . . .*' or 'It's too sweet, our affair, it's too sweet to be happy'. The light from the kitchen did not reach far into the dark interior, where the frozen carcasses of various game (rabbits or hares, maybe even a small deer, but Nestor preferred not to investigate further) were faintly visible. '*C'est trop beau notre aventure/c'est trop beau pour être heureux.*' He had forgotten the rest of the words, so he continued whistling the tune and amused himself with this joyful rendition for a few seconds before going back out to get the rest of the boxes. Just a few seconds: the space of a breath, but some breaths last an eternity.

When Chloe came into the kitchen, she stopped in her tracks for a moment. Then she saw that the door of the cool room was open and heard a happy whistle emerging from within. As she approached she could hear noises, as if someone was in there moving things around. But it was a different sound that attracted her, drawing her towards the shiny metal surface. It seemed the trick mirror was speaking to her: 'Here I am, Clo-clo, come over here, don't be a coward. Come on.'

The whistle from the cool room sounded joyful. How could anyone extinguish such a happy, innocent whistle? But that's silly, Chloe wasn't going to kill anyone; she just didn't want to miss her chance again. She was convinced that Eddie had told her to come downstairs, and that he would be looking at her from the other side of the mirror. So, to see Eddie's eyes in her reflection, Chloe had to move the door, not shut it, just give it a bit of a push. You're not going to trick me this time, are you, Eddie? You'll be there when I look, won't you? And sure enough, when she dared to look, for a moment Chloe saw her brother's unmistakable dark eyes in her own reflection. She couldn't help reaching out towards those eyes, which seemed to be smiling and asking for a kiss. And as she leant against the cold surface, the door swung shut with a *click*.

'Bloody brilliant, but it *can't* be true . . .' thought Nestor, since incredulity often precedes fear, and then: 'But *for Heavens' sake*, I can't have been in here more than two minutes, three at the most, stacking away these boxes of chocolate truffles.'

The following minutes went by in a blur, both inside and outside the cool room. A blur for Nestor who started beating on the door with his hands and then his feet. Holy Virgin of Loreto, Merciful Mother of God, Santa Maria Goretti and Don Bosco . . . I forgot to pull down the bolt so the door couldn't swing shut. Meanwhile, outside, Chloe was thinking: There must be a way, there has to be a way I can make Eddie stay for longer, instead of playing this cruel hide-and-seek. What can I do to make you stay for ever? What game do you want to play?

Let's see, I have to keep calm and think straight. Who could help me? Who's left in the house? wondered Nestor on the other side of the metal door. There's Karel and Carlos, and then four others I'm not so sure about:

Ernesto and Adela Teldi, young Chloe Trias, and of course Serafin Tous. Nestor called out their names:

'Tous! Teldi! Trias!'

But the cold was gradually becoming unbearable, making his teeth chatter, so his tongue stumbled over the Ts and all that came out was an indistinct stuttering.

Chloe Trias was holding her hands over her ears. I heard you, I heard you, just be quiet, please, she said, not out loud or in her usual tone of voice, but mentally, the way she talked to her brother. She had to do it silently like that, it was crucial, otherwise her imaginary world might evaporate. So with that mute voice in her head, she begged the captive to wait a moment. Just a moment, Nestor, I can't open the door now, you have to understand, he'd go away for ever. And Chloe couldn't let that happen, it would be too stupid to let him disappear again like that afternoon when he set off in search of emotions, barely twenty-two years old, the age she would reach very soon.

This time the magic of the mirror promised to be more generous and lasting, so, to make the most of it, she decided to replay what had happened on that last afternoon, in the hope of changing the ending. Tell me a story, she begged, as she had done years before, adding something she should have said then but hadn't: Don't go. Please, please don't go. Stay with me. And this time her brother's dark eyes seemed to be smiling at her, although he said nothing. Or maybe he *was* saying something. Staring into his eyes, her eyes, Chloe could see a kind of anger in them, like the rage welling up in her, and she refused to believe that death could snatch away a young life just like that, with all its promises unfulfilled. What happens to all those dreams and plans when death intervenes? They can't just disappear. They must go somewhere.

The banging on the other side of the door interrupted Chloe's speculations and reminded her of the chef. He's such a bore, she thought. Just shut up, unless you want me to leave you in there for good. Maybe you could work this one out for me: is there a way of fulfilling a destiny that death has cut short?

But Chloe was talking to herself, so no-one could hear or help her, least of all Nestor, who could feel the cold gradually numbing his will and his mind, dulling all his senses. Which is why he had come up with an original form of insulation, to stop the icy torment creeping into his skull. Somehow, he needed to block off all his bodily orifices, to stop the ache from driving him mad. Santa Madonna de Alexandria. He had managed to get his moleskin notebook from the pocket of his jacket, the little book in which he had recorded a wealth of trade secrets: so many little indiscretions jotted down in his tiny hand. Don't give up, Nestor. You have to stop your brain freezing. The paper will block out the cold and keep your mind from seizing up. That's all you can do for the moment. And destroy an irreplaceable collection of dessert recipes? Worse still, you'd be destroying all the secret details of those . . . little indiscretions. Now there's proof your neurons are freezing up, you old fool. What use is all that to you now? Come on, it's going to be all right. Remember what the witch said: 'You have nothing to fear until four Ts conspire against you.' And that's impossible, so don't give up. Keep banging on the door. Someone's bound to hear.

* * *

Chloe was about to open the door.

OK, OK, for fuck's sake, she said to herself. So I have to risk losing Eddie again because of some old fool. Doesn't he realize that as soon as the mirror moves, Eddie's eyes will disappear? You'll go away, won't you, Eddie? Like you always do, leaving me on my own. You'll say you have to go off somewhere to look for some stupid story like you did that afternoon, and I won't be able to stop you. That's what ghosts do, isn't it? They repeat what they did on the last day of their life? Over and over, for ever. That's what Miss Liau Chi was telling me, something like that. Or was it that people who die young find a way of coming back to finish off the destined path cut short so brutally? Now Chloe dearly wished she had paid more attention to what Liau Chi had said, though it had sounded like bollocks at the time. She wished she could turn back the clock, rewind and listen to the ghost lady's mad theories again, but all she could hear was Nestor's banging and his muffled shouts.

He was kicking now. And she was confused: it wasn't a ghost; it was coming from inside, and the door was shaking, so the image blurred and she could hardly see her brother's eyes.

'Nothing's going to happen to me,' said Nestor, trying to convince himself, just a few centimetres away in the darkest and iciest of hells. I'll come through this; I know. I just have to stay calm until someone hears me. And someone will, because somewhere here, near the door, thought the cook, feeling around in the dark, there's an alarm bell, and with all this banging I must have pressed the button. And when they hear it, one of them is bound to come and save me: Teldi, Tous, Trias, T . . .

If I could turn back the clock, find an explanation . . .

sooner or later, people who die young come back to accomplish their destiny . . . the things they left unfinished. All these confused thoughts seemed to be swimming on the dark surface of the shiny door, which shook as Nestor thumped it, while Chloe stared at the blurred image until it all seemed to come clear, as if a brilliant solution were written there, in unequivocal letters, for her to read.

And now that she knew exactly what to do next, she burst out laughing.

Laughter. On the other side of the door, Nestor clearly heard someone laughing. My God, there's someone out there, and that means it wasn't an accident, he thought, launching into a panicky deduction. That's when the penny dropped: three names beginning with T (and counting two Teldis, that made four Ts). Madame Longstaffe's words came back to him: 'Nestor has nothing to fear until . . .'

. . . And they're all here, the four of them together, just as the witch foresaw, he thought with the lucidity of those who are about to die. Teldi, Teldi, Tous, Trias: four Ts. Why didn't I see it before? I'm such an idiot. The cold felt thick and heavy, pressing in from all sides, filling his lungs. In his mouth it had the bitter taste of poison. He wanted to let go. There was no point struggling now, but the cold had not yet extinguished the last flicker of reason in his mind. Wait a minute, hold on; there's something that doesn't make sense. Why would those four want to hurt you? You of all people: you've always been a model of discretion. You've never meddled with other people's lives.

Absurdly, he could feel a sneeze coming on, rising and rising: Achoo! The paper he had stuffed in his ears felt as if it were exploding in his head. All those little indiscretions, those little secrets, trying to escape, he thought with a shudder. Of course, that's it, *cazzo*. You know their shameful secrets: an adulterous affair that led to a death . . . cries in the night . . . an unspeakable desire . . . Adela Teldi, Ernesto Teldi, Serafin Tous . . . they all seem so respectable, but you know what they're ashamed of. And that's enough to get you locked in a cool room with someone laughing on the other side of the door.

The cold kept pressing in, turning Nestor's fingers into claws gripping the notebook. Those claws would never straighten out again, nor would his legs, which had turned to ice, and had lost all feeling so that Nestor hardly noticed when they buckled and let his rigid trunk drop to the floor of the cool room. His mind, however, felt as if it were boiling, and with the blind hope of those who are about to die, he thought: Hang on, it'll be all right. It can't happen like this. Listen, it can't, because the prophecy hasn't been completely fulfilled. I know shameful secrets about three of them, not about all four. I know Ernesto's story, and Adela's and Serafin's, but the fourth T, Chloe, what can she have against me? She hasn't done anything shameful, as far as I know, so why would she be part of the conspiracy?

Another laugh. On the other side of the door, Chloe laughed again, but under her breath, so it sounded to Nestor like a sort of fizzing, or a hiss, like a series of TTTTTTTTTTTs promising that all would be well.

'There are only three Ts, three Ts, three Ts . . .' he said, repeating himself like a frightened child. Good old Madame Longstaffe made it perfectly clear: my time has not yet come, so I will get out of this. Just hang in there a bit longer, old boy, just a bit longer. The door will open. So just hang on.

And then Nestor Chaffinch heard the life-saving *click*.

You see? I told you it would be all right in the end. Madame Longstaffe may be a crooked old witch, but even crooked prophecies are bound by the laws of fate, and there were only three secrets this time.

Every muscle in my body is frozen, thought the cook as he heard the door begin to open. Holy Mary, Mother of God, Santa Gemma and Don Bosco, I can't move a finger, but my brain is still working perfectly. It's OK. It's over now. A *click*, and then another *click*.

Not a moment too soon, just when the cold was getting to me, filling my head with stupid thoughts and fears.

5

A Ray of Sunlight on Nestor Chaffinch's Body Bag

A serendipitous accident, thought Ernesto Teldi, alone in his room at The Lilies. Several hours had passed since they had all gathered around Nestor's body in the kitchen. The police had spoken with each person present at the time, after dusting the door of the Westinghouse cool room for fingerprints, which, as one might have guessed, was not very helpful given the number of prints they found. Nestor's for a start, brown from the chocolate, then those of Carlos, Karel and Chloe (lots of Chloe's), and finally a smaller number of prints left by Adela, Serafin and Ernesto. 'It's what you'd expect in this sort of case,' said the detective, scribbling in his notebook.

'You were all in the kitchen yesterday. Now what we need to know is whether any of you saw anything suspicious that might help us in our investigation.'

But they all remained silent, because the only thing that might have been considered suspicious, that is, the sheet of paper Nestor had been clutching, and on which was written

especially delicious with cappuci
lso be served with a raspberry coul
which prevents the mering
not to be confused with frozen chocolate
but rather with iced lemon

was sleeping innocently between the pages of the chef's copy of Brillat-Savarin, while Karel, the only one of them who might have remembered that piece of paper and linked it with the death of his friend, was not trying to solve the mystery but admiring the serene beauty of Chloe's face. Somehow that morning she seemed more mature, as if she had suddenly grown out of the 'Pierce my tongue, not my heart' T-shirt she had just put on.

The kitchen was empty again. The police and the magistrate had finished their investigation, concluding that the death was due to an accident in the home, an unfortunate bit of carelessness. 'There's nothing more we can do here. They can take the body away now.' Looking out of his bedroom window, Teldi was dazzled by the unseasonably strong sun reflected off the shiny plastic body bag in which Nestor was being transported. He watched the bag proceed towards the garden gate, carried on a stretcher by two men in green coats. Resting on the dead man's feet (or perhaps on his head) was a bunch of flowers that had been cut and gathered at Ernesto Teldi's request. A naïve observer interpreting this as a kind gesture on the part of a thoughtful employer would not, in fact, have been too far from the truth. Perhaps it was not kindness exactly that prompted Teldi to have the bouquet made up, but it was a kind of elegance: when an enemy abandons the field, or better still, has the good manners to die before one is forced to kill him, the very least one can do is send him off with a tribute.

Roses, wisteria, petunias . . . a simple but elegant bouquet, he thought, watching the flowers bob up and down on the mortal remains of his enemy. He even found the scene rather moving. It had a certain grandeur that reminded him of his treasured works of art, and, in particular, his most recent acquisition.

He moved away from the window, reached into his pocket, took out the love letter he had bought from Monsieur Pitou the previous evening and examined it. There could be no doubt: it was definitely Oscar Wilde's handwriting, his signature, his particular way of writing the letter c. All the signs were there, clear as day. How could I ever have thought, even for a moment, that it was a fake? he wondered, genuinely surprised. Because now that Nestor was dead, Ernesto Teldi could hardly even remember the inexplicable and uncharacteristic attack of insecurity he had suffered the previous evening, when he had started to panic, imagining that his colleagues might be trying to cheat him. Him of all people! How absurd! Who would dare? Teldi was a collector with a reputation, and so he would remain until his dying day. His credentials were impeccable . . . The insecurity he had felt seemed remote to him now, as remote as the possibility that his reputation could have been threatened by that chef who was, at that very moment, being carried off in a body bag as if he were wrapped in foil. All that worrying, the cold sweats, the terrible thoughts that had passed through his mind for a couple of hours, it all seemed like a bad dream, as distant and harmless as the screams he heard each night in his sleep.

How neatly it has all worked out, thought Teldi with a smile. Had he believed in such things, he might have attributed his good fortune to the helping hand of a sardonic god with a fine aesthetic sensibility. But Ernesto Teldi didn't believe in gods, not even sardonic ones with aesthetic sensibilities; he believed only in himself, and that was why he had the bouquet made up, to congratulate Nestor, and himself, on such a happy (and sensible) ending.

The funereal procession was already approaching the entrance gate. Ernesto slipped Oscar Wilde's letter lovingly back into his pocket, giving it a little pat. Life had to go on and things were looking up: tomorrow he'd be flying to Switzerland for a meeting of collectors at the Thyssens' house. Next week he was off to London to do a difficult valuation (who else could they rely on?), and next month the Gulbenkian Foundation would be rendering him a well-deserved little tribute. Life is sweet, thought Ernesto, unable to resist the cliché, and he was so absorbed in his pleasant meditation that at first he didn't hear the knocking at the door.

'There's a man downstairs who would like to talk to you,' said Karel Pligh when Teldi finally opened the door.

But Teldi was still envisaging delicious projects and triumphs so, rather than rushing down, he gazed over the boy's head, appreciating the tasteful decor of the stairwell. It really was quite charming: the curtains gave off a subtle fragrance of lavender, while the yellow walls of the landing provided the ideal backdrop for a set of beautiful still-life paintings. Perfect, just perfect.

'What is it about, young man?' he asked, returning (how dreary!) to mundane matters for a moment. 'Don't tell me there are more policemen, I'm thoroughly sick of men in uniforms.'

But Karel Pligh said he didn't think it was a policeman.

'He must be about seventy, an average-looking man, and he insists on seeing you today. Of course I didn't let him in just like that. I told him to wait at the door, so he wrote this note (it wasn't easy – his fingers are all twisted) and he said he was sure that when you read it you'd want to see him immediately.'

Karel was not familiar with Teldi's refined ways, so he had not used the letter tray to deliver the note. He was holding it in his hand, and his fingernails were not quite as clean as the collector might have wished. But Ernesto didn't notice these details, nor did he pay any attention to what Karel told him about the stranger's appearance, because as soon as he saw the writing on that card, he was mesmerized by the green, scribbly letters that seemed to be peering back at him like a row of parrots on a wire.

It was not by chance that the rooms occupied by Carlos and Adela at The Lilies were one above the other. Yet the walls and floors were so thick that no sound filtered through, making it impossible even to guess what was going on up- or downstairs. Had it not been so, Adela and Carlos would have been surprised to discover that while Nestor's body was going out through the gate of The Lilies for the last time, they were simultaneously performing the same actions in their respective rooms, like a pair of dancers following the same choreography.

At the same moment both came to their windows to bid the chef a last goodbye, and then leant pensively on the sill. Although their movements were the same, their motives were quite different. Carlos was moved by sorrow, Adela by relief, one might almost say gratitude.

Suddenly a ray of sunlight struck the body bag and the reflection was so dazzlingly bright that Adela had to step back. Take a good look, Adela, she said to herself. Don't turn away. There goes the last obstacle to your ultimate happiness. Take a good long look, the way you stared so intently at his lifeless face in the kitchen earlier, to ensure his lips were sealed for good, to be certain his eyes would never witness your foolish passion again. For better or worse, you are a free spirit: the contents of that frozen brain are no longer a threat to you. However shameful secrets are, they die with the people who keep them. So take a good look, Adela, and thank your lucky stars. This is the first day of the rest of your life.

Goodbye, my friend, thought Carlos, standing at the window of his attic room, watching the shiny bag as it was carried away, containing a body that had once been Nestor Chaffinch. But no longer, because the corpse of a friend is already a stranger. So Carlos had discovered, observing Nestor's face that morning. And, as the hours went by, he noticed other changes that confirmed his theory about the transformation of corpses: before long, he could hardly find a trace of his friend in that grey remnant. The head seemed to have shrunk, as if death had been brought by a zealous member of the head-shrinking Amazonian Jivaro tribe. Carlos preferred not to kiss that wretched mask – it seemed so alien to Nestor. The death of his father had taught him memories keep more happily when not associated with a dead body. The less one looks at the dead the better, because it's not easy to wipe out what the eyes have registered, and those who have spent hours looking at the lifeless face of a loved one often find that image superimposing itself on their fondest memories. There is no such danger, however, in paying one's respects to an anonymous, shiny body bag. Goodbye, Nestor, goodbye, my friend. And now, if you'll excuse me, I have to start collecting my things.

Even after a death, the living have their chores to do, thought Carlos as he turned away from the window to start packing. He cast an eye over the room he had shared with Adela last night. It didn't feel like his room at all, but why should it? The only things in it that belonged to him were two shirts, a waiter's uniform and a pair of jeans. Even the objects on the bedside table were not his but hers. Sitting on the unmade bed, Carlos reached out to pick up the watch Adela had left behind and lifted it to his lips. A lover's belongings are passion's strongest and most faithful allies, often more faithful than their owners. Tick-tick, said the clockwork, beating like a heart. Everything will be all right, tick-tick. And Carlos put the watch back where he had found it: yes, it would all work out in the end.

Then his fingers encountered the green cameo, which Adela had left behind along with her watch. Carlos had not noticed it before, as it was hidden by various other objects. It was beautiful, it was hers, but somehow he was not inclined to kiss it, perhaps because cameos do not beat like hearts.

In a few hours' time I'll leave all this behind me, thought Adela, sitting on her unmade bed like Carlos upstairs. Beside her was an old wooden box she had just taken out of the wardrobe. She opened it. Adela was not a romantic. Throughout her life she had been careful to keep sentimentality out of her love affairs. It's far more sensible; it saves you pain. So for years she had not examined the contents of that box, in which she had piled up letters, passionate words, declarations of love, souvenirs, photos . . . the memories of many, many years. Adela preferred not to look at them, since each letter, each object, represented a piece of her life that was gone for ever, and each reminded her that the years had fled like her looks, and that she was no longer the woman who had inspired those beautiful words. Beautiful and dead, Adela. All you have is the future. Love while you can. But first . . .

Before leaving it all behind, The Lilies and her memories, Adela had one last thing to tie up. She sat down at the little table in front of the window to write a farewell letter to her husband. A rather nineteenth-century way of doing things, cowardly too, but without doubt the simplest solution. An unwritten but longstanding rule of their marriage was that they both avoid all embarrassing displays of emotion, particularly the distasteful and inconvenient sort of scene that would go with announcing one's departure after twenty-something years of convenient co-habitation. So she wrote:

The Lilies, 29th of March

Dear Ernesto

(Then she paused, searching for the right words.)

Carlos, on the other hand, had no difficult letters to write or old memories to say goodbye to. His attention was focused on relics of a much more recent past: the objects Adela had left behind the previous night. What should I do with this? Should I put it in the case with her clothes? Should I take it with my things? They had agreed not to leave together. They would meet up later, in Madrid, after a few days, when things had settled down a bit. At the Phoenix Hotel perhaps. Things would be perfect: they could start again where it all began. Carlos looked at his watch and then at Adela's: there was five minutes' difference between the two. No doubt hers was showing the correct time. It was getting late. He picked up the few things that were left, and last of all, the cameo.

Dear Ernesto,

I don't know how to begin this letter. You will probably think I have gone mad, or, worse still, that I have turned out to be just as stupid as those deluded, romantic women we used to make fun of.

Adela stopped again, suddenly conscious of her thumbs. A superstitious fear made her check for Hecate's symptom that warned her when something bad was about to happen, but she could feel nothing. Relax. Everything is all right. The chef is dead. No-one can go delving into your past now.

As he picked up the cameo and put it in his pocket, Carlos realized that, since the moment he had seen it pinned to Adela's dress, he hadn't given it another thought. But that was hardly surprising; so much had happened since then, such terrible things. Before putting it away, he wrapped it in his handkerchief. It had an odd glow, but there was no reason to interpret that as a bad omen, he thought. And besides, he should have been grateful, really, because today, or maybe in a few days' time, when they were reunited forever at the Phoenix Hotel, he would be able to ask Adela and find out how that cameo had forged such a beautiful link between them long before they met. 'You tell me where you got that cameo, and I'll tell you a story you won't believe.' That's what he would say to her, and they would probably end up having a good laugh about the invisible threads that for years had been drawing them towards one another. Even if Adela's cameo isn't the same as the one in the picture, thought Carlos, it's such an odd coincidence, it's enough to make you believe in Madame Longstaffe's prophecies. But it *is* the same cameo. It has to be. I'm sure of it.

As if sensing the danger, Adela Teldi's fingers tightened on the pen and began to tingle. Without realizing it, she wrote, 'By the pricking of my thumbs, something wicked this way comes,' in her letter to Ernesto, and then had to cross it out, because it had nothing to do with what she wanted to tell him. Come on, Adela, just forget about those stupid premonitions, you're never going to finish the letter this way, and it's getting late.

. . . Adela's blond hair, so much like his grandmother's . . . the resemblance between The Lilies and Number 38 . . . a portrait kept in a wardrobe for years, and the blue eyes of a girl who must have been Adela . . . Carlos had thrust the cameo to the bottom of his pocket, but he couldn't stop thinking about it. He had gathered all his things and was walking across the landing. As he passed the door of Nestor's room (Goodbye, my friend), the thoughts that were troubling him crystallized as questions: Why was the picture of Adela banished from the yellow room? Why did his grandmother forbid his father to enter Number 38? Why had his mother Soledad died in Buenos Aires, of all places? And why hadn't he recognized Adela as the woman in the picture, when he had been looking for her in every woman he saw?

'Something wicked this way comes . . .' Now that Carlos had left his room, Adela could hear him walking across the landing upstairs. The steps were young and curious and full of dangerous questions: Who is this woman? What exactly happened? Where and when? Of course she could not actually decipher or even guess what those steps were asking, but her witch's thumbs knew. The pricking was painful now, and it continued until, suddenly, the steps upstairs came to a halt. Who are you? Why? How did it happen? Twinge after twinge, as Adela tried to guess why the steps that sounded so resolute and dangerous a moment before had suddenly stopped.

Since Adela was not possessed of Madame Longstaffe's extraordinary powers, which would have been particularly handy for understanding this scene, she would never know that as Carlos went past the door of Nestor's room, his mind a welter of ever more clamorous suspicions, something the cook had said the previous afternoon came back to him. He had already remembered it once, on seeing Adela in the salon of The Lilies, wearing that cameo from the painting: '*Cazzo* Carlitos,' (it was as if Nestor were there, whispering in his ear) one day you'll learn that in life there are times when it's best not to ask questions. Especially when you suspect you'd be better off not knowing the answers.'

'. . . So goodbye, Ernesto, I don't expect you to understand,' wrote Adela. She was writing fluently, her fingers relaxed now, not a trace of that premonitory pricking. Her pen flew across the paper, finishing off the highly conventional, bourgeois farewell letter to her husband: 'I'm sorry, believe me. I don't regret a moment of the years we have spent together and I hope you won't either. I wish you all the best and I bid you goodbye with . . .' As she was finishing this sentence, Adela raised her head, as if defiantly, and looked out the window, but being short-sighted she did not see the object falling from the floor above.

So she would never know that on her last day at The Lilies, just before she walked out and left it all behind, upstairs in Nestor's room Carlos had decided to get rid of the green cameo so that its lustrous sphere, bulging with troublesome questions, would disappear among the various shades of green in the garden of The Lilies. And there it remains to this day, among the leaves and branches, if anyone should care to confirm the veracity of this story.

From his window Serafin Tous also saw Nestor's body taken away, but he didn't have flowers cut, like Ernesto Teldi, nor did he pause to watch the sun sparkling on the shiny body bag, as both Adela and Carlos had done. Rather than observe the goings-on in the garden, the mild-mannered magistrate preferred to busy himself packing his bags. Serafin Tous was intending to leave that day. The Lilies was a nice enough house, but not the sort of place in which he was inclined to linger – too many unpleasant associations.

Fastidiously, he began to fold his clothes, starting with the trousers, following the method his late wife had taught him, so that they would be impeccable when he got home. He took them from the hangers, checked the alignment of the creases, then packed them away: the blue on the grey and the beige on the blue. But as he was folding the beige pair, he realized that there was still a very noticeable sherry stain in the crotch. That was from yesterday, when Nestor had appeared on the terrace and given him a shock. A silly little accident, nothing serious . . . But it is remarkable, he reflected, how accidents can happen, and just at the right time too, occasionally. He was no longer thinking about his mishap on the terrace but another, much more serious, and for him, much more fortunate, household accident: the door of the cool room happening to swing shut while that bothersome chef was inside. It couldn't have come at a better time, thought Serafin. He realized that death by freezing was no trifling matter, of course not, but he couldn't help wanting to shout: Thank God for household accidents!

Serafin Tous proceeded to pack away his shirts. First he put them into the very practical and handsome covers he had brought with him (another one of his late wife's ideas), which he then smoothed and laid in the bottom of the suitcase: there, excellent. Nora would have been proud of him. Household accidents are quite unpredictable, thought Serafin, who was beginning to find this line of thought most reassuring. And they happen all the time, much more often than people think, all sorts of accidents, from major disasters to tiny slip-ups, often just silly things. Anyone can give themselves an electric shock with a toaster or start a fire with a pan full of hot oil, say. It can happen to anyone, anyone at all. And yet, as Serafin Tous admired his perfect shirts, he felt a little thrill of pleasure, as if the sight of them so neatly piled had revealed something to him. Suddenly it seemed there was something different, unique, about the accident that had set him free. Something, but what? Serafin didn't know quite how to put it: the way it had happened, the place, the circumstances . . . there was something curiously domestic and benevolent about it . . . motherly, you could almost say. Yes, that was it.

The mild-mannered magistrate was counting his pairs of socks now: five of them, each folded in two, each bearing a discreet little label on which the name of their owner, Serafin Tous, was written in navy blue, black or blood red. It was another of his late wife's practical ideas, to prevent the pairs from getting mixed up in the wash or lost in hotels. Among many other things, Nora was a superlative housekeeper, he thought proudly. There wasn't a stain she couldn't remove or a household mishap she couldn't set right, such was her skill. Serafin always admired the way she directed those invisible but indispensable manoeuvres that transform married life into an idyll. With Nora, everything in the house seemed to run itself. Her organization was perfect: no detail was neglected; the meals were always done to a turn and delicious, and it all seemed to happen effortlessly. There was never an unpleasant cooking smell in the house, never an object out of place, and Nora herself had the rare virtue of being unobtrusive. It's only now that I really notice you, my dear, said husband to wife, now that you are gone, now that I need you, my treasure. The people we really miss are those who quietly filled our lives with pleasure, not the noisy fools we couldn't fail to notice when they were alive.

Serafin Tous had gone into the bathroom to gather his toiletries and as he packed them away – the impeccably clean razor, the tube of toothpaste rolled up from the bottom, just like Nora used to do it, to save him the trouble – an idea began to take shape in his mind. He found himself marvelling once again at the neat, domestic way in which all his problems had been tidied up. Domestic and practical at the same time, he thought.

It bore the mark of a woman's touch, or rather, the delicate touch of a ghost, because there was something about this accident that reminded him of Nora. So as he put his razor and his other toiletries away, Serafin wondered if the souls in the next life could shut the doors of earthly cool rooms, and finding in favour of this conjecture, he couldn't help exclaiming: 'It was you, Nora, wasn't it, my darling?'

As the body of Nestor Chaffinch was being carried through the garden to the gate of The Lilies, Chloe was sitting in front of the window at a makeshift desk, with a look of girlish concentration, as if she were preparing to note down all her observations like some sort of record-keeper. A little black moleskin notebook lay open to her left, and she was holding a pencil, which every now and then she raised to her lips. Now the pencil stopped half way, as if she were trying to work out some particularly difficult problem.

An observer of human behaviour watching her at that moment through the window would have been able to see how, behind the elaborately neat desk, the room was in a complete mess, with the contents of Chloe's backpack spilt on the bed and her clothes scattered all over the place, while among the rumpled sheets lay the red case containing the photograph of her brother Eddie. Yet if that same busybody had happened to be in the bedroom just a few minutes earlier, he would have witnessed an even stranger scene. He would have seen Chloe striding up and down the room like a child throwing a tantrum, leafing through the notebook, then rummaging around in her backpack until she found the photo of her brother, as if she wanted to confront one object with the other, absolutely furious, as if those objects, photo and notebook, were to blame for a betrayal, or worse still, a pointless murder.

But there was no curious observer looking in through the windows of The Lilies, just a cockroach on the mat outside the front door, wiggling its antennae knowingly, as if it understood the quirks of human psychology. But who can really understand what makes a capricious girl like Chloe tick? Or how she might come to believe that she could modify the destiny of someone who died before his time. Or why she might think that sooner or later he would return to this world to complete the life he left unfinished. Few can fathom such irrational thoughts, but that doesn't stop them from existing and explaining why Nestor was now inside a shiny body bag on the way to the cemetery, while Chloe observed his departure with a smile.

'And you got what you deserved, old fool,' she said. Put me back in the same situation and I'd do exactly the same thing again, every time, she thought, relishing each detail of what had happened in the kitchen the previous night, like a triumphant artist or the perpetrator of a perfect crime.

With her pencil still suspended in mid air, as if she were choosing which part of the perverse story to relate to her non-existent readers, Chloe decided to leave aside what had happened in the small hours of that morning, when she had heard Nestor whistling in the cool room. She preferred to evoke what she felt a little later on, looking into her brother's dark gaze reflected in the mirror, searching for an idea, a message, some way of making him stay close to her. Chloe remembered how gradually she came to the conclusion that the only way to revive the memory of the dead was by fulfilling the desires they had had when they were alive. A simple, obvious idea that gathered force as she stared at herself in the mirror. On the last day of his life, Eddie had gone off on a motorbike because he had this mad idea that to be a writer he had to 'live fast, have loads of experiences, get drunk, fuck hundreds of girls, kill someone or something . . . Clo-clo, you wouldn't understand, you're too young.'

And when she had asked him what would happen if it turned out he didn't have the guts to do any of those terrible things that were supposed to give him the experience he was looking for, he replied: 'Well then, Clo-clo, I'll just have to steal someone else's story, won't I?' That's what he had said, her brother Eddie, but he didn't carry out his plan, instead he went away for ever, leaving it all unfinished.

But she was here now, young Chloe, little Clo-clo, the same age as Eddie when he died, ready and willing to do all those things he would have done if he'd had time. She hadn't planned what had happened the previous night at The Lilies, nor did she have any grudge against the chef, with his pointy moustache and his little notebook full of the scandals and secrets he'd been privy to, or so he said: a treasure-chest, in other words, of real-life stories, cruel and perfect, better by far than anything a writer could invent.

'OK, I'm opening the door, you old fool, it's OK,' she had said. But when she finally opened the door to help Nestor, there he was on the floor holding that little book, as if he were offering it to her, while her brother looked on. All Chloe could think about was helping Eddie to fulfil his dream. That's why she snatched the book from the chef's outstretched hand: that's where they were, all those stories of love and crime that Eddie would have loved to write.

The opportunity had presented itself; exploiting it was

easy. Easy to find a justification for what she had just done, to shut the door again, pretend not to hear, dream of Eddie, wait for the cold to silence the chef's cries forever, and then go up to her room as if nothing had happened . . . it had all been very easy. And now she realized that she, the little sister, had succeeded where her brother had failed, because now she would be able to fulfil the destiny that death had snatched away from him. 'Those who die young always find a way to come back to this world and finish off their destiny,' that's what Miss Liau Chi had said to her, and she believed it. Wasn't she holding the proof in her hands: the very thing Eddie had gone looking for the day he died?

Little Indiscretions, that was the title Nestor had given to the collection of anecdotes he was writing. It was bound to be full of really juicy gossip, terrible, shameful secrets: exactly what she needed to live out Eddie's mad idea of writing books about other people's lives.

So, the previous night, without checking the contents of the notebook, Chloe had gone off to sleep peacefully, pretending that nothing had happened. And she believed it – she had fooled herself. It's the best way to fool others, after all.

Sitting in front of the window now, Chloe Trias remembered all this as well as something far worse that had happened just a few minutes earlier when she opened up her treasure-chest and discovered what the chef had really written in his moleskin notebook. What the fuck?!

She couldn't believe her eyes. She read the sentences over and over, stunned: 'The secret of a chocolate mousse . . . the trick for making a perfect île flottante . . .' Jesus fucking Christ! 'The scandalous flavour of a mango sorbet . . .'

She looked out of the window. The funereal procession was approaching the garden gate now. The bright sunshine seemed to be mocking her as she tried to spot Nestor's body. She wanted to shout something obscene at that lying, cheating, pompous chef. She even opened the window. But then she stopped. There's no point abusing the dead, so she went back to leafing through the notebook, as if she were hoping a magic spell might grant her the power to find something she hadn't noticed before. But all she could see were Nestor's culinary indiscretions, written down in that neat, rounded hand of his, stubbornly occupying the pages. A pointless murder, another broken dream.

Karel would be coming to get her soon. It was nearly time to leave The Lilies. She would have to pick up her clothes and stuff them into her backpack. Another chapter of her life would come to an end and she would be alone again. As usual, she thought. And yet, as she was about to stand up, something outside caught her eye and made her stop. She sat there watching a ray of sunlight shining on Nestor Chaffinch's body bag, the same ray the other characters in this story had seen from their respective windows. The way the plastic of the bag reflected the sunlight reminded her of all those mirrors and their sparkling reflections, and, suddenly, she was laughing again, as happy as she had been when staring at the closed door of the Westinghouse, as if her brother's dark gaze had returned to her eyes. Life had not been kind to her, true: stealing what she loved, deceiving her and laying traps. And it was true that luck had just played the cruellest trick of all: the substituting of recipes for all the stories she had planned to use to live out a dream. And yet despite all this, she still smiled as she said goodbye to Nestor's body bag, because she had just realized that there might still be a way of beating destiny. She had a story that no-one could ever take away. The story of a little or perhaps a not-so-little indiscretion: her own story, what had happened to her at The Lilies. And realizing what she has, like a boy with a head full of dreams who has just completed the first twenty-one years of a long, ambitious life, Chloe began to tear out all the pages on which Nestor had written. Nestor's culinary secrets were scattered in a flurry of paper – after-dinner petits fours, ginger truffles, ice-creams and sorbets – until only blank pages were left and the title page, which read:

LITTLE INDISCRETIONS

Once she had removed all traces of cookery, underneath the title inscribed in Nestor Chaffinch's tiny, round hand, Chloe noted down the first lines of a story. She would work out how it ended later on. This is how it began:

> His moustache was stiffer than ever, so stiff a fly could have strolled out to the end, like a prisoner walking the plank on a pirate ship.

She stopped to take a breath and think about what to say in the next sentence of *Little Indiscretions*, a novel by Eddie Trias.

And as she continued her draft:

Except that flies can't survive in a cool room at thirty below zero, and neither could the owner of the blond, frozen moustache: Nestor Chaffinch, chef and pastry-cook, renowned for his masterful way with a chocolate fondant.

Chloe discovered that, with a real death and a couple of basic ideas, it's not so hard to spin a story of passion, secrets and malice, because lies can be perfectly convincing if they contain an element of truth.

So where do I go from here? she wondered, before writing:

And that's how he was found hours later: eyes wide open in astonishment, but with a certain dignity still in his bearing. True, his fingernails were scratching at the door, but a dishcloth was tucked into the string of his apron as usual, though looking dapper is hardly a major preoccupation when the door of an 1980s-model Westinghouse cool room, two metres by one and a half, has just shut automatically behind you with a *click*.

But as she drafted the first paragraphs of *Little Indiscretions*, unbeknownst to Chloe, on the doormat of The Lilies a cockroach was wiggling its antennae.

THE END